SORC

Recin looked out at the fields. "If there's no magic, then what's that?" He pointed over the wall at the approaching globe of blue-white fire.

Crossbows thrummed as several of the Viashino let bolts fly, but their shots only vanished into the glow. Others leaped from the wall and ran crying into the night. The sphere, now almost as big as the city itself, reached the wall and swallowed it like the tide moving over a castle of sand.

For a moment it seemed that every throat in the city joined in a scream of terror. Recin squeezed his eyes shut and threw his hands up to protect himself. The light was everywhere, burning so brightly that even through his closed eyelids it seared. Heat washed over him, and he could smell the awful odor of his own hair scorching . . .

Look for
MAGIC: The Gathering

<u>Novels</u>
Arena
Whispering Woods
Shattered Chains
Final Sacrifice
The Cursed Land
The Prodigal Sorcerer
Ashes of the Sun*

<u>Anthologies</u>
Tapestries
Distant Planes*

From HarperPrism

* coming soon

MAGIC
The Gathering™

THE
PRODIGAL
SORCERER

Mark Sumner

HarperPrism
An Imprint of HarperPaperbacks

HarperPaperbacks   *A Division of* HarperCollins*Publishers*
10 East 53rd Street, New York, N.Y. 10022

Copyright © 1995 by Wizards of the Coast, Inc.
All rights reserved. No part of this book may be used or reproduced in any manner whatsoever without written permission of the publisher, except in the case of brief quotations embodied in critical articles and reviews. For information address HarperCollins*Publishers*,
10 East 53rd Street, New York, N.Y. 10022.

Cover illustration by Dennis Nolan

First printing: November 1995

Printed in the United States of America

HarperPrism is an imprint of HarperPaperbacks.
HarperPaperbacks, HarperPrism, and colophon are trademarks of HarperCollins*Publishers*.

❖ 10 9 8 7 6 5 4 3 2 1

THE PRODIGAL SORCERER

CHAPTER

1

TALLI PRESSED HER CHEEK AGAINST THE
cold dark stone, squeezed her eyes shut, and breathed
in the tower's dry, earthy smell.

The fear that slowed her pace was growing stronger
with each step, and the pride that had kept her moving
all morning was nearly exhausted. The tips of her fingers were raw and bleeding from hours of running
them along the abrasive crystalline face of the rock.
Her legs trembled, and her feet felt bruised inside her
leather boots.

She opened her eyes just a crack. The western valley
of the River Nish stretched out before her—miles of
forest broken by a patchwork of fields along the banks
of the river. Talli could see the tall white walls of
Berimish in the middle distance, and the gray-brown
smear of the Great Marsh beyond.

The army that her father had led through the valley
was no more than a spot on the green expanse of fields.
Tamingazin looked peaceful, even neat.

But it wasn't the breadth of the view that bothered

Talli, it was the depth—in particular the hundreds of feet of vertical cliff face that separated her perch on the tower from the safety of the flat ground below.

"Were you planning on moving soon?" said a voice at her back.

Still shaking, Talli turned and saw Rael Gar standing behind her on the trail. He stood calmly, with his arms folded across his broad chest and the loose hood of his soft black clothing casting a shadow over his flat triangular face. Rael Gar's head barely reached Talli's shoulder, but his height didn't diminish the impression he gave of strength. The Garan's shoulders were almost impossibly wide and every visible inch of him—even his fingers and neck—was corded with lean muscle.

Rael Gar's large silver eyes showed flashes of green. Talli had been around him long enough to know that the color was either impatience, or the beginnings of anger. It was only those shifting colors that revealed anything of his emotion. No Garan elf would dare let fear show on their faces over something so trivial as the prospect of falling to their death. Talli fully expected that if the path crumbled from beneath them, Rael Gar would keep that calm expression all the way to the ground.

She was also quite certain that, given a good reason, the Garan would have pushed her from the trail without a second glance. The thought didn't make her feel particularly good about sharing the trail with him.

"Just looking at the view," said Talli.

"Well, it will only get better," the Garan replied. He raised his eyes to indicate the mass of dark stone yet to climb.

Talli drew a deep breath. "Oh, yes," she said. "Wonderful."

She raised her right foot and cautiously moved it to

the next step, then followed it with the left. The stiff boiled-leather soles of her boots crunched against small pebbles and sand on the trail. They did not slip, but Talli was sure they were always *about* to slip. About to slip and send her tumbling head over heels, screaming . . .

She drew in another long breath of the cool air and balled her hands into tight fists. She had conquered a dozen opponents in battle; she wasn't about to be defeated by her own fears. Talli moved on up the winding path.

The tower was made from thousands of hexagonal pillars of shiny black basalt. Each of the pillars was little more than a stride across, and whoever had hewn out the spiral path to the top had carefully cut each column slightly higher than the one before to form broad six-sided steps. The course went round and round the bulk of the tower, climbing perhaps a hundred feet with each turn of the spiral and turning a thousand feet of climbing into miles of walking. It was not a steep ascent, but it was a long one. Talli's climb from the warm grasslands below had begun while it was still dark; now it was near noon and there was still several hundred feet of tower—and thousands of steps—ahead.

Though it sent jabs of pain up her raw fingers, Talli kept her left hand on the comforting bulk of the stone as she climbed.

She concentrated only on the next step, and studiously did not look down at the distant ground. The only sound was her breathing, the shuffling of her boots, and the irregular grating of her sword hilt across the rock. Behind her, Rael Gar was silent.

Occasionally, she caught glimpses of her father and his advisor, Karelon, working their way along the trail ahead. Talli wished she had confided with her father about her fear of heights. If he had known how frightened she was of the drop at her side, Talli was sure that her father would have stayed closer. But she had not told him. Tagard Tarngold had seen his daughter raise her sword bravely in a dozen battles. He had no reason to suspect that this peaceful climb would be the most frightening day of the long war for Talli.

The curving path took them around again to the shaded side of the tower. It was noticeably cooler than it had been on the last circuit, and chill drops of water clung to the stone. A silver coat of mist gathered against Talli's woolen leggings and weighted the mass of her pale hair. The soles of her boots grew slick with the moisture. To make matters worse, a few more steps brought her into a heavy layer of cloud, where Talli could see only a vague shadow of the steps ahead. She hesitated at the edge of the shifting mist, her legs trembling with tension.

"Do you need aid?" asked Rael Gar.

Talli shook her head. "No, I'm going." She moved carefully into the fog, feeling for the invisible stairs with her feet.

With each advance, the swirling grayness tightened around her. Talli moved over one unseen step, then another. The clouds were actually not so bad. In fact, without the dizzying view to her right, she felt better than she had all morning. She stood up straighter and took a confident step forward.

A strong hand clamped down on her shoulder. Startled, Talli tried to pull away, but Rael's voice cut through the mist.

"Don't move," said the Garan.

"Why not?"

"Because, the path ends here. The only way you can go now is down." Despite the import of his words, Rael's voice was flat. He squeezed beside Talli on the narrow shelf and pointed through the fog. "I wouldn't recommend going that way."

The clouds rippled, then flowed apart for a moment to reveal a heart-seizing glimpse of the ground far below. The ragged edge of the path was only a foot away. Then the mists closed in again and Talli was left gasping for breath. "One more step," she choked out, "and I'd have fallen a thousand feet."

"More like a hundred," said Rael Gar. "Then you would have hit the next turn of the path below. Of course, you might have bounced." If the idea caused the Garan any concern, it wasn't obvious in his voice.

Talli had a grim thought. "If the path ends here," she said, "then where did my father and Karelon go?"

She half-expected the emotionless Garan to gesture at the long drop, but instead he took Talli by the shoulder and turned her toward the tower of stone. She squinted into the fog, seeing little but a patch of darker gray in a world of gray. Cautiously, she stretched her hands toward the wall. Instead of the hard stone, she found only air.

Talli stretched a little farther and found the edges of a doorway cut into the tower. Beyond was a dank tunnel where the gloom faded to almost total darkness. She stepped inside and found stairs leading upward as the tunnel cut directly into the heart of the stone tower. The passage of untold numbers had worn the edges from the stairs and left each stone step with a shallow depression in the center. Talli's fingers found the dangling end of an iron handrail, but water and time had turned it into a crumbling length of rust. She reached past the rail and put her aching hand against the unyielding stone. Then she started up the stairs.

The stairs were steeper than the winding path, steep enough that within a few minutes of climbing, Talli had a whole new set of aching muscles. But she was glad to suffer the pain and darkness instead of facing the precipice outside.

They climbed on in silence for long minutes. Talli's mouth filled with the sour taste of her exhaustion, but she tried her best to keep up the pace. Finally a dim light appeared above. Another ten minutes of climbing, and the faint glow ahead turned into the distinct bright blue of daytime sky. Holding up a hand to shield herself from the brightness, Talli emerged blinking from the tunnel and stood shivering in a brisk wind.

Rael Gar emerged from the tunnel and stood at her side. "It seems the stories are true," he said.

Talli squinted against the light. As her eyes adjusted to the scene before them, her mouth dropped slowly open.

The entire top of the stone tower was covered in a crazy quilt of buildings. They ranged in size from tiny huts to huge soaring structures larger than any Talli had seen before. Their styles were as varied as their sizes—dark wood walls, windows of colored glass, towers of clean white stone, domes of burnished metal—all crowded together in no apparent order. In the narrow space between buildings, gardens covered every available foot of ground. Despite the cool weather at the top of the tower, the gardens were verdant and choked with ripe fruit and brilliant flowers.

At the very center of the tangled mass of structures stood a dark pyramid carved from the same black stone as the tower on which it stood. It loomed over the other buildings like a thunderhead rising above the plains.

Talli had grown up in the gray stone halls of Farson Hold, one of the oldest of the human keeps. She had always thought that the intricately carved designs on those ancient walls made Farson the most beautiful place in all the valley. Now she knew better. The city atop the tower of stone was like something from one of the stories her mother had whispered when Talli had been a child. The pyramid alone was large enough to swallow Farson Hold entirely and leave plenty of room for expansion.

"Tallibeth!" called a strong voice.

Talli saw three figures approaching from among the nearest buildings. Even if she hadn't been able to see the crown of yellow hair and the bright gleam of ceremonial armor, she would have known that the central figure was her father just by the speed and purpose of his stride. The slight, dark figure to his left had to be Karelon—the woman who had first championed her father as leader of all humans, and who had been at his side throughout the war. At first Talli took the third figure to be another human, but as the shapes approached, she saw that it was strangely hunched beneath its robe and its gait was quick and mincing. It was a Viashino.

Instantly, Talli's hand went to the blade at her belt, and her lips peeled back from her teeth. As the cloaked figure drew closer, she could see the Viashino's long neck and its narrow head with its jutting snout. She saw its scaly and clawed hands. She saw its yellow eyes. Her fingers tightened on the hilt of the blade, ready for attack.

"I see you survived the climb," Talli's father said. The chilly air had made Tagard's cheeks ruddy, but he seemed none the worse for the long ascent.

"It was . . . invigorating," said Rael Gar.

Talli nodded without taking her eyes off the Viashino. Ever since her mother's death, Viashino had filled Talli's nightmares. Her mother had gone to gather fruit from a grove downslope from Farson Hold. The Viashino who claimed ownership of the trees had killed her for a basketful of green utulpa—and the great crime of being a human on Viashino land.

The long, bloody war had only reinforced Talli's hatred for the scaly people of the valley. Though some Viashino now fought under Tagard's banner, it did not make her trust them any more. Talli had been only a child when her mother died, but she had not forgotten—or forgiven.

The Viashino returned her stare, but she could not read its expression. Viashino faces were as hard and immobile as stone, unreadable to human eyes. Its huge yellow-orange eyes looked out from deep bony sockets, but they too gave no clue to the creature's thoughts.

"This is Oesol," said Karelon. "He's going to take us to the king." Like Talli, the dark-haired woman had never had any love for the scaly creatures. It was one of the things that brought her close to Talli from the moment they met.

"Not king," said the Viashino. His voice was soft and liquid. "We have no king here."

Karelon shrugged. "Your leader, then," she said. "Whatever you call them, it comes to much the same thing." Her distaste for speaking with the Viashino was beginning to show in her voice.

Oesol shook his muzzle from side to side. "Not in this place. We have no hereditary ranks or titles of conquest. Each of us casts lots for those who—"

"That's wonderful, really," Tagard said, cutting off the Viashino's speech. "Why don't we go and meet this leader, and you can tell us more about it as we walk."

Oesol's head bobbed at the end of his extended neck. He turned and started toward the cluster of buildings. His long stiff tail jutted out from under his gray robe, moving slightly from side to side with each step. The gravel of the carefully raked path crunched softly under his three-toed feet.

Tagard followed close behind the Viashino, and Karelon came at his side. As she fell in behind her father, Talli found her gaze slipping from the splendid buildings and the hated Viashino to the woman who walked at her father's side.

It had been nearly ten years since Talli's mother had died. Almost from the moment of that tragedy, Karelon had been at Tagard's side. And over the years, Talli had become closer to the woman than she was to anyone but her father. She was a small woman, shorter than Talli by several inches, and very thin, but despite her size, she was not without considerable strength and speed. She had been the leader of her own hold long before Tagard had united the people of the hills. Her skill on the battlefield was unmatched.

For years, Talli had been attempting to make her father see Karelon as something more than an advisor. From the way the men spoke in the camp, Talli knew that the dark-haired woman was not unattractive, and ten years was a long time for a leader of their people to go without a mate. Finally, Talli's work seemed to be paying off. Tagard was beginning to notice that the woman at his side *was* a woman. There had been talk among the soldiers that as soon as the war ended, Tagard would make his military partner into his marriage partner. Talli looked at the two of them walking close beside each other up the path. Their hands touched, and for a moment their fingers twined together. Talli smiled.

They reached a group of buildings, and Oesol moved to what looked like a smooth stone wall. A soft tap from the Viashino's clawed hand sent a section of the wall sliding inward to reveal a narrow, dimly lit hall. Oesol moved inside, and the entourage of three humans and one Garan followed.

Talli was disappointed with the interior of the building. After the impressive size and breathtaking design of the structures, she had expected the inside to be filled with exotic furniture and opulent tapestries, but the hallway was completely bare. Were it not for the occasional sign or plain wooden door, there would have been nothing but cold naked stone all along their path.

The hallway turned and twisted, and the stone went from pale marble to red granite to dark basalt shot through by threads of white. Every few dozen strides their small hallway crossed larger passages. At many of these junctions, the small group of visitors encountered more residents of the tower. A few of those they passed were human. A few more were Viashino. But the vast majority came from races that Talli could not even name. Some were tall, with scarlet skin and glowing blue eyes. There was a trio whose hairy faces were highlighted by curving tusks, and a whole group of creatures with heads as smooth and featureless as casperjay eggs. One shaggy, hulking form was so wide, they were forced to press themselves against the wall to let the enormous figure pass.

A few of the strange faces turned to glance at them as they went by, but most ignored the little delegation from the valley floor.

Finally the hallway ended at a door of pale wood. Oesol tapped his claws against the frame, then pushed the door open and stepped inside. The chamber beyond was large, but like everything else they had seen, bare of any decoration. The walls and floor were carved from jet black stone. From somewhere far overhead came a warm yellow light.

Waiting in the center of the room was a small white-haired man dressed in another of the shapeless gray robes. He had a lengthy white beard and a large nose that dominated his narrow face. He sat cross-legged on the floor of the room, without even the benefit of a rug between himself and the cold stone.

Before him was a tiny device made from red and gold wires. The object seemed to have some vaguely familiar form, but Talli couldn't quite puzzle it out.

"These are the ones who climbed the tower," said Oesol.

The man on the floor lifted the twisted mass of wire and got to his feet. Despite his apparent age, he moved quickly and smoothly as he walked across the room and faced the four visitors. "Welcome," he said. "Welcome to the Institute for Arcane Study."

"Thank you," replied Talli's father. He stepped ahead of the other three and touched his forehead in a gesture of respect for the older man. "I am Tagard Tarngold, king by the acclamation of both human and Garan. These others are Sachem Karelon Frie of Valiton Hold, war leader of our forces; Rael Gar of the Garan; and Tallibeth, my daughter and a member of my council."

"King, War Leader, Gar," said the white-haired man. His gaze drifted from one visitor to the next. "Very impressive titles. Very impressive." The man's dark eyes peered at Tagard with new interest. "There is a tradition of . . . humbleness, here. So I'm afraid I have only my name to offer in return. I am Aligarius Timni."

The sorcerer gave his name with an air that was anything but humble. Though there were no wizards in the army, Talli had seen several of them over the years. Most of them seemed to wear elaborate clothing and carry fancy staffs or other signs of their trade. In his plain gray robe, the old man did not look very impressive.

"Are you the leader here?" asked Karelon.

"Oh, well, not *officially*, you understand," said Aligarius. "We aren't much for leadership of any sort." He drew himself up straighter. "Though we do recognize ability and expertise."

"As do all people of wisdom," said Tagard. "We need some of your expertise today."

Aligarius turned to the Viashino, who still stood near the door, and held out the wire object. "Friend Oesol, would you be good enough to take this back to storage and have some cushions brought to this room? I'm sure that our guests are not used to the privations which we impose on ourselves."

"Please," said Tagard, "we're content to stand."

Talli groaned inwardly. After the long climb, she wanted nothing so much as a chance to sit down and rest her legs.

"Nonsense," replied Aligarius. "As one of the most senior members of the institute, I am expected to show the less-seasoned members the proper way to free the mind for magical research, but there is no reason for you to suffer." He gave an elaborate sigh. "I only wish we could offer proper chairs."

"Thank you," said Tagard. "I'm sure cushions will be fine."

The sorcerer nodded to Oesol. The Viashino took the wire object from his hand and moved toward the door. "And have someone bring over food and drink," Aligarius called after him. "These people have had quite a climb to get up here. They're bound to need some refreshment."

Talli decided she liked the old man.

The white-haired man turned his attention back to the four visitors. "I apologize that we aren't better prepared for you. But, situated as we are, few make the effort to call on us."

After a few moments, Oesol and another Viashino appeared with thin pillows made from the same gray cloth as the robes which everyone at the institute seemed to wear. The two Viashino moved around the room, arranging the cushions in a single long row in front of Aligarius. Talli thought that her father and Karelon looked slightly silly as they folded their legs and sat on the cushions. Their ceremonial armor was clearly not meant for such a pose. She was glad she had chosen to wear her best woolen leggings instead.

Talli eased down onto one of the cushions with a sigh of relief. Even before reaching the tower, they had been on the march for days, and the nights had been filled with meetings instead of sleep. She hid a yawn behind her hand. Just sitting down felt so good she thought she might drop off to sleep.

The two Viashino moved away from the cushions to stand at the side of the room. With their knees jointed in the other direction, Viashino did not sit like humans, and Talli had heard that they rarely laid down, even when sleeping. Instead they rested against the wall, propping themselves in place with their stiff tails. Talli turned her head slightly to keep the two scaly beings in sight. Karelon was whispering quietly with Tagard, and the others seemed to be taking no notice of the Viashino, but Talli felt a deep wrongness at being in the same room with the creatures that had been the enemy for so long.

Aligarius folded his legs and returned to his place on the cold stone floor. "Now, while we wait for refreshments, perhaps you can tell me the reason for your visit."

Tagard nodded. Talli could tell that her father was relieved to get to the real discussion. For Tagard, the only thing to talk about that was worth talking about was his great crusade. The brief exchange with Aligarius had exhausted his limited store of tolerance for pleasantries.

Evidently, it wasn't only Tagard who was anxious to get to the heart of the matter. Karelon suddenly leaned forward on her cushion, the leather bindings of her armor creaking as she moved. "We're here to ask your help," she said.

"Of course," said Aligarius. "We will render what aid we can. Providing comfort to travelers has always been among the functions of our institute."

"We're pleased to hear that," said Tagard. "I'm sure that you know of our efforts to bring all of Tamingazin under one banner . . . "

"Actually," said the sorcerer, "we hear so little of what goes on below. You are the first visitors we have had in over a season."

"A great struggle goes on at your feet," said Tagard. He paused and Talli noticed that her father's blue eyes had taken on the same glint they acquired when he was giving a speech before the armies. "For centuries, our land has been divided by walls of race. Humans and Garan have been restricted to the high country, while the Viashino toiled in the central valley. Conflict has kept us apart. We seek to knock down those barriers, end the fighting, and unite all our peoples."

"A noble aim," said Aligarius. "And one to which we have no traditional opposition." He ran his fingers through the long whiskers at his chin. "Do you seek access to our libraries? Will you be sending members of your staff to study the knowledge we have gleaned?"

Tagard shook his head. "At this moment, our army prepares to move on Berimish, the last point of resistance to unification," he said. "Though we've been victorious up to this point, our enemies have marshaled their forces behind the stone walls of the city. The coming battle will decide the fate of our long war. I'm afraid we have no time for study."

"Then what is it you want?" asked the wizard.

"We need someone who can lend sorcerous aid. With your help, a just end to this war can be assured."

"We cannot help you," said Oesol from his place by the wall.

Every head in the room swiveled toward the Viashino. "What makes you say that?" asked Tagard.

Oesol gave a flick of his tail and pushed himself away from the wall. "The institute cannot interfere directly in these matters." The Viashino raised his arms and spread his clawed fingers. "This place is dedicated to learning, not to war. We have sworn to forsake all things but our study of the arcane. It is our charter."

Tagard opened his mouth to reply, but at that moment a trio of figures appeared at the doorway. "Ahh," said Aligarius, "it seems our refreshments have arrived."

The food bearers, one human and two who were of some tall, skeletally thin race, bent to place platters of flat bread and vegetables on the floor in front of the visitors. Another human followed them into the room, this one a young girl laden with a tray of cups and squat stone jugs. The girl looked to be about Talli's own age, but with pale skin and very dark hair, not the sort of coloring usually found in Tamingazin. Talli wondered how the girl had come to be at the institute.

Just looking at the cups and jugs reminded Talli how thirsty she was. As soon as the girl put them down, Talli took one of the jugs and poured herself a cup of a milky yellow liquid. She had the cup halfway to her lips when the girl suddenly put a hand to Talli's wrist.

"The juice is ellinvine," warned the girl in a soft voice. "It's one of the few things that grows well up here."

Talli wrinkled her nose. Ellinvine grew wild near her home, and any child who had the misfortune to pop one of the bright green berries in her mouth could not forget that it was among the most bitter of fruits. But her thirst was strong, and she took a tiny sip. The liquid was tart, but not nearly so bad as she remembered. She took a longer swallow and felt the cold drink roll down her throat.

"It's fine," Talli said.

The girl nodded. "Just don't gulp it," she said, making a face like she was swallowing a handful of the berries. "It'll make you pucker till your cheeks cave in."

Talli laughed. "I'll be careful."

"Friend Kitrin," Aligarius said in an impatient tone. "Please hurry and do your job. There are others waiting for their drinks."

The girl smiled at Talli for a moment longer, then hurried to serve the other visitors. Talli wished that they could have talked longer. There were few humans of her age in the army, and her position in the council put a wall between Talli and most of the soldiers. The chance to discuss anything but supplies and marching orders would have been welcome.

Her father was in no mood for food or drink. As soon as the servers left the room, Tagard turned his attention back to Aligarius. "Is what Oesol says true?" he asked. "Will you give us no aid?"

Aligarius looked uncomfortable. "I'm afraid that Friend Oesol is *technically* correct," he said. "It's always been the policy of the institute to remove itself from the struggles below. We don't interfere directly."

Karelon made a sound of disgust. "But you're the ones that raised the magewall around us all. How can you say that you don't interfere?"

Talli looked from Karelon to Aligarius in surprise. She hadn't known that the institute had anything to do with the magewall. From what Talli had been told, the shifting barrier of light which surrounded Tamingazin on all sides had been there since before the founding of the holds. It forced all who passed through to move with the difficulty of an insect struggling in tree sap, and left any army that tried to enter the valley so vulnerable to attack that none had seriously tested it in an age.

"The magewall was raised for the protection of everyone in Tamingazin," said Oesol, still standing near the wall. "It has ensured peace."

"Peace?" said Karelon. "There's been no peace. This valley has seen nothing but war." She pointed a slim finger at the Viashino. "Your magewall kept anyone from bringing an army in here and taking your precious institute, but it hasn't kept the rest of us from tearing at each other's throats."

"We have not forced you to fight," said Oesol.

"We are penned in like beasts in a cage," said Tagard. "The human lands are farmed out. Each year brings a smaller harvest and greater hardship. The way of the Garan has always been hard, and it is growing harder still. But if either of us move toward the valley, the Viashino attack us. What do you expect, that we should stand quietly and die?"

There was a strained moment of silence. Talli set down her cup and slowly moved her fingers toward her blade again. If the Viashino decided to stop talking and attack, she wanted to be ready.

"We're not asking you to win the war for us," Tagard said, his voice pitched low and calm. "We'll win this war whether you help us or not."

Oesol moved closer to Aligarius, the clawed toes of the Viashino's feet clicking against the hard stone floor with each step. "Then you've no need of us, and it's just as well. We cannot give you the help you want. We can't interfere in what—"

"You've already interfered," Tagard said. He rose to his feet, his blue eyes level with the yellow ones of the Viashino. "Karelon is right. Your magewall has

ensured your safety, but kept this valley walking a
knife edge of turmoil and pain. All we ask now is that
you help us attain peace."

Oesol shook his head sharply; it was a gesture that
all the races of the valley shared. "No, we cannot help."

"Oh, perhaps we can," said the soft voice of
Aligarius. Oesol started to protest again, but the old
man raised a hand to quiet him. Still sitting on the
floor, Aligarius looked up at Tagard. "Finish what you
were saying before," he said. "Tell us exactly what kind
of aid you need."

Tagard bent one knee and kneeled down close to the
white-haired man. "There are more than forty thousand people in Berimish. Viashino, mostly, but humans
as well."

Aligarius nodded. "We have some initiates here who
came from Berimish."

"Most of the Viashino forces have moved within the
walls of the city. We must take it to end the conflict,"
Tagard continued, "but if we're forced to scale its walls
and take Berimish by force, there'll be many deaths on
both sides." He paused for a second and leaned in
closer to Aligarius. "What we are asking is that you
help us take the city without the use of torch and
sword. You're an experienced, powerful sorcerer. Help
us end this war without needless death."

Oesol looked down his long snout at the two men.
"It violates the charter, Friend Aligarius. We cannot
do it."

Aligarius shook his head. "I'm not so certain," he
said slowly. "They have a point. The magewall has
affected their lives."

"It only kept others out," said the Viashino. "It
didn't force them to fight among themselves."

"Regardless. It was interference." The wizard
extended a hand to Tagard, and together the two men

rose to their feet. "I will go with you to Berimish and see the situation for myself," said Aligarius. "Perhaps there is something that can be done."

"You cannot," Oesol repeated. "This is wrong. If we're to do something this important, we should call a meeting of the whole institute."

Aligarius looked at him calmly. "You have only a few years of study to your credit, Friend Oesol, I have more than a century. I am only doing what I think best for both the institute and the valley."

The old man went to get his things. Talli got to her feet and stretched her legs. Karelon glanced over at her and smiled. The meeting had gone well. Talli was glad that her father had gotten what he wanted, but she was not looking forward to the long walk back down along the treacherous trail.

The girl who had brought the drinks earlier reappeared in the doorway and went to gather the jugs and glasses. "That was a short concourse," the girl said as Talli handed over her cup. "These wizards will usually keep you talking all day."

"Aren't you a wizard?" asked Talli.

"I suppose," the girl said with a shrug of her shoulders. "But I've only been here a couple of years. You've got to be here a century or two before they notice you around this place."

Talli smiled and was about to reply when Aligarius called from the hallway and the visitors filed from the room. Last in line, Talli reluctantly said her good-byes to the girl and started after the others.

She was almost through the door when a clawed hand took her arm. Cold fear washed over Talli as Oesol's muzzle moved in close to her face.

"Listen to me, young human," said the Viashino. "This is wrong."

"Let me go," Talli said, her voice little more than a

hoarse whisper. Her hand closed on her blade and she
eased it silently from its leather sheath.

"This is wrong," the creature said again. "The institute has great power, and only strict obedience to our
charter has kept that power from wrecking this land."
He released Talli's arm and looked away. "For your
own sake, for your people's sake, do not let the power
come into the hands of those who would use it."

Talli raised her blade, then paused and returned it to
its sheath. Oesol stepped past her and vanished down
the long hall. Talli hurried to join her father.

In another day, they would be in Berimish.

CHAPTER
2

RECIN SLID DOWN THE POLE, TWISTED through the narrow door, jumped over the counter, raced out into the alley, squeezed past a man working leather into pouches, and emerged onto the main street of Berimish without allowing a single redberry loaf to slip from the bundle in his arms. He was forced to slow to a walk among the crowds and heavy carts that surged down the street, but he walked impatiently, straining for a chance to get ahead.

The sun was setting, staining the whitewashed walls of the city with ruddy light. In the narrow alleys that branched from the main road, shadows had already drawn together. On a normal day, the streets would be growing quiet as shops closed and families prepared the evening meal. But there was nothing normal about this day. Everyone had heard the rumors: the enemy army on the move, the city soon to be surrounded.

The knowledge filled the soft evening air with a current of uncertainty and excitement. Soldiers, both human and Viashino, hurried along in knots of three or four. Merchants hawked their wares at prices that would have been outrageous on any other day, but today people snatched up food, clothing, and everything else with hardly a grumble about the cost.

As he made his way up the street with frustrating slowness, Recin noticed the enticingly sweet smell that leaked from the paper-wrapped bundle in his arms. There was no doubt in his mind that redberry loaves were the best thing that his mother and Aunt Getin made in the huge stone ovens of their bakery. The smell of the loaves he was carrying was almost enough to tempt him into sneaking some bread for himself, and every minute of delay made the temptation stronger.

But with the price that food was bringing in the market, it would have made for a very expensive feast. Since Tagard had taken the villages along the river, the city had depended on food imported from the islands or countries to the south. Everything cost ten times more than it had only months before. Money had always been short in Recin's home, now it was especially dear—dearer even than the sweet taste of redberries. Recin sighed and kept his appetite in check.

He craned his neck, trying to see over the crowds of tall Viashino. At last he reached the spot where his mother had set up her simple stall and saw her selling a large stack of rolls to a well-dressed Viashino. It appeared that Recin had arrived just in time, as the sale left the booth totally empty of wares.

His mother took the offered gold and slipped it into the cash box. As she straightened, she spotted Recin coming down the street and raised her hand in welcome. "How did the last batch turn out?" she called.

"Here they are," he said as he put the bundle down on the rough wooden plank at the front of his mother's stall.

She picked up one of the loaves and pursed her lips. "A little overdone," she said. "But not bad. Did Getin do these?"

Recin shook his head. "I did most of them."

His mother nodded. "We'll make a baker out of you yet."

"Uh, great," said Recin. He tried to smile, but his effort only brought a flash of blue to his mother's changeable gold eyes.

"I've never seen the Garan yet that aspired to baking," she said, "but it's a good job. A lot better than many I could name." She pushed a mass of brown curls away from her face and looked down the street. "Why don't you get back to the house? As soon as I sell these loaves, I'll join you."

Recin frowned. "There's nothing left to bake. I was hoping to go see Heasos."

Now his mother's eyes lost their usual warm golden color and shifted to a flat gray. "With the attack coming, won't Heasos be on the wall?"

"Well, probably," admitted Recin.

"You don't need to go up there tonight. It's dangerous, and you'll only be in the way." His mother turned to sell a pair of loaves to a human man whose singed leather apron marked him as a smith.

"Bey Tagard's army is still a long way off," Recin protested when she finished her business. "Everyone says they won't be here until tomorrow."

His mother turned quickly back to him. "*Bey* Tagard? Where did you hear that name? Who said this man from the hills was bey?"

"I don't know," Recin said with a shrug. "It's just what everyone is calling him."

"Well, Lisolo is the only bey in this valley," she said, "and I don't want you saying otherwise."

His mother's face might have looked emotionless,

and her voice seemed calm, but Recin had no trouble reading the anger in her shifting eyes. Bey Lisolo had accepted her family into the city at a time when all Garan were looked on as enemies. She would brook no comment that might be taken as an insult to the Viashino leader.

"I didn't mean anything by it," said Recin. "I just want to visit Heasos."

His mother reached behind her head and ran her fingers through the mass of her curly brown hair. "After this Tagard is sent running, I hope things will get back to normal."

"Sure they will."

Like almost every citizen of Berimish, Recin had no doubt that Tagard's attack on the city was destined to fail. Berimish was defended by thick stone walls three times the height of a human—four times as tall as most Garan. Even in times of peace those walls were topped by better than a thousand city guards. Now that number had been almost doubled by soldiers who had fled from the captured villages of the valley.

There was no way the ragged army could defeat that number of armed Viashino firing from defended positions. Besides, Berimish was *the* city. All the rest of the valley was just small villages and pitiful little hovels like the human holds. Even before the war had forced refugees in from the countryside, almost as many people had lived within the protection of Berimish's walls as lived in all the rest of the valley. That Tagard's army had conquered the rest of Tamingazin was quite a surprise. But the idea that his little collection of hill humans, Garan elves, and a few traitorous Viashino could capture Berimish . . . it was unthinkable.

"If I go see Heasos, I can take some bread to the soldiers," Recin suggested. It was a gamble that had worked in the past. His mother was prone to giving any leftover bread to the city guards, and such an offer had often gotten him excused from chores around the bakery.

This time, she was not so easily convinced. "It's too dangerous," she said with a quick shake of her head. "Besides, we have to get ready for tomorrow. We need to bake at least two more batches to keep up with the demand. Getin will need help getting the supplies, and I—"

"It'll only be for a minute," Recin said. He picked up two loaves of the bread. "With the way everyone has been hoarding food, I bet no one else has brought anything to them."

His mother's eyes swirled between gray and green. "I don't know . . . "

"And I'll stop by the brew house on the way home and pick up a pot of yeast. That'll make things easier for Getin."

"I suppose a few minutes wouldn't hurt." Recin started to dart off, but his mother caught him by the arm. "Just be sure that the bread makes it to the soldiers."

Recin looked at the sweet redberry loaves and sighed. "I won't eat a bite." He started to leave, but his mother didn't loosen her grip.

"And make sure that the only thing you get at the brew house is yeast."

He nodded reluctantly. Finally his mother's fingers loosed their grip and Recin dashed off into the milling crowd.

By the time he reached the wall, the sun had set. He stared at the notched poles leading up to the wall and wished for the hundredth time that Viashino looked more favorably on stairs. But Viashino feet were better suited for ropes or poles. The only place that stairs

were to be found in Berimish was in the human section
of town. Recin resigned himself to the climb and did
his best without crushing or dropping the bread.

He expected the wooden ledge that ran along the
inside of the wall to be crowded with troops, but it was
all but deserted. He had to walk most of the length of
one side before he found where Heasos was stationed.
The young Viashino saw Recin approaching and
favored him with the sharp lift of the chin that passed
for a greeting among his people.

"What are you doing up here tonight, baker?" called
Heasos. "Don't you have ovens to clean?"

Recin pretended to be wounded by his friend's jibes,
but he knew Heasos was only joking. The young
Viashino had lived in his small home next to the bakery ever since he left his hatchling group, and he and
Recin had been trading friendly barbs for years.

"They say an army's only as good as its cook," Recin
said as he tossed one of the loaves to Heasos.

The Viashino caught it nimbly in a clawed hand and
lowered his muzzle to sniff at the loaf. "Looks like we
must be a pretty good army," he said. He opened his
long mouth and snapped off a third of the bread in one
bite. A lump slid down his narrow throat. "Give my
thanks to your mother."

Recin nodded. "So why are you all gathered down at
this corner?" he asked. "Aren't you supposed to be
watching the east wall?"

"Yeah, but there's nothing to look at over there,"
said Heasos.

Recin squinted into the growing darkness. "What is
there to look at over here?"

The Viashino pointed a claw to the northeast.
"Riders. Five of them."

He moved back from the side and Recin took his
place. But no matter how long the young Garan stared

out into the night, he could see nothing. "You sure they're out there?"

Heasos made a hiss of disgust. "I thought Garan elves were supposed to have good eyes." He reached into the pouch that hung at his side and pulled out a spyglass. "Here. Try this."

The spyglass was not the best quality, but through the ground waterglass lens Recin at last made out a line of dim figures.

They were seated on riding beasts in the fields outside the city, near an empty farmhouse whose owner had chosen to wait out the war inside Berimish's walls. As far as Recin could tell, the riders were motionless.

"Are they from Tagard's army?" he asked.

"Illis thinks one of them is Tagard himself."

Recin examined the distant forms as best as he could, but he could see nothing more than shapes in the darkness. If the Viashino could really make out faces at this distance, then their eyesight was truly amazing. After a few more minutes, Recin gave up and handed the glass back to Heasos.

"So, if it is Tagard," he said, "then isn't he taking a big risk, putting himself out here in front of his army?"

Heasos started to answer, but another Viashino approached. From his size, almost two feet taller than Heasos, and the heavy scales along his throat, Recin could tell the newcomer was an older male. He looked nearly ready to retire to the breeding house.

"Who is this?" asked the Viashino. "What's he doing on the wall?"

"It's only Recin," said Heasos. "His family lives in the city."

The older Viashino held his head low, a sure sign of irritation. "I don't like it," he said. "A Garan on the walls on this night. How do we know he's not working with the ones out there?"

Recin felt a stirring of anger. There were enough humans in the city that the Viashino majority accepted them with little thought, but the population of Garan in Berimish began and ended with his family. There were many who looked on them with suspicion. He fought down his anger and smiled. "I brought bread," he said, trying to defuse the Viashino's fears. He held out the remaining loaf.

The old Viashino continued to stare at Recin for a moment. Then he snatched the loaf of bread with long claws and walked slowly away down the wall.

"Sorry," Heasos said as the other Viashino moved away. "There's a lot of raw nerves up here tonight."

"You expecting a fight tomorrow?" Recin asked.

Heasos shook his head. "I doubt it. They'd never get up these walls. I expect they'll go to surround us, then try and starve us out."

"It won't work," Recin said. "The city can get all the food and water it needs for months right out of the river, and they can't lay siege to the river."

"I know it won't work," said Heasos. "But they don't know it. I expect they'll be a month or two finding out."

There was a sudden commotion among a knot of Viashino a dozen yards to their right. Heasos stretched out his long neck and cocked his head to listen, then he snatched the spyglass from his pouch and trained it back on the dark fields.

"What is it now?" asked Recin.

"More people coming," mumbled the Viashino, with the spyglass still pressed to one eye. He moved the glass back and forth over the field, then let out a long hiss.

"Do you see something?"

"I see something all right. I see the whole of Tagard's army gathering out there in the darkness." As he finished speaking, the Little Moon rose in the west and began its swift transit of the sky. But it was scarcely more than a brilliant spark in the black of night, and its light was too faint to do anything to illuminate the fields outside the city.

Recin took the spyglass from his friend. With its help he could see movement in the distance, but little else. He wished that the Great Moon would rise and light up the night, but that was still hours away. "What are they doing moving around at night?" Recin asked.

"I don't know," said Heasos. "Maybe I was wrong, maybe they're going to have a go at the walls after all."

"Tonight?"

"Who knows?" Heasos reached behind his back and pulled out his long, narrow crossbow. "Maybe you better get down," he said. "It looks like something is going to happen."

Recin was still peering at the gathering forces. "I'd like to stay," he said. "If they really start to—" There was a distant flash of light. He moved the spyglass slightly and saw a ball of blue-white fire rising from the dark ground. For a moment, he could clearly see a figure dressed in pale robes and another figure in brightly polished armor. Then the ball of light rose higher in the air and began to move slowly toward the city.

"Magic!" he cried.

"What?"

Recin shoved the spyglass into the Viashino's hand. "It's a magical attack. Something's on its way right now."

Heasos turned and shouted to the nearby group of Viashino. "Illis! A magic attack coming!"

The other Viashino stopped talking and looked their way. A middle-aged male detached himself from the group and walked down the planking in their direction. "Can't be no magic," he said. "Tagard's got no wizards."

Recin looked out at the fields. The ball of pale light was now close enough to be seen without the spyglass. "If there's no magic, then what's that?" He pointed over the wall at the approaching globe of blue-white fire.

The Viashino glanced into the field, and his yellow eyes bulged in their sockets. He threw back his head and let go a booming trill of alarm. All up and down the wall, heads turned. In moments, others had seen the slowly approaching ball of fire. Hundreds of Viashino stood watching helplessly as the sphere of light drew near.

Recin stood with them, frozen by the sight of the approaching sphere. It took several seconds for him to realize that the ball was not just getting closer, it was growing larger.

When he had first seen it rising from the dark field, the sphere had been no bigger than a melon. Now it was greater than a barrel, and it was swelling ever faster. When it was two hundred strides away, it was the size of a wagon. When it was one hundred strides away, it was larger than a building. The brightness was also increasing, growing to the point that just looking at the sphere was quickly becoming painful. Even in the streets below, people stopped in their tracks and faces turned up toward the strange glow. Still the sphere grew closer and larger, blotting out the night, filling the sky.

Crossbows thrummed as several of the Viashino let bolts fly, but their shots only vanished into the glow. Others leaped from the wall and ran crying into the night. The sphere, now almost as big as the city itself, reached the wall and swallowed it like the tide moving over a castle of sand.

For a moment, it seemed that every throat in the city joined in a scream of terror. Recin squeezed his eyes shut and threw his hands up to protect himself. The light was everywhere, burning so brightly that even through his closed eyelids it seared. Heat washed over him, and he could smell the awful odor of his own hair scorching.

Then the light was gone, and the night air was cool again.

Recin opened his eyes. At first he saw nothing but a throbbing red mist. It took him a moment to realize that he was no longer standing and another to recognize the rough boards of the ledge under his hands. He felt around, found the edge of the wall, and slowly got to his feet. Being careful not to step off the ledge, Recin leaned against the reassuringly solid stone of the wall. Gradually, his eyes recovered and shapes swam out of the red fog. Heasos lay sprawled across the ledge on his left, more Viashino were tumbled in a heap on his right. None of them moved.

In the streets of the city below, Viashino lay fallen at every angle. From his high vantage point, Recin saw a single human go staggering down the street. Except for that one lonely figure, the whole city lay still and quiet. Recin bent down beside Heasos and put his hand on his friend's finely scaled neck. He could feel no pulse, and for a moment he was cold with fear, but then he saw that the Viashino's chest was still rising and falling with his breath. Heasos was alive.

Recin stood and looked at all the other fallen Viashino. If Heasos was alive, then the rest of them were probably living, as well. The ball of light had put them to sleep, but it hadn't killed them. At least, he hoped so. But before he worried about everyone else in the city, he had to make sure his mother and aunt had survived the attack.

He started for one of the climbing poles, but before he had taken two steps, a sound from outside the city drew his attention. It was a strange sound, both rumbling and shuffling—like a herd of riding beasts moving at a slow walk. Recin leaned over the stone wall and peered into the darkness. What he saw there made his throat tighten in sudden fear.

Troops were moving outside the city. Hundreds—thousands—of humans were marching through the fields, close enough that Recin could have thrown a loaf of bread into the midst of them. They marched along the perimeter of Berimish without even a glance at the battlements, moving with the confidence of an army on parade in the cold light of the Great Moon.

It wasn't until that moment that Recin realized the Great Moon was even in the sky. When he had looked out at the approaching fireball, the moon had not yet risen. Now it was halfway to its zenith. Recin doubted that Tagard's wizard had the strength to move the moon. Though it seemed only moments had passed since he first saw the ball of light approaching the city, it had to have been hours. So the magical ball must have put Recin to sleep while the Little Moon finished its flight across the heavens and the Great Moon rose.

The thought that he had been put to sleep for hours was frightening enough, but the thought that in those hours no one had awakened and rallied the defense of the city was terrifying. It suddenly struck Recin that the enemy soldiers were marching to the south, toward the largest gate in the walls. If there was no one there to protect the gates . . .

Recin raced back to the sleeping Heasos. As fast as he could, he loosed the Viashino's bolt sling and snatched up his heavy crossbow. Then he ran along the guard platform, his feet clapping against the wood and making loose boards bounce as he tried to beat Tagard's army to the gate.

When he was still a hundred strides away, Recin

heard the squeal of the gate ropes slipping around their pulleys, and the rasp of the iron outer gate sliding up into the wall. He slowed to a walk, fitting a bolt into place with trembling fingers. A ladder had been thrown up against the wall beside the gate, and Recin could see that the outer doors had been fully raised. Two dimly seen figures worked in the shadows at the base of the wall. In another few seconds, the inner doors would open, and Tagard's army would flood into Berimish unopposed.

Recin moved slowly to the edge of the elevated walk and raised his weapon. He had fired one of the complex Viashino crossbows only once before, back when Heasos had been first training to be in the guard. Now, frightened and working only by the light of the Great Moon, Recin struggled to turn and set the bands of tough, stretchy abex hide that gave the bow its power. He lifted the weapon in his arms and centered the thin blade of the sight of one of the figures below. His finger tightened on the bone trigger.

A fist struck the side of Recin's head with such force that for a moment he thought someone had turned a bow on him. The weapon fell from his numb hands. Its deadly bolt snapped into the hard wood at his feet. He staggered back, ears ringing. He had not even managed to turn and see his attacker when a second blow rang against the back of his skull. Recin tripped, stumbled, and fell from the guard platform.

He landed flat on his back on the paving stones. All the air was driven from his lungs in a painful burst. A shock of pain rolled around his battered head.

Recin was still lying on the ground, fighting to draw in air and hold down rising bile, when the inner doors opened and Tagard's forces stepped into Berimish.

He watched as a handful of men ran quickly through the doors and moved out in all directions. Close behind them came a larger group, headed by a man with tight blond curls over a thin, sharply defined face. Recin tried to get up, but a wave of nausea and dizziness swept over him, and he fell to his hands and knees.

"Looks like this one is awake," said the man.

"Only the Viashino will be held through the night," said an older man with a robe as gray as his beard. "Most of the humans are free by now."

Recin managed to draw a painful breath. The world stopped spinning quite so fast, and he made another attempt to get to his feet. He was frozen between the desire to run and the need to stand up to the invaders who had come into the city under cover of both night and magic. He wished he still had Heasos's bow, but it was out of reach up on the guard platform. Not that it had done him a lot of good even when it was in his hands.

A girl stepped out from behind the blond man. She was tall, as tall as Recin or taller, and Recin did not doubt for a moment that the man at the head of the army was her father. She wore gleaming amulets of polished stone and metal, which, together with her strange clothing, gave her an exotic appearance quite different from that of the human girls Recin had known. Her hair was a great mass of curls and ringlets so pale they were almost white. Despite everything that had happened, his first thought was that this girl was painfully beautiful.

"You're a Garan elf," she said.

"Yes," Recin croaked. He added a nod of his head, which only brought back his dizziness.

"I thought there were no Garan in the city."

Recin started to reply, but before he could there was a sudden streak of movement from above and a figure dressed all in loose black clothing landed almost silently on the ground at his side. A hand seized Recin's upper arm in a painfully strong grip.

"This one was about to put a bolt through you," said the dark figure, his voice muffled by the hood he wore over his head.

The blond man stood beside his daughter and fixed Recin with a stare that was more intense than any he had ever experienced.

"I don't think this boy will be hurting anyone now," he said.

The dark figure reached up and pulled the hood from his head, revealing curling brown hair and small features. "We should make sure of that," he said flatly.

Recin looked at the figure in black and felt a shock almost as great as his fall. It was a Garan, the first that he had seen outside his own family. "You're . . ." he started. Then he shook his head and looked back at the blond man. "You're not welcome here. I'm sorry, but you're not wanted."

Laughter ran through the front line of soldiers. "We're used to that," said one of them.

"We should kill this one," said the Garan. The flatness of his voice made his words all the more chilling. "Or at least see that he doesn't get in our way."

The blond man shook his head. "No, Rael, let him go. I think it's a good thing this one showed up when he did." He turned his attention back to Recin. "Do you know where the palace is?"

"Palace?" said Recin.

"The bey's home. The place where the city is governed."

Recin wanted to say no, but under the blond man's stare, he nodded. "I know. It's called the Splendent Hall."

"Good. Then you can show us." The blond man put

a hand on Recin's shoulder, his grip much more gentle than that of the Garan. "What's your name, boy?"

"Recin."

"Well, Recin, I'm Tagard. I think you've probably heard of me."

Recin nodded.

Tagard smiled and the severe features of his face were at once transformed into something infinitely warmer. "Recin, we intend to march to this Splendent Hall tonight. Right now. We want to get this thing over with once and for all. You can show us the way, or we'll find it for ourselves. But if we have to find it for ourselves, it could be a lot more trouble for everyone. Understand?"

"I can't show . . . "

Another figure stepped from the group of soldiers. This time it was a woman with dark, severe features and a jacket of heavy gray and black armor. "If you don't tell us, we'll just have to ask someone else," said the dark woman. "And if they don't tell us, we may just have to kill them. And burn their homes. And maybe a few other homes besides."

"Karelon," said the blond man softly.

"We need to know," the woman turned to him. "If the Viashino wake up before we're in position, it'll cost more than a few lives, and not all of them might be Viashino. Burning a few scaleheads now would be better than that."

Recin hesitated for a moment. He didn't want to be a traitor, but he couldn't see any way that his refusing to show the way would help Berimish or Bey Lisolo. "I'll show you where to find the bey," he said. "Follow me."

He turned and started along the street toward the Splendent Hall, ancient home of the Viashino bey. He had no idea if he was causing the death of his city, or if his actions were preventing even more damage. Too many things had happened too quickly. He no longer knew what to think. He simply walked, passing through street after street where Viashino lay insensible on the ground while Tagard and his army followed close behind.

The whole procession was amazingly quiet. The soldiers did not laugh, or joke, or sing as did the Viashino soldiers Recin knew. The silence only increased his feeling that, despite the all too real ache he still felt from his fall, all this was not actually happening; in the morning he would awaken in his cot on the roof of the bakery and find the walls of the city intact and Bey Lisolo firmly in charge.

At last they reached the plaza surrounding the Splendent Hall.

In the moonlight, the white stone walls looked cool and serene. Recin had been there several times. His mother liked to send gifts of warm bread and desserts to the bey in remembrance of the charity he had shown in taking them into the city, and Recin was often charged with delivering those gifts.

Unlike most buildings in Berimish, the entrance to the Splendent Hall was not open. Tall doors of dark wood strapped with iron guarded the entrance to the interior. Still worrying about his own guilt, Recin grasped the handles of the doors and pulled. The heavy doors didn't so much as rattle.

Recin felt a surge of relief. "It's barred. I can't get in."

"Don't worry," said Tagard. "We'll get inside."

He signaled to a woman trooper and she moved forward. "Hinges on the inside." She ran a hand over the door. "Brasswood. This will take a while."

"Go as fast as you can," said Tagard. He turned to the pale-haired girl. "Take a maniple and move around the building. There have to be—"

Before Tagard could finish his sentence, there was a solid thump from the other side of the doors. With a rumbling squeal, the doors split and opened on darkness.

"Get back!" shouted Tagard. "They're awake!"

Recin stood frozen as the hands of all the humans went to their weapons.

There was movement in the shadowed gap of the open doors. Then a floppy pink hat and a narrow, bearded face appeared. The strange human scanned the faces outside the door and settled on the tall man. "Ah," he said. "You must be Tagard."

"And who are you?"

The man stepped out of the doorway and revealed a tunic even more gaudy than his headwear. Even in the dim light, the stripes of color were almost blinding. "I'm Ursal Daleel," he said. "Ambassador from Suderbod. I suppose you're looking for Bey Lisolo?"

Tagard nodded. "Is he inside?"

"Yes," said Daleel, "though he's asleep at the moment."

"Can you lead us to him?"

"Of course." The Suder disappeared back into the darkness of the Splendent Hall and the humans streamed after him. Recin was bumped and pushed as he followed behind the leaders of the invading army. They walked past dozens of passageways and open rooms, but Daleel led them straight through the maze of confusing passages, through the outer courts, and down the corridor to the bey's audience hall.

It was a large, round chamber, with glass panels in the ceiling that let in the cold light of the Great Moon. Viashino, armed with crossbows still gripped in their hands, lay scattered across the stone floor. More Viashino lay in a heap near a raised dais that was strewn with cushions and surrounded by a padded rail.

On this raised platform, the Viashino Bey could rest against the railing, or more rarely, lie upon the cushions, as he listened to grievances and issued his rulings. Now the bey lay sprawled among the pillows with his clawed feet dangling over the edge of the dais and his long neck limp across the cushions.

"Here is the bey," said Daleel.

Recin felt a surge of emotions he could not even name. The bey was Berimish. Seeing him lying helpless before the humans seemed worse than anything else that had happened.

Tagard stepped past the others and walked across the still chamber to the side of the Viashino leader. Recin expected the human to draw a sword and slay his enemy. Instead, Tagard knelt at Lisolo's side and rested his hand on the smooth scales of his neck in a gesture that was surprisingly gentle.

Tagard's daughter moved to Recin's side. "This place is beautiful," she said.

Recin looked around the chamber at the carvings and hangings which decorated the walls. "It's the bey's home," he said.

"I don't mean just this room," said the girl. "I mean everything, the whole city. It's so different than I thought it would be."

"Thank you," mumbled Recin. "I guess."

King Tagard moved his hand to the ornate band around Lisolo's neck. He lifted the Viashino's head from the cushions, then slid the band free. He stepped onto the dais and stood looking down at them all.

"The struggle is over," he said.

His voice was not loud, but in this silent room in the center of a silent city, it carried to everyone that could hear. He lifted the band and held it high over his head.

"The valley is one," said Tagard. The soldiers of his army broke their silence with a roar that echoed through the city.

Recin closed his eyes and wondered how everything could be turned upside down so suddenly.

Interlude

FOUR-FINGERED HANDS

There are four fingers on each Viashino hand: two in the center and two "thumbs" on each side, each of which ends in a sharp claw. One might think, given eight digits, that they might do their counting by eights, but they—like all the races of this valley—count in tens.

Eight does show up here and there. There are eight measures in a grainweight. There are eight days in Kalas, their great celebration of the spring rains: Pres, Salas, Atas, Kwes, Cas, Lul, Shuss, and Liss. There are eight roads which run out from the plaza east of the Splendent Hall. It may be that these incidents of eight are a remainder from an earlier time, a lingering shadow from a time before the language and habits of all the races in Tamingazin became inseparably tangled.

Perhaps in the language of their temple they still count by eights—untainted by their five-fingered neighbors. But no human can speak the language of the Viashino temples. They do not try to keep humans from their sacred places. Knowing how important an understanding of these creatures could be to our mission here, I have stood in the back of the temples for hours on end, leaning against the prop rail and listening to their recitations. Still, I have not learned so much as a single word, or fathomed the meaning of their odd gestures. And on this one thing, they will give me no assistance.

That much, they have kept separate. And whether they count there by eights, or by eighty and eights, I do not know.

*—From a dispatch by Ursal Daleel, Ambassador to
the Valley of Tamingazin from the Court of Hemarch
Solin, Conqueror of Suderbod.*

CHAPTER
3

ALIGARIUS TIMNI WAS BORED. HE FOUND IT strange that after a lifetime spent in quiet contemplation within his bare room, or weeks studying in the grand library of the institute, that he should be bored among crowds of people in the heart of a city after only a few days. But he was.

"This is a marvel," said Tagard. He tapped his finger on the sheet of paper that lay spread across the table. "A true marvel. I've never seen anything like it."

Lisolo nodded to the man who had taken his city. "With this sanitation system, Berimish has much less disease than in the past."

Aligarius sighed to himself. Sewers. A meeting about sewers.

Since the night he had used magic to bring Tagard's army into Berimish, there had been nothing but meeting after meeting. Tagard met with the Viashino bey, Lisolo. Tagard met with Rael Gar and Karelon. He met with the clownish little ambassador from Suderbod, the squat hairy delegate from Skollten, towering representatives of the En'Jaga, and delegations of business owners from the city. He met morning, noon, and night. And at every one of these meetings, Aligarius was expected to be present, ready to offer his advice and the position of the institute.

The trouble was, Aligarius had no idea what the position of the institute might be. Or rather, he knew all too well. The truth was that the institute had no position. It was a far too diverse and disorganized place to ever speak with one voice. All the sorcerer offered was his own thoughts on the matter, and he was not sure that his thoughts were worth the air it took to speak them.

Aligarius was an expert on the institute's collection of artifacts. No one anywhere on the vast globe could best him at his knowledge of the Spheres of Le'Teng, or the Magewall Hub, or the Amulet of Kroog. On any of these, he could lead a discourse lasting hours. But no one sought his advice on these matters. Instead they asked about political alliances, and military affairs, and sewers, and a hundred other things of which he knew nothing. All he could do was nod and try not to look like an utter old fool.

He hated feeling foolish. Several times a day, he considered returning to the institute, where he could continue his studies and get the respect he deserved without suffering through meetings and inane questions. And he would have gone back to the institute but for three things: the food, the wine, and the beds.

He had eaten more in the last ten days than he had in the month before. He was slightly embarrassed by his gluttony, but the celebrations surrounding Tagard's victory seemed to all be followed by grand feasts, each more lavish than the one which came before. The food was just so much better than what he was used to at the institute. There were meats which he had never before tasted and spices of which he had never even heard. He was heartily glad that his robe was loose enough to hide the roll of flesh that was quickly developing around his formerly flat stomach.

Food alone was enough of a temptation, but the wines were another thing. There was no proscription against the drinking of wine at the institute, but the weak concoction that they made from fermented berries had never caught Aligarius's tastes. Now he discovered that there was a universe of drink in the world, made from every kind of berry or fruit that could be eaten, and from several that could not.

Meals at the institute were a regular part of the day, something that lay between study and sleep. But in Berimish, Aligarius found himself looking forward to each meal with an almost painful longing. It was not the discussions with the king or his advisors that the sorcerer looked forward to, it was the supper table.

And after a table loaded with heavy foods and heady wines, there was a real bed, padded with abex fur and covered in soft, woven sheets. When he thought about the hard wooden plank where he had slept back at the institute . . .

Aligarius suddenly realized that both Tagard and the Viashino leader were looking his way with an air of expectation. Evidently, he had been asked yet another question.

"Yes," he said quickly, hoping that this question, whatever it was, would be amenable to a yes or no answer. "I think we can be of some help in this matter."

Tagard smiled. "You see," he said cheerfully, "with the aid of the institute, we can make this system work even better."

Aligarius groaned inwardly. He was still not sure what he had agreed to, but he worried that he had now committed the institute to provide magical sewage disposal. Tagard clapped a hand on his shoulder.

"Are you feeling well, sorcerer?" asked the king.

"I am a bit tired," said Aligarius. "Perhaps it would be best if I could go and rest?"

"Of course," said Tagard. "I'm sorry if we have been asking too much from you."

Lisolo stepped forward, his muzzled face held high. "I can send a physician to your room if you are feeling poorly," he suggested. "I assure you he is quite adept at treating humans."

"No, no," said Aligarius. "I'm sure rest will be enough." He smiled at the man and the Viashino, stood up, and left the room as quickly as possible. His smile slipped away as soon as the door closed behind him.

He had decided. Food or no food, he was going back to the institute right away.

The hallways of the building the Viashino called the Splendent Hall were bustling with people of all races. Tagard had said that he was trying to build a government that united the whole valley, and to the surprise of almost everyone, he had done just that. In the corridors of the Splendent Hall, human military officers arranged supplies with Viashino officials. Human soldiers pitched their sleeping rolls on floors in the same rooms where Viashino troopers reclined against sleeping racks on the walls. No Garan seemed to be inside the city, but from what Aligarius understood, they were now guarding the borders of Tamingazin side by side with Viashino forces.

Aligarius had hardly taken a step toward his room when the ambassador from Suderbod appeared and fell in at his side. "Amazing, isn't it?" said the man. He was dressed in stripes of bold pomegranate and puce. Compared with the robe Aligarius was wearing, the man's clothing was garish, but the wizard also recognized that it was costly and well made. No matter how the ambassador might appear, he was a man of some means.

Aligarius cleared his throat. "What did you say?"

"I said it was amazing. Better than anyone would have believed. Quite the coup."

"Coup," mumbled Aligarius. The man was talking about more politics. Aligarius had already heard far too much on that subject. Now that he had made up his mind to leave, his thoughts were on getting home again. He hurried his steps in the hope that the ambassador would be left behind.

"A united Tamingazin," said the ambassador. "Quite a thought." He shook his head. "I can tell you we never expected this."

"No, I suppose not." Aligarius reached the door to the room where he had been staying and was about to go inside, but the ambassador slipped around and blocked his way.

"You must be quite tired of this place by now," said the small man. "Let me take you out of here."

"Out of here?" Aligarius was surprised to find the ambassador's thoughts running so close to his own. "Where would we go?"

"Out to see the city!" The man spun around, sweeping his arms up over his head in a gesture that took in all of Berimish. "True, this is not Grand Sudalen, but there are things in this city that you can scarcely imagine. Entertainment. Experiences. Food and drink that make palace fare seem like grass."

A rumble went through the sorcerer's stomach. Better food than he had already experienced? There would undoubtedly be an evening meal in the dining hall, or perhaps even another celebratory feast. But those things were hours away.

"Food?"

The ambassador's smile grew wide. "Certainly," he said. "Inns, bakeries, and food sellers abound in this city. Come out with me, and we will sample only the best. Why, I know of one inn where they prepare such delicious and exotic treats that . . ." He mimed taking a bite of food, and smacked his lips with exaggerated gusto. "No one who tastes their fare is ever the same again."

Aligarius released his grip on the door handle. "Will it take long? I wouldn't want to be gone if Tagard should need me."

"Need you for what? Magical help on getting rid of garbage?" The Suder leaned in close and spoke confidentially. "King Tagard has been placing far too many demands on your valuable time and putting the institute's great power to trivial use. He can do without you for one afternoon."

The words touched a chord in Aligarius. With all he had done, a few hours in the city wouldn't hurt. Besides, if he was leaving in the morning, this would be his only chance to see what the city was like outside the walls of the Splendent Hall.

"I'll come with you," he said decisively.

The ambassador smiled and led the way through the maze of corridors to the side of the hall. Aligarius blinked in the afternoon sunshine. It was the first time he had been outside of the bey's home since the night they had come into Berimish. He was surprised to see that the city appeared to be carrying out its business normally. Crowds of Viashino moved through the streets. The booths of merchants, both Viashino and human, lined the main thoroughfare.

As Aligarius and the Suderbod ambassador stepped away from the hall, many of the merchants turned toward them.

"Gold," cried one scarred, dark-skinned human,

holding up handfuls of rings and bracelets. "Precious gold, all the way from Acapiston!"

In another booth, a young Viashino waved a length of twisted, dark, tree root. "Urbak!" he called, his voice almost a scream. "A spice, a dye, a medicine, a powerful totem. Urbak!"

He continued to call and wave his dark piece of wood as the two men passed. Aligarius stared at the root curiously and fingered his beard. He was not familiar with any magical root called urbak. He thought about purchasing a bit so that the botanical magicians at the institute might examine it, but he suspected it was no more than some useless folk medicine.

They passed other stalls and were offered all sorts of trinkets, cloth, and craftwork. The sheer number and variety of items was baffling to Aligarius, and he found the shouting merchants and tight press of the crowds in the street more than a little disturbing. He was greatly relieved when the ambassador pushed aside a sheet of cloth and waved Aligarius through the door.

With one step, he left the hot, crowded, noisy street and entered a cool, shaded courtyard where casperjays sounded in the branches of sheltering trees. High, white walls blocked all view of the rest of the city. A smooth, stone path led from the humble entrance through which they had passed to a much grander doorway across the courtyard.

"What sort of place is this?" asked Aligarius. He had few conceptions of what an inn was like, but this place fit none of them.

"This is a special place," said the Suder. He moved past Aligarius and slapped his palm against a sheet of burnished bronze that hung beside the inner door.

Before the noise of the metal died, the door popped open and a Viashino of middle years emerged. He looked different than any of the other Viashino that the sorcerer had seen. He was extremely gaunt—so thin that the bones of his neck and shoulders pressed sharply against his scaly skin—and his scales were dotted with patches of pale green.

As soon as the strange Viashino spied the ambassador, his chin rose and he threw up his clawed hands in an expression of happiness. "Daleel!" He reached out one claw and tapped it lightly against the shoulder of the Suder. "I was hoping you would come today."

"Of course I came," the ambassador said. "Would I disappoint you?" He turned and gestured to Aligarius. "Do you have room for a new guest tonight?"

The Viashino tilted his head and looked at the sorcerer. "Who is this?"

"This," said the Suder, "is the most illustrious representative from the Institute of Arcane Study—the renowned conjurer, Aligarius Timni."

"The sorcerer," said the Viashino slowly. "You're the one who magicked the whole city."

Aligarius felt uneasy. He had not considered how the population of Berimish viewed him. Thousands of Viashino might well blame him for the capture of their city. He took a half-step back from the thin Viashino. But instead of attacking, the creature only looked at Aligarius with an expression the sorcerer could not make out.

"Well, Ohles," said the ambassador. "Are we coming in?"

The Viashino stepped back from the doorway. "Certainly. Come in. Come in."

The ambassador ushered Aligarius through an outer chamber hung with bright swatches of cloth. From there they went down a gentle slope into a large round room. There were no windows, and the only light came from bits of flaming wick drifting in plates of scented oil. There were several Viashino in the room, dining from bowls of all colors. The sorcerer was surprised to see that rather than leaning against a wall or table, as all the Viashino that he had known did at mealtime, these creatures rested on cushions strewn about the floor.

"Let's go over there," said the ambassador, indicating a empty portion of the room. "That way, we can talk in private."

Aligarius was about to say that he wanted to leave. This place was simply too odd, and it made him nervous. But then a smell reached his nose. At first it was the smell of meat smoking slowly over coals, then it was something more exotic—and far stronger. Aligarius realized that he was quite literally drooling at the aroma. Embarrassed, he quickly drew his sleeve across his lips and followed the ambassador to a seat in the round room.

They had scarcely left their feet when the thin Viashino appeared with a loaded platter.

"Ahh," said the ambassador. "This is one of the things I wanted you to try." He reached into a shallow bowl, drew out a slice of yellow fruit dripping a golden sauce, and handed it to Aligarius.

"My thanks, ambassador," said the sorcerer. He was a little disappointed. The Suder had promised exotic dishes, but this looked like nothing more than a slice of marshglobe.

"Daleel," said the smaller man. "Call me, Daleel."

Aligarius nodded. "Daleel." He put the fruit in his mouth.

With that one bite, Aligarius realized the things served at Tagard's table were no better than mud. And the food he had eaten all his life was not fit for worms. This was real food. This was the only food worth eating.

"Do you like it?" asked the thin Viashino.

"Oh, yes," said Aligarius. He reached into the bowl and plucked out another bit of the fruit. If anything, it was better than the first. "I've never had anything like it before," he said around the mouthful of food.

The ambassador—Daleel—rocked back and forth with laughter. "Of course not. You may think that you know magic up in your tower, but the real magic of the kitchen belongs only to Ohles."

The Viashino blinked his eyes in embarrassment. "You flatter me." He set the bowl down on the table and stepped away.

Aligarius reached out and took another piece of the yellow fruit. Then another. He ate greedily, crunching bit after bit between his teeth and savoring the cool feeling of the juice as it flowed down his throat. When he reached into the bowl and found it empty, the disappointment was almost a physical pain.

"Still hungry?" asked Daleel. "Well, don't worry. This is only the first course of many."

"Good," said Aligarius. "That's good." If anything, he felt hungrier than he had before he started.

The Suder leaned back on a stack of pillows and linked his fingers behind his head. "The food here *is* quite wonderful," he said. "It's a shame it's so expensive."

"Expensive?" It had not occurred to Aligarius that he might have to pay for the meal. He felt terribly embarrassed that such an obvious point had escaped his attention.

"Oh, yes." The Suder shook his head. "What you've had already could cost more than many earn in a handful of days."

Daleel drew a rough gold coin from the purse at his belt and turned it over in the light of the lamps. "Of course, I'm sure that Tagard is compensating you well for your great efforts on his behalf."

"Well, actually . . ." Aligarius looked down at the food and felt his stomach twist with desire. "Actually, I've not been paid."

"Not paid!" The Suder ambassador rocked back on his cushions and threw his hands into the air. "Tagard has the most powerful, most knowledgeable sorcerer in the world at his side, and he provides no compensation?"

"What I did here was done for justice," said Aligarius. Though he tried not to show it, he was warmed by the Suder's praise.

Daleel smiled. "Of course, of course." He waved a hand over the table. "In any case, you don't have to worry about the cost of anything this evening. Tonight, you're my guest. Eat all that you please."

"My thanks."

The ambassador waved a dismissive hand. "It's nothing." He leaned in closely and spoke in a whisper. "And do keep in mind that there are some who know that talent such as yours deserves a reward." Before Aligarius could reply, the man leaned back again and smiled. "I believe our friend Ohles is returning. Let's see what he has for us now."

The Viashino brought a plate laden with slivers of roast attalo. The pink meat was brushed with the same golden sauce that had accented the fruit. Daleel chattered away while the meat dish was served, but if he said anything important, Aligarius didn't hear it. He was far too intent on the food.

After the meat, there were balls of fried bread stuffed with chunks of fish and vegetables. Like everything else, they were glorious. Aligarius managed to stuff down only a few before his stomach was quite full, but he kept on eating through that course and two more. Only when he was so painfully stuffed that he felt he might literally die did the craving for the food begin to lessen.

"Had enough?" asked Daleel.

The sorcerer looked down at the remaining food on the plate. Even as full as he was, he felt an urge to stuff in just one more bite, but his stomach felt overwhelmed at the thought.

"Yes," he said. "No more."

The Suder stood and stretched. "Well, friend, now perhaps we should return to the bey's home. It is late, and I'm sure King Tagard will be worried if you should be found missing."

"Late?" Aligarius looked around the room, but the flickering glow of the oil lamps gave no clue as to the time. "Surely it can be no later than sunset."

"It is far into the evening," said Daleel. He reached down and offered a hand to the older man. "We are still under the curfew which Tagard announced on the day of the city's capture. If we hope to get back without explaining ourselves to a patrol of soldiers, we should leave now."

Aligarius nodded and took Daleel's hand and let the man help him to his feet. Had he really lain in this room for hours, eating all the time? It seemed only moments had passed. His stomach was so full that he swayed as he walked slowly up the ramp to the front of the strange inn. The two men stopped near the door, and the ambassador handed a sizable stack of coins to the skinny Viashino, Ohles.

"Did you enjoy your meal?" the Viashino asked, staring at Aligarius with wide, dark eyes. Like his spotted skin, his eyes were a different color than any other Viashino the sorcerer had seen.

"It was wonderful. I've never had anything like it."

Ohles made a soft sighing sound. "Of course. Of course." He gave an upward bob of his head and walked back down the ramp into the round room.

Aligarius had a sudden thought. All through the

evening, while he had eaten dish after dish, he could not recall seeing the ambassador put one bite of anything in his own mouth. He looked at the small man, then over his shoulder at the other customers, who still lingered on the soft cushions, slowly eating the bits of fruit and meat. Despite the painful fullness in his gut, he felt a sudden surge of desire for more of the food and its delicate golden sauce.

"Are you sure you've had enough?" said Daleel.

"Yes." The sorcerer forced the hunger from his mind and patted his full belly. "Enough for a week," he said.

The Suder laughed. "It's a strange thing, but no matter how much of Ohles's food you eat, you're always hungry again soon."

He pushed open the door, and Aligarius followed him into darkness.

CHAPTER
4

"HUNDREDS OF PEOPLE HAVE DIED IN YOUR
service. For what? We have taken the whole valley,
and now you are trying to give it away!" Karelon
leaned over the polished stone table with her black hair
spilling across her shoulders and her face flushed with
consternation.

Tagard stirred in his chair. "That's not what I'm
saying."

The lines of dismay only deepened on Karelon's face.
She slapped her palms against the table, then she
turned and stomped out the door, leaving Tagard
frowning at her back.

Talli watched the war leader leave with a stab of
despair. Ever since they had come to Berimish, the warm
sparks between her father and Karelon had been drown-
ing under a flood of disagreement. The months it had
taken to bring them close were coming undone in days.
And it wasn't only Tagard's personal relationships that
were fraying. The alliance that had seen them through
the years of war was growing weaker at every seam.

Talli glanced across the room. Her eyes met those of
Rael Gar as he sat on a long bench next to the wizard,
Aligarius. As usual, the Garan's face was expressionless, but there were uncounted emotions in the play of
colors in his eyes.

Tagard turned and looked from one of them to the
other. "Surely you can see it must be done?" he said.

Rael Gar shook his head. "No. That you might not
want to kill him . . . yet. That much I can see. But I
can't see returning him to any position of power."

"Sorcerer," said Tagard, "what do you think?"

Aligarius was slow to respond. Talli had noticed that
he seemed distracted all morning. Finally he looked at
Tagard and shook his head. "I don't know," he said.
"I'm not sure that this is something that the institute
should be involved with."

Tagard frowned. "But wasn't the institute's reason
for being involved in this conflict in the first place to
see that Tamingazin was shared by all its people?"

Again, Aligarius sat in silence for several seconds
before finally answering. "I don't know."

"You don't know," Tagard said. There was an edge
of exasperation in his voice. He turned to Talli. "Well,
let's hear it. What are your thoughts?"

"I . . ." Talli hesitated, then she stood and shook her
head. "I'm sorry, Father, but Rael Gar and Karelon are
right. We fought this war to win. Why give back everything that we've gained?"

"I'm giving away nothing," Tagard said. He balled
his fist and struck it hard against the table at his back.
"Lisolo knows this city, and the people here know him.
If we make him an equal member of the council, it will
benefit us all."

"If you make him a member of the council, a hundred men will leave us," said Talli. "Maybe more. And
if Karelon leaves . . . "

"Karelon will not leave," Tagard replied angrily.

Talli faced him squarely. "If Karelon leaves, over half your men go with her."

Tagard held her gaze for a moment, then turned away. "I've told you from the beginning what I meant to do. This fight was for all the people of the valley. I said it a thousand times. Did none of you bother to listen?"

"No one thought you meant the Viashino would be included in the council," said Talli.

Rael Gar shifted in his chair. "For ages, we've lived in the harsh lands of the plateaus and seen the game we lived on grow more sparse with each passing year," said the Garan. "While we suffered, the Viashino enjoyed the fruits of the valley floor and the rich trade of Berimish." He fingered the dark wood of his chair and looked around at the room. "It is only right that we should have our turn."

"Our turn?" said Tagard. "Our turn at acting as badly as they did?"

The Garan nodded. "If that is how you must think of it. The Viashino, and the traitors who have lived with them, have to pay for what they've done."

"It's only fair, Father," Talli said.

Tagard squeezed his eyes closed and put his fists against his forehead. "It's not fair. It's never fair." He turned his back to both of them.

"Leave me," he said. "I need to think."

Rael Gar rose immediately and left the room without a backward glance. Aligarius got to his feet more slowly and followed the Garan out the door.

Talli bit her lower lip and looked at her father. Through the bitter war, even after her mother's death, she had not seen him in as much pain as he had suffered since their victory.

"Everyone knows that when you win a war, the loser

must bear the price," she said. "The Viashino lost. They're the enemy, Father."

The king turned to his daughter with a grim smile. "They were the enemy, Talli. The war is over."

"But . . . "

"Do you want to fight the war every day of your life?" He stepped quickly to her and put his hands on her shoulders. "I know that you want revenge for your mother's death," he said. "But I don't think hurting thousands of people is the kind of memorial that would have pleased her."

"We can't forget her," Talli said fiercely.

Tagard shook his head. "This isn't about forgetting. This is about doing what's right." He turned his head for a moment, then looked back at Talli. "Come over here and see this, maybe it will help you understand."

He led Talli to the table, where large sheets of paper nearly covered the gleaming stone surface. The top sheet showed broad swaths of pale shades. The names of Tamingazin and surrounding lands were inked on it with large expressive letters. Before Talli had a chance to do more than glance at this sheet, Tagard pushed it away to reveal a larger page. This one had been inked in dozens of colors, and fine lines twisted and snaked over the pages. Writing almost too small to read was crammed into all corners and ran in as many directions as the lines.

Talli tilted her head and studied the paper, but it was not like any scroll or harvest record she had ever seen. "What is this?" she asked.

"This is Berimish."

"How can this be Berimish?" asked Talli. "Berimish is a city, this is only paper." She looked at her father curiously, wondering if there was more wrong with him than just his inability to make the Viashino pay for their acts.

Tagard pointed to one of the dark lines on the paper. "This is a street—the street right outside, in fact." He moved his finger to a pale blue line that crossed the first. "And here's a passage that runs beneath it."

Talli's brow wrinkled as she looked at the lines. "How . . ."

"It's a map, Talli," said her father. "It's like a plan of battle. Except instead of troops and weapons, this map shows streets and buildings and sewers and drains. Here, look at this one." He flipped through the stack of paper and found the sheet that had been on top first. Talli noticed that in addition to the words, it was decorated with drawings of tiny mountains, trees, and ships at sea.

"This shows the relationship of Tamingazin and the surrounding lands," said Tagard. "See, here is Skollten to the north, and down here across the marsh is Suderbod."

"I think I see," Talli said after a moment. She turned the paper around on the table and tapped her finger near its right edge. "This is where you would find Farson Hold."

"Yes." Her father pulled out the larger, more complex sheet and returned it to the top of the stack. "And this map is the same, only it shows a smaller area with much greater detail."

Talli pointed to a large gray square. "If that line is the street outside, then this is the Splendent Hall, where we are now."

"Right."

She frowned. "But how can these other lines be tunnels? How can we see the things that are underground?"

"We can't," said Tagard. "But we can draw them."

"I . . ." Talli blinked and squinted at the lines. Battle plans were simple, usually nothing more than a few symbols drawn out on the ground, and even the map of Tamingazin was like a picture drawn by someone standing on a very high mountain. But this Viashino thing, with its thousands of snaking lines and dozens of colors, was enough to make her dizzy. "I'm not sure I understand."

Her father sighed. "Well, you already grasp it better than Rael Gar or Karelon. And I have to admit it took some time for Lisolo to explain it to me."

Knowing that she was better at something than the others cheered Talli. Lately, she had felt all but useless. While in the field, she had organized raids that gained them valuable supplies. She had scouted Viashino positions. She had led her own band of troops in battle and acquainted herself well with the sword. But now that the war had ended, all those jobs were gone, leaving Talli feeling about as worthless as an earring for a Viashino.

She studied her father's face. "What I don't understand is what this has to do with how you should treat the Viashino."

"How far is it from here to the western gates?" asked Tagard.

Talli shrugged. "I don't know."

"Lisolo does. What if there was a fire in the Splendent Hall? Where would we draw water to fight it?"

"I don't—"

"Or what if we should need to get troops from the south wall to the north? What is the fastest way?"

Talli shook her head. "I don't know."

"Lisolo knows all those things and a hundred more," said Tagard. "He can read these maps and he knows what to do." He left Talli's side and walked over to the window. Sunlight streamed through the open shutters and blazed in his pale hair. "This is no tiny hold in the mountains, or some farming village. This is a real city.

If we mean to keep it under control, we'll need the help of those who know its secrets."

"But we've already won the war," Talli said again. "No one can take the city from us."

Her father shook his head. "We defeated the city guard—and we only managed that with Aligarius's help. But there are scarcely two thousand people in all our army. This city holds more than forty thousand. What do you think will happen if all of them rise up?"

Beyond her father, Talli could see the rooftops of the city. "They would kill us."

Tagard nodded. "At any rate, they could make the city ungovernable."

Talli frowned. "But that's exactly what Rael Gar and Karelon have been saying, and what I've been saying— we have to put restrictions on the Viashino to make sure that they can't hurt us."

"No," Tagard said firmly. "Never in a thousand years could we manage to make ourselves safe through punishment. We have to make sure that they don't want to hurt us. And that's going to be altogether more difficult."

He went back to the table and gathered up some of the large maps. "I have a new job for you."

"What?"

"I want you to become my expert on this city." He handed over the bundle of paper. "Get yourself a local guide and visit every square foot of this town. Learn to read those maps. The next time I ask you anything about Berimish, I want you to be ready."

Talli felt a spark of hope. Perhaps she could gain new respect on the council and stop her father from this madness with the Viashino at the same time. "If I learn about the city, will you get rid of Lisolo?"

"You learn the city," said Tagard, "but Lisolo is still going on the council."

"You will lose a hundred men," said Talli. "Maybe more."

The king nodded. "Lisolo is worth more to me now than a hundred men."

"And if you lose Karelon's people, or the Garan?"

Tagard sighed. "I'll talk to them again. Now, find yourself a guide that knows their way around and learn this city."

Talli staggered out the door with the clumsy bundle of papers in her hands. She had a new assignment. She wasn't sure if her father really thought the job was important, or if he was just trying to get her out from underfoot. At least it might take her mind off Lisolo, Karelon, and the council.

Just as she was thinking of Karelon, Talli saw the war leader standing at the junction of two hallways. Talli looked at the woman and bit her lip. Surely it wasn't too late to mend the damage that had been done between the dark-haired woman and Tagard. Talli went over what she might say as she walked down the hall toward Karelon.

But as she drew close, she saw that the war leader was not alone. The ambassador from Suderbod was with her. Their voices echoed between the stone walls of the hallway, but Talli could not hear what the two were saying. Whatever it was, the Suder was waving his arms around, obviously excited.

Ever since they had gotten to Berimish, the ambassador had been asking for one audience after another. He was probably complaining about not getting enough time to talk with Tagard.

Talli backed away. There would be time to talk to Karelon later. Maybe by then she would have figured out what to say.

She reached the end of the hallway and paused to roll the maps into something a little easier to handle. A courtyard was visible ahead, and she watched for a moment as some of Karelon's people unloaded a wagonful of ripe marshglobe. The sticky sweet smell of the yellow fruit filled the air. Talli drew in a deep breath.

Getting out of the hall sounded like a wonderful idea—Talli had never cared much for spending a day indoors—but going outside would mean walking among crowds of Viashino. Not only that, but Tagard had insisted that she select a local guide. She wrinkled her nose at the idea.

Then she had a thought that brought a grin to her face. Her father had only said that the guide had to be local. He had not said it had to be a Viashino. She would get a human to guide her.

She knew that there were supposed to be hundreds of humans living in Berimish, but they did not seem to live near the Splendent Hall. At least, she had not seen them around. Someone had to know where they lived. She was about to approach the men who were unloading the wagon and see if they might know when the solution to her problem stepped into the courtyard.

The same young Garan who had led them to the bey on their first night in the city was crossing the courtyard with a bundle in his arms. He walked behind the wagon and entered the dim mouth of another hallway.

Moving as quickly as she could with her clumsy burden of maps, Talli trotted across the courtyard and followed him into the shadows. She almost lost the boy in the long, twisting halls, but he was even more burdened than Talli, and eventually she caught sight of his slim figure a few strides ahead.

"You there," Talli called. "Garan!"

The boy turned and looked at her with wide brown eyes. "Me?"

Talli stepped closer to him and nodded. "You're the one that showed us how to get here, aren't you?"

The young Garan swallowed nervously. "Yes, that was me." Seen up close he was thinner and taller than Talli remembered—quite a bit taller than most Garan, and within a hair of Talli's own height. He also looked older. His wide eyes were a deep liquid gold, not hard silver like Rael Gar. He still had the distinctive sharp-chinned face, pale skin, and wide eyes of a Garan, but in his colorful city clothing he looked exotic and, thought Talli, not unattractive.

"I thought it was you," she said. "How long have you lived in Berimish?"

"All my life," he replied. Talking to Talli obviously made him nervous. The threads of violet that worried the gold were not a color she had ever seen in Rael's eyes, but this boy was not good at disguising his emotions.

"Then you must know it well," said Talli.

The boy shrugged. "I guess. As well as anybody."

"Perfect," said Talli. "I need a guide to show me around the city. Will you do it?"

His eyes went even wider, and their color changed from gold to indigo. "I don't know," he said after a moment. "I mean, I'd like to, but my mother and aunt, they'll have work for me."

Talli frowned. She could probably force him to do what she wanted, but that didn't seem like the best way to start with someone when they might be together for days.

"I could pay you," she suggested at last.

He nodded. "If you would, they'd probably let me go. At least, I can ask."

"Then let's get started," said Talli. She raised the roll of maps. "From the look of these papers, we've got a lot of ground to cover."

The Garan looked down the hallway, then held up the clothbound bundle in his arms. "I should deliver these rolls first," he said. "My mother made them special."

"Who are they for?"

"The b—" He stopped suddenly and blushed a furious red. It was the first time Talli had ever seen a Garan show such emotion. "I mean, Lisolo."

Talli pressed her lips together. "My father is the only leader here now," she said firmly.

"I know," the boy replied. "It's just hard to change when you've been used to something for so long." He looked down at the bundle again. "Is it all right? Can I give Lisolo the rolls?"

"My father's men feed the Viashino," Talli said, her irritation growing. "He's not starving."

"I'm sure he's not," said the Garan. He was regaining both his composure and his normal coloring. His eyes regained their gold tone. "But Lisolo helped my family once, probably saved our lives. My mother likes to send him things."

Talli felt her anger begin to fade. "I guess I can understand that. Go ahead and deliver the rolls."

She stayed well back as the Garan went to the suite of rooms at the end of the hall and handed the rolls over to the men who were guarding Lisolo's chambers. The Viashino leader had been allowed to remain in his own rooms after Tagard took over— another of Tagard's ideas to which many objected. Talli did not even know what the Viashino's quarters looked like.

The Garan exchanged a few words with the men, then started back toward Talli. Behind him, Talli saw one of the soldiers peel back the cloth wrapping and pull out a roll. She wondered if any of the gift would actually make it to Lisolo.

"Our bakery is near the northeast corner of the city," the Garan said as they turned to leave the Splendent

Hall. "We'll have to go there first so I can tell my mother what I'm doing."

"Sounds like a plan," said Talli, "but before we leave, I think I should at least know your name." She smiled at him. "That way, when I get lost, I'll know who to blame."

The boy smiled back, another expression that she had never seen on a Garan face. "I'm Recin."

"Recin. And the second part of your name?"

He shook his head. "There's no second part. Just Recin."

"I never met a Garan without two names," said Talli. This city Garan was nothing like she expected. "Anyway, my name is Tallibeth Tarngold, but just Talli is fine."

"I know," said Recin. "Everyone knows who you are."

That thought made Talli feel a little uncomfortable. If she didn't like the Viashino, she was sure that at least some of them felt the same way about her. "Do you think everyone will recognize me when we're look-ing around?" she asked.

"You're kind of hard to miss," said Recin. "I mean, you don't look like someone from Berimish."

The idea of going outside the hall was starting to look even less attractive. "Do you know where I can get some local clothing?" Talli asked. "Maybe if I were dressed like the people around here, I wouldn't stand out so much."

"We can probably find you something." He looked her up and down. "We'll have to do something about your hair, though. I don't know anyone in Berimish with hair like that. Maybe we can get you a hat."

Talli put a hand to her unruly mane of flaxen curls. "Fine," she said. She peeled off some of her burden of maps and handed them to the boy. "Let's split these up. Otherwise, I'm going to fall on my nose."

They stepped out into the sunshine and went down the ramp that jutted from the hall into the broad main street of Berimish. On the other side of the road was a small lake bounded by walls of white stone. In its blue waters, a group of young Viashino splashed and swam while an older male looked on. Not far away from them, a young human girl stripped off her clothing and leaped into the waters.

"This is one of my favorite places," said Recin. "When it's really hot, I like to come down here and swim."

Talli eyed the water suspiciously. The lake was small, but the water looked deep. "I don't know how to swim," she said.

"Really?" Recin seemed surprised. "Maybe I can teach you."

This time it was Talli who blushed. Perhaps it was the custom in Berimish, but she was not about to take off her clothing in front of this Garan boy—much less the whole city.

They walked past the pool and down the street. At regular intervals they passed knots of human guards. Several of the guards nodded to Talli, and one old veteran favored her with a formal salute. Except for the soldiers, the streets were filled almost exclusively with Viashino. The crowds of Viashino made Talli keep one hand near her blade. There were more of the creatures in the streets of Berimish than she had ever faced on the battlefield. All her instincts screamed for her to defend herself. Only the soothing presence of the human guards helped her fight down her fears.

Most of the scaly people were no taller than Talli, though they passed an occasional ancient who towered far above the crowd. Talli soon learned that she had to stand well back of walking Viashino or risk an accidental slap from their long stiff tails. The Viashino they passed either looked away, or lowered their long necks as they spotted Talli. Their yellow eyes would not meet her gaze.

"Do they hate us?" she whispered to Recin. "Do they hate me?"

"I think they did at first," he replied. "I know I did."

Talli looked at him in surprise. "And now?"

Recin shrugged. "Before you took the city, they said that you would just loot and burn everything, and kill people, and make slaves of those that lived." He gestured at the busy street. "But it hasn't been that way. Things have gone on pretty well as they always have, and the soldiers aren't being nearly as rough as people expected."

Talli nodded. Looking at all the streets filled with Viashino, keeping them happy didn't seem like such a bad idea. Maybe her father wasn't completely wrong in what he wanted to do.

Many of the buildings along the wide central street were two or three stories tall. Talli watched in surprise as Viashino moved from floor to floor on dangling ropes or poles. The size of everything—windows, doorways, walls—was different than what she was used to. The shapes of the Viashino buildings made her feel slightly dizzy, like looking into a poorly made reflecting glass.

She called to Recin to stop and tried to find their position on the map. But they had already left the area on the piece of paper that showed the Splendent Hall, and without that landmark, she could make little sense of the maps.

"Do you know how to read these?" she asked Recin.

The Garan looked over her shoulder and shook his head. "I've seen maps before," he said, "but these are really complicated. Maybe when we get to the bakery we can spread them out and have a good look."

As they moved on along the street, Recin described many of the buildings they passed, pointing out places where precious metals were traded and where ships could be hired for the journey downriver to the sea. "There are customs houses over there," he said, pointing to a series of low buildings near the wall. And that big one is the dockmaster's house. When a ship comes in from Suderbod or the islands, they stop there to report what they've brought back."

Talli looked at the buildings, wondering if they were still staffed by Viashino or were now being run by her father's people. She saw no one go in or out as they passed. Perhaps no one was operating them at all.

Along a stretch of river just past the docks, Viashino stood shoulder to shoulder, casting lines into the roiling green waters of the Nish.

"What are they trying to catch?" asked Talli.

"Attalo," said Recin.

"A fish?"

"Something meaner," he said simply. "They get as big as a rowboat and have a head as big as a human. They've got a shell that'll stop a crossbow bolt, and they can bite an oar in half with one snap of their beak. Catching them is not the safest way to make a living. That pile on their left is made of the shells they peel from the attalo when they bring them on shore."

Talli watched the Viashino work as they went past, but she didn't see anyone catching anything. "Do people swim in the river, too?"

Recin laughed. "Have you ever seen an attalo feeding?"

"No."

"If you had," said the young Garan, "you wouldn't ask about swimming in the same waters with them."

The farther north they went in the city, the more humans they ran into. Their stalls appeared in the clutter at the side of the street. Human children ran laughing through the crowds. The buildings in this section of the city were less well tended than those near the hall and looked older. Wooden or metal doors gave way to sheets of cloth or leather. Tiled roofs gave way to tarred strips of bark.

As they passed a series of alleys, Talli caught a glimpse of a gray robe and silver hair among the crowds. She paused, trying to see over the heads around her.

"What's wrong?" asked Recin.

Talli shook her head. The figure she had seen was gone. Aligarius, if it was Aligarius, must have slipped into a doorway. "No," she said slowly. "I don't think so." She told herself that it was probably not the wizard anyway. Many people in Berimish wore robes, and surely some of them had to wear gray.

"Is this where all of the humans live?" asked Talli.

"Most of them," said Recin. "The northern market is just ahead, and that's where a lot of humans sell their goods."

Talli's eyes stung as they hurried past the door of a tannery, then a few strides later she stopped and watched in wonder as a glass blower formed delicate goblets from orange masses of molten glass. Glass was rare in Farson Hold, but in Berimish it was common enough that some buildings even had windows covered with it. A crowd of children stood nearby, watching the man shape his glowing wares. Talli and Recin moved to join them. The man molded and twisted the viscous liquid glass with movements that were both economical and as smooth as the substance he worked. To Talli, it seemed almost as magical as the sorcery of Aligarius.

Suddenly, a woman ran in front of Talli, grabbed a small boy by the arm, and drew him quickly to the side. Talli looked away from the glass blower and saw that the crowd around them had drawn back. Across the street, she saw women whispering together behind their hands, and a child pointed her way while tugging his father's arm. A passing Viashino turned away, but not before Talli saw a flash of teeth in its long, hard muzzle.

Her nervousness at being unguarded and alone in the city surged and her hands again itched to hold her sword. "I think we better move on," she said.

"Good idea," said Recin. "When we get to my home, we'll see about making you look more like a native."

Another block brought them into a wide square that was lined with stalls and stands of all sizes and crowded with people. Talli was about to ask another question when she suddenly stopped and drew a ragged breath.

At the center of the square stood a figure that made an adult Viashino look no bigger than a field lizard. It was more than twice as tall as any human, and it bartered with two women who stood no higher than its knee. Its scaly neck and head were the dirty gray of old metal, its teeth as long as Talli's hand. Though she had never seen such a creature before, she had heard enough tales to know what it was.

"En'Jaga," she said.

Recin nodded. "They come here to trade. Most of them live in the mountains to the west, or across the magewall in the Great Marsh. But there's one here every few days."

The En'Jaga turned their way, and it seemed to Talli that it was looking right at her. Unlike the golden yellow eyes of the Viashino, the En'Jaga's eyes were unbroken black. A heavy, forked blue tongue flicked out between its slotted lips and slid back inside. Talli shuddered.

Abruptly the En'Jaga turned and stomped away, parting the mixed crowd of humans and Viashino like a person fording a stream. It moved quickly, and in a few seconds its large gray head was gone behind a building.

"I've never seen one before," Talli said numbly. It was one thing to be told about the En'Jaga, it was another to actually see one of the beasts. It seemed incredible that the Viashino had actually defeated numerous attacks by the huge creatures.

"You'll see plenty if you stay here," said Recin.

He led the way through the busy market and down a smaller street. A final turn into a twisting alley brought them to the bakery where Recin's family made their living. It was a two-story structure, but quite narrow. Like most buildings in Berimish, its walls were plaster white, but unlike the Viashino homes, there was a staircase running along one side and the door was of a shape that Talli thought to be normal.

"We live on the upper level," Recin explained as he went to the door. "That way we get the breeze in the summer and the ovens help keep us warm in the cold season."

"It seems like a nice place," said Talli. Even from outside the smell of baking bread was enough to make her mouth water.

A Garan woman was bent over a pan of rolls when they entered. She was small and, even with a splash of flour in her dark brown hair, quite pretty. She had the even, fine features that were common among Garan women. With her large eyes and smooth pale skin, she reminded Talli of the dolls that some children back at Farson Hold played with. She looked too young to be Recin's mother, but then, Garan hid their years well.

The woman looked up at Recin and her eyes turned from metallic gold to a welcoming warm brown, then her gaze shifted to Talli and the brown became freezing gray. "What are you doing with this one?" she asked.

"Her name is Tallibeth," Recin said.

The woman gripped her rolling pin so tightly that the knuckles of her hand went white. "I know who she is. I'm asking what you've got to do with her." Her sharp-chinned Garan face was expressionless, more like a mask now than a doll, but she made no effort to hide the anger in her voice.

Talli was shocked by the strength of the woman's emotion—especially coming from a Garan. "I asked for his help," she said.

"No." The woman took one hand from the rolling pin to brush her hair from her face, leaving another streak of flour in it as she did. "You'll get no help here."

"Aunt Getin—" Recin started.

The woman stepped around the counter. "I know we're supposed to be nice to these murderers, but if they want to come into my home, they'd better bring a sword." Streaks of sour yellow entered her large eyes, and her lips were pressed into a hard white line.

"But Aunt Getin . . . "

"But nothing," said the woman. "What would your mother say if she saw you with this girl?"

"I'd say, what is all the racket about?" said a voice from the back room. A second Garan woman entered the room. Like Recin, she was taller and thinner than most of her race. The natural angles of a Garan face were softer in this woman, almost human, but her eyes were huge. Her golden eyes caught reflections of the room, throwing back colored images of Talli and Recin. Fine lines edged those eyes and gathered at the corners of the woman's mouth, and there were a few streaks of gray in her dark brown hair. Where Getin was only pretty, this woman was strikingly, inhumanly beautiful.

No one spoke as she crossed the room and took the

rolling pin from Getin's hand. Then she turned to Talli and inclined her head politely.

"I'm Janin. Welcome to our dwelling, Tallibeth Tarngold," she said. Her voice was calm, soft. Like Rael Gar, Janin kept her emotions behind a calm mask. But where the Garan leader gave an impression of cold calculation, this woman's stillness spoke only of serenity.

"Thank you," Talli said. "I'm sorry if I caused a problem."

Getin continued to glare. "There's no reason to be nice to her. I'm not scared of them."

"There's no reason to be rude, either," said the taller woman. She set the rolling pin on the counter in front of Getin.

"Just as there's no reason to be ashamed of fear when fear is justified."

"I didn't come here to make anyone afraid," Talli said.

Recin stepped closer to his mother. "She wants to offer me a job," he said.

"Working with the enemy!" cried Getin.

"Hush, Getin," said Janin. Her golden gaze moved from Talli's head down to her feet and back again. Though the Garan woman was only a baker, and Talli was now one of the rulers of the city, the inspection made Talli flinch. Even in her common robes, Janin had an air more regal than any of the women at Tagard's court. "What kind of job did you have for my son?" she asked.

"My father wants me to learn my way around the city," Talli said. "I thought Recin could help me. I can pay him."

The Garan woman nodded. "You've made a good choice. I doubt anyone else knows all the alleys and nooks of this city as well as my son. And we could use the extra money." She stopped and touched one long finger to her lips. "But Getin is right," she said after a moment. "Our family is pledged to aid and protect Bey Lisolo. I swore this oath myself. To do what you want may be a violation of that pledge."

Talli frowned. She had only known Recin for the space of their walk across the city, but already she liked him. She hated the idea of trying to find another guide. "My father wants to put Lisolo on his council," she said, searching for something that might win the woman's approval.

Recin's mother looked hard at Talli. "But you don't want him to do this, do you?"

"No," Talli admitted. She felt a blush creep into her cheeks and looked down at the stone floor of the bakery.

"Is it only the bey you fear, or is it all Viashino?"

Talli looked up sharply. "Who said I was afraid?"

"You did," said Janin. "You said it in your tone and in the way you hold yourself."

A spark of anger quickened in Talli. "A Viashino killed my mother," she said. "I have a right to dislike them."

Recin's mother nodded. "I know what it is to have someone taken from you, and what it is to hate. My husband fell years ago, and some days I still want my revenge on the one who took him."

"Who killed him?" asked Talli.

"I did," said a voice from the door. Rael Gar stepped into the room and pushed his way past Talli. He faced Janin and placed his hands and feet in a position Talli recognized from a dozen battlefields. It was the stance Garan took only when they were preparing to kill.

"If you want your revenge," he said, "now is the time to take it."

Interlude

GUARDED BY PAIN

From my seat here in the city of Berimish, the Garan remain the most mysterious of the races in Tamingazin. There are few of them in the city—no more than a single household—and their representatives from the mountains visit here to trade only once in a great long while. If the handful that I have seen are any key to the rest, then they are a people of great beauty, with large eyes and dark hair over pale skin. But beauty, of course, is not their reputation.

The transient colors of the eyes, the cold high places, the night-black clothing, the deadly blows of hands and feet—these are the things that people remember about the Garan. Even when I was a small child far south in Cresino, my dagger instructor, Asham, spoke of the people who would handle no blade, but who made their own bodies more deadly than any sword. They were a favorite subject of his.

Cresino could not tell me why the Garan would not use weapons, but the Viashino in this city have a story they tell. Perhaps there is knowledge here we can use.

"The Garan come from the north, from a place beyond the Skollten Apes, and beyond even the Umber. They are an old people, sliced from the root of all elves far back at the beginning of time. Some say they have human in them, as their appearance is so close to that of human. But an attalo looks much like a tortoise and is still a hundred times more deadly.

"They did not always shun blades. Before they came to Tamingazin, they were great swordsmen. They could make a long sword whistle through the air with such speed that the end of it would pop and crack like a drover's whip. No one, and no thing, could stand before them.

"But their love of fighting turned on itself. In anger and iron, Garan made war on Garan, and only by a whisker did any live.

"Those who survived shunned all weapons and put aside the rage that had driven them to kill their own kind. They left their ancestral homes and came to live in the mountains that border Tamingazin. There they made a ritual of fighting and taught themselves the skills of hand and foot. From birth they teach their children the painful lessons of weaponless combat, and some may die from these lessons before they learn how to defend themselves. They did all this that killing would not be so quick or so easy, and that if they would be destroyed, it would not come from their actions."

There is far more to the story, and many variations. But whether it is true, I do not know.

But it may be that we can find a way to use these people.

—From a dispatch of Ursal Daleel, Ambassador to the Valley of Tamingazin from the Court of Hemarch Solin, Conqueror of Suderbod.

CHAPTER
5

RECIN TIGHTENED HIS FINGERS INTO FISTS.
Blood pounded in his ears, and he felt a heat on his
skin. When he had been younger, his mother and aunt
had talked about the man who killed his father. Since
Recin had come of age, they no longer spoke of this
man in front of Recin. That didn't stop Recin from
thinking about him.

Now that same man stood in their front room,
within an arm's length of Recin's mother, with his
hands raised in a fighting stance. The killer was short,
a full head shorter than either Recin or his mother, but
that didn't mean he was not imposing. His shoulders
were very wide, and his every movement spoke of
power under tight control. His face was lost in the
shadows of his hood, but Recin could see the sparkle
of cold silver eyes. In his soft black clothing he looked
as dangerous as a rampaging En'Jaga.

Recin simmered as his mother studied the intruder.
If she was surprised at the Garan's sudden appearance,
she gave no sign.

Even her eyes remained a calm shimmering gold. She made no move to either flee or defend herself.

"I knew you would pay us a visit sooner or later," she said. "You were never able to resist gloating."

The man pushed back his hood. His eyes churned and shifted like a pot of boiling lead. Recin had no trouble recognizing the warrior's hard, sharp face. He was the same Garan that Recin had encountered on the night of Tagard's invasion, the one who had beaten him and knocked him from the wall—the one who had wanted him dead.

"I'm not gloating," said the warrior in a voice that was little more than a dry whisper. "It is my duty to be here." He made an odd, sharp gesture with his hand. "But then, those kind of things have always eluded your family, haven't they? Duty. Honor."

"We understand sacrifice well enough," said Janin.

Beside her, Aunt Getin looked paler than the dough on the table. Though she managed to keep her face expressionless, her eyes had gone a pale frightened gray. She reached for the rolling pin, but the pin beat a tattoo against the countertop.

"Rael Tak," she said, her voice a choked whisper.

"What's going on here?" Talli stepped to the center of the room and put herself between Rael Gar and Recin's mother. Recin had almost forgotten the human girl was in the room. "Why are you here?"

A crimson tinge washed across the warrior's eyes. "My business here is my own." He moved around Talli and stood closer to Recin's mother.

Recin had none of the training that made the mountain Garan such feared fighters, but he was facing the person who had killed his father. That same person now threatened all that remained of Recin's family. He could not just stand by and watch. He took a breath and prepared to leap.

With a whisper of cloth, the warrior was suddenly there, one hard palm pressed against Recin's chest. "I see your family traditions continue in many ways," said the warrior in his dead whisper. "This boy could not sneak up on a stone, and his emotions are more clear than the sky in midwinter."

"Let him go, Rael Tak," said Janin. "He's not a fighter."

The Garan nodded. "I can see that," he said. "And it's Rael Gar now, just as you are now nameless, without position in the Garan Agnate." He took his hand from Recin's chest and stood in a more relaxed pose.

Recin saw his mother raise an eyebrow in surprise. For her, it was an extreme reaction. "Rael Gar," she said slowly. "Congratulations."

Rael Gar. Now Recin had both a face and a name to go with his dreams of the killer.

Talli put a hand on Rael Gar's shoulder. "Stop this," she said. "Tell me what you're doing here."

Rael Gar shrugged off her hand without bothering to look at her. "It's strictly a Garan concern," he said. "And what are you doing here, daughter of the king?"

Talli drew herself up and leaned over the shorter Garan. "I'm here on the king's business. These people are helping me."

If Rael Gar was either upset or intimidated, he didn't show it. "These people are Garan—my people," he said. "And they're under my charge." He crossed his arms over his broad chest and turned to Talli. "My business here is justice. It's business that concerns neither you nor your father. Surely there must be somewhere else you can do the king's work."

Talli's eyes didn't change like the Garan, but her tan skin went white with anger. "Are you asking me to leave?" Her right hand crept to the blade at her belt.

"Asking?" said Rael Gar. "No, I'm not asking."

Recin's mother stepped forward and swiftly pulled Talli back. "Getin," she said, "why don't you take our guest upstairs? I'm sure she'd be interested to see how the citizens of Berimish live."

Talli shook her head. "I want to know what he's doing here. I am a member of the council in my own right. What goes on in this city is as much my business as it is his."

Rael Gar faced Talli and curled his hands into claws. Recin had seen many colors in the eyes of his mother and aunt, but until that moment, he had not known Garan eyes were capable of boiling bloodred. The anger in Rael Gar's eyes was so raw that Recin was sure the man was about to attack.

Then Rael Gar lowered his hands to his sides and made the slightest of bows. In an instant his eyes changed to a flat iron gray.

"I have overstepped," he said softly. "Forgive me. Though your father is king, and we are all allies, there are still matters which must be carried on only among the Garan. This is one of those matters."

"He's right," said Janin. "I ask you as a favor. Please go with Getin."

There was an awkward moment of silence before Talli finally nodded. "All right. I'll go." She pointed one long finger toward Rael Gar. "But these people are under my protection," she said. "If anything happens to them, you'll answer to me."

For a moment, Rael Gar's eyes were again bloodred. "We'll see," he said in his dry voice.

Getin, her eyes still pale with shock, stepped around the counter and headed for the door. As she passed Rael Gar, a noticeable shiver ran down her body and she hurried her last few steps out of the room. Talli glanced over at Recin, then followed Getin from the bakery.

"I want you to go, too, Recin," said his mother.

Recin blinked. "Why?"

"The boy stays," said Rael Gar. "He should hear this."

There was a blur of movement so fast that Recin could see nothing but its direction. Then his mother was standing with her face only inches from Rael Gar's. The flat blade of her fingers was hard against the skin of the intruder's throat.

"You are gar, now," she said softly. "But we're not part of your agnate. Not anymore. My son does what I say."

Recin felt his mouth drop open and he could do nothing to stop it. He had never seen his mother move so fast—he had never seen *anyone* move so fast—and he had certainly never seen anything like the crimson glow of her eyes as she faced Rael Gar.

"It doesn't matter," said Rael Gar. "I've said all I need to say. I know where you are."

He stepped back from her hand, spun around, and walked quickly from the bakery. Recin's mother sagged. Her eyes returned to their normal green and she leaned back against the counter.

Recin ran to her side. "Are you all right?"

She nodded. "Go see to the human girl and your aunt. If you're not there to watch them, they may come to blows. I'm fine."

"What if he comes back?" asked Recin.

"He will," said his mother, "but not for some time. Midwinter day has passed and midsummer is months away. If Rael Gar wants to call a convocation, he'll have to wait till then."

"A convocation?" Recin raked his memory, but he didn't think he had ever heard the term before.

"A meeting of the gar and the lesser positions in the agnate . . . the tak, the kan, the warrior ranks." She drew in a deep breath and stood up straight. Carefully she smoothed the wrinkles from her pale green dress. "They don't have a convocation often, but Rael Gar will need one if he wants to keep this according to tradition."

Recin shook his head. "Keep what to tradition?

"Rael Gar considers me a traitor, Recin. Probably all of us. I disobeyed the rules of the agnate, and now they want us to pay."

"I don't understand," he said. "What rule did you break that was so important?"

His mother sighed. "We'll discuss it later. To the agnate, we are renegades. Dangerous."

"What do they want from us now?" asked Recin.

Janin looked away, but not before Recin saw her eyes go pale. "You better hurry to the human girl," she said quickly. "If your aunt forgets about Rael Gar, she might remember to be angry with the girl."

Recin frowned. It was obvious that the Garan leader would want to do more than talk with them, and it was just as obvious that his mother didn't want to talk about it. "Are you sure you'll be all right?"

She nodded. "Go on, before they begin to throw things at each other."

The narrow alley outside carried echoes from the market and the crowds along the main street. It seemed strange to Recin that the city's business had continued while Rael Gar had been in the bakery. But the heart of Berimish had hardly paused for the change in kings. Should one small family of Garan elves vanish, it would not even miss a beat.

He climbed the stairs to their home on the second floor of the building. When he pushed aside the heavy cloth that served as a door, he was surprised to find Talli standing before the reflecting glass in the main room. He was even more surprised to see that the

human girl had shed her heavy mountain clothing for a
simple gown of pale orange. It was the kind of clothing
that was common in Berimish, but on Talli it looked
anything but plain.

Aunt Getin fussed around her, adjusting the fit.
"Hold still."

Talli looked down and frowned. "Are they all this
short?"

"Where did you get that?" Recin asked.

The girl turned to him with a grave expression. "Is
Rael Gar gone?"

Recin nodded. "He's gone."

Aunt Getin paused in her work, closed her eyes, and
gave a sigh of relief. "He'll be back, though," she said.
"I know he will."

"That's what Mother says, too." He pointed to Talli's
gown. "Where did you get the clothes?"

Talli fingered the orange cloth and frowned. "It's
one of your mother's. I said something to Getin about
not wanting to stand out so much, and she came up
with this." She looked down at her bare legs and wrinkled her nose. "I feel silly."

"Hold still," said Getin. "You'll feel even sillier with
a pin through your leg."

"You look fine," said Recin. In fact, he thought she
looked wonderful. In her heavy leather and woolen
clothing, she had an exotic, wild look that was not
unattractive. But dressed like a woman of the city, he
thought she was simply beautiful. Freed of her padded
cap, her golden curls were a cloud around her head.
He had never seen hair like it.

Getin went to a table and brought over a length of
scarf colored to match the gown. "Now if we cover up
that hair . . . "

Talli's gold ringlets disappeared under Getin's careful wrapping. A few bright strands were still visible,

but only on careful examination. "Will I pass?" she asked.

"You look like you've lived here all your life," said Recin. He was disappointed that her hair was covered, but he had to admit that without it the rest of her disguise would have been useless.

Talli touched the thin fabric of her gown. "If I wore this back at the hold, I'd freeze to death."

"It took me and Janin a bit to get used to it, too," said Getin. "You're not in the mountains now. It's warm in Berimish, and you'll find this a lot more practical here than your heavy winter clothes." She finished her inspection of Talli's clothing and nodded her approval. "Now, if you two are about to run off, I'd best get back down and help Janin with the bread."

Recin stood aside to let her out the door, but Getin grabbed his arm. "Watch yourself," she whispered. "This girl has something to do with Rael Tak. If you should come on him in the street . . ." She stopped and shook her head. "Make sure you stay away from him." Getin released his arm and slipped through the cloth-covered doorway.

Recin glanced at Talli. "Do you think Rael Gar will do anything right away?"

"I don't know," said the girl. "He sent Samet Tak and the rest of the Garan down to guard the border. If he really wanted to try your mother before the agnate, wouldn't he want some of them here?"

Recin frowned. "Maybe."

"Well," said Talli, "are we going to see the city?"

"Sure." Recin wanted to show her Berimish, but he also wanted to go down and talk with his mother. It was obvious that there was much more to the story of his father's death than he had been told. But he knew from experience that it was a subject neither his mother nor his aunt would discuss.

"Well," he said, "I suppose we should get going. Like you said, we have a lot of ground to cover."

"I feel like I'm going out in my underdress," said Talli.

"You'll be grateful for that gown when the sun really heats up." Recin went to the door and pulled aside the cloth. "Are you ready?"

Talli nodded. She went to the table where her clothes were piled up and pulled out her sword belt.

"What are you going to do with that?" asked Recin.

"I was just getting my blade," Talli said. She started to buckle it around her waist.

Recin smiled. "You put that on, and you really will look ridiculous."

"So what am I supposed to do?"

"Leave the sword here," he said. "You can pick it up before you go back to the hall."

Talli looked stunned. "You want me to go around the city with no weapon?"

"Everyone does," Recin said with a shrug. "Except for the city guard, no one in Berimish carries a sword."

"I don't know. I've carried a weapon every day for as long as I can remember." Talli ran her fingers over the hilt of the blade.

Recin nodded. "If you take it, you might as well put your old clothes on and forget about fooling anyone."

Talli frowned. "All right. I'll leave the sword." She put the weapon back on the table and picked up the bundle of maps. Then she reached into a fold of the crumpled clothing and drew out a smaller knife. Carefully, she concealed the blade behind the belt of her gown. "Now I don't feel quite so naked."

When they went outside, the sun was almost directly above and the usually dim alleys were filled with light. Recin hesitated at the door to the bakery, but there were several customers inside and his aunt and mother were busy selling fresh bread. His questions would have to wait.

"Where do you want to go first?" he asked.

"I don't know." Talli turned the stack of maps around in her hands and squinted at the tracery of lines. Then she rolled up the maps and looked at the buildings around them. "I'm supposed to get familiar with the city. Do only humans live in this area?" She looked at him and smiled. "Humans and Garan, I mean."

"No," said Recin. "Even here there are a lot more Viashino than anything else." He pointed to the building next to the bakery. "Three Viashino live over there. One of them is a friend of mine."

Talli looked at the narrow building. "Are they all from the same family?"

Recin looked at her in surprise. "Family? Viashino don't have families."

"How can that be?" she asked. "I've heard lots of strange things about the Viashino, but everyone has a family. Even Viashino have to have parents."

"Maybe so, but I've never seen them together." He looked up at the top room in the building. "I can't tell if Heasos is in, but I've been up to his room a hundred times. I don't think he'd mind if I took you there for a look."

Talli didn't seem very excited about the idea. "I'm not sure learning about the city means breaking into a Viashino house."

"We won't be breaking in," said Recin. "And if you're supposed to learn about the city, shouldn't you learn something about the people who live in it?"

The blond girl nodded. "All right, let's go."

Recin walked to the front of the building and grabbed the knotted rope that dangled from the side of the building. "The Viashino don't like stairs."

"I've noticed that," said Talli. She looked up the rough wall. "I don't think I'll have any problem climbing."

"Would you like to go first?"

Talli looked at him and raised an eyebrow. "In this clothing? No, I think I'll let you lead the way."

Recin laughed and began his climb. He thought about Talli as he made his ascent. The human girl was not at all like he had expected. He had thought she would be swinging her sword every few minutes, pausing only to give orders. Back in the corridors of the Splendent Hall, she had been more than a little intimidating, but once away from the bey's home and its hundreds of soldiers, she had become much easier to talk to. Recin wondered how much of this was really a difference in Talli and how much was his own nervousness.

He reached the top of the rope and stepped onto the platform outside the wide door. Talli was only a moment behind him. She stepped lightly onto the boards and looked at the cloth drapes.

"Are there no thieves in this city?" she asked. "I've not seen one door in this section that deserved the name."

Recin leaned against the wall and grinned. "You remember the nice pool of water we passed? The one where all the children were playing?"

"Yes."

"The city guard drowns thieves there each Restday. If someone steals something particularly valuable, they add some rostiworms or attalo to the water before they put the thieves in." Recin made a long slurping noise. "I think you can say we have a few thieves, but very few old thieves."

It was Talli's turn to laugh. "So if you don't have real doors, how do you knock?"

"Knock?"

"How do you let someone know you're here?"

Recin shrugged. "Like this." He went to the door, leaned in, and shouted, "Heasos! Are you home?" He brushed aside the cloth over the wide door and stuck his head inside.

"Heasos?"

The single room of Heasos's home held only a few pieces of furniture. There was a large heavy table in one corner, a stack of cushions held in place by padded ropes, and a fireplace with a mantel of dark wood.

With the lamps snuffed out and only two small windows, it was dim and cool inside. Like almost every home in the city, the primary smell was that of wood smoke, but there was also a sharp odor that Recin recognized as bronze peppers. He grimaced at the thought. Bronze peppers were a favorite with many of the Viashino, but they were far too hot and much too bitter for either humans or Garan.

Talli stepped around him and peered into the shadows. "I thought Viashino slept standing up," she said, pointing at the stack of cushions.

"They usually do," said Recin. "But if they're feeling sick, or just really tired, they'll sprawl out on pillows. Heasos injured one of his legs during the flood season, and it still hurts him sometimes. I think that's why he keeps the cushions handy."

The girl nodded and went over to the fireplace. There were a number of small objects lined up across the mantelpiece, but in the dim light, it was difficult to make them out. Talli lifted down one of the objects and took it closer to the window. Suddenly, she looked up in surprise.

"It's a figure of a woman," she said. "A human woman." She held the object toward Recin. "What's a Viashino doing with this in his home?"

"Heasos likes humans," said Recin. "I mean, he likes the way we look." He walked over to Talli and took the small statue from her hands. It was a figure of a young human girl with a billowing mane of hair, all carved from a single piece of freckled marshwood. "I've seen this one before. I think it's Heasos's favorite."

Talli shook her head. "I don't understand. The Viashino are so different from us. Why would they like to look at statues of humans?"

"I've asked Heasos that," said Recin. He took the small statue back to the mantel and carefully set it in its place. "He says we do the same thing."

"We do not," the blond girl said with a distinct air of distaste in her voice. "At least, I've never seen a human keep any kind of image of a Viashino."

"Maybe not of Viashino, but how about riding beasts, or mountain cats, or casperjays? I'm sure you've seen decorations with some kind of animal in them." He shrugged. "People find a lot of animals nice to look at. Some Viashino think humans are nice to look at, that's all."

"But it's not the same," said Talli.

"Why not?"

"Cats and 'jays, those are just animals. Humans are people."

Recin nodded. "I'm just telling you what Heasos tells me."

Talli went back to the mantel and bent in close to inspect the other figures. "These are all humans."

"Some of them are Garan, actually, but it's hard to tell humans and Garan apart in the dark."

The remark drew a sharp reaction from Talli. She straightened abruptly and folded her arms across her chest. Then she stared at Recin with such force that all the nervousness he had felt in the Splendent Hall came rushing back.

"What is that supposed to mean?" she asked.

"It means . . ." Recin started, then he drew a quick breath and started again. "Just that its hard to tell the human statues from the Garan ones."

Talli stared at him for a moment longer. "Yes," she said at last. "I suppose it is." She gestured at the row of figures on the mantel. "All of these are statues of women."

Recin nodded. "Heasos thinks female humans are more attractive than male humans." He started to add a comment about how he agreed with his friend, but decided against it. "I see a lot more women in all the statues Viashino make of humans."

The girl glanced at the statues again, then shook her head rapidly. "It's wrong. There's something wrong with a male Viashino sitting around looking at statues of human women."

"Oh," said Recin. "Heasos isn't a male."

She looked back at him with a puzzled expression. "You mean this Heasos is a female? You said 'he' when you were talking about Heasos before."

"I only said he because that's what Heasos asked me to say. When you want to know what to call a younger Viashino, the polite thing is to ask." Recin held out his hands in a gesture of uncertainty. "But as to whether he's a male or a female, I don't know."

"How can you not know?" she asked. "I thought Heasos was your friend."

"Even Heasos doesn't know yet," he replied. "He won't be mature for another three or four years, and until then, no one can tell."

Talli pressed her hands against her temples and shook her head. "The Viashino are so strange," she said. "I don't think I'll ever understand them."

"Well, I won't claim to understand them completely," said Recin, "but I know enough to answer some questions." He snapped his fingers. "I know," he said. "You want to see some really good Viashino art? Some that has humans, and Viashino, and En'Jaga, and everything else in it?"

The girl shrugged. "I guess so," she said. "We had carvings on some of the stones back in Farson Hold, but it was all old. I've seen some of the wood carvings that the Garan troops do around camp. I like those."

"My mother makes carvings, too," said Recin. "I think it's something that the Garan do when they're bored or worried."

"Are the Viashino carvings like that?"

"Different. But if you like those, you'll like this. Come on."

They left Heasos's home and went down the rope. Recin, who went first, resisted the temptation to look up as Talli worked her way to the ground in her short gown. The destination he had in mind was near the western wall, and he set a brisk pace across the city. Along the way, they passed through several street markets and took shortcuts down a number of alleys where both Viashino and humans lived.

"I think your aunt's clothing is working," Talli whispered as they went around a group of Viashino who were bickering over a cartload of ellinberries. "No one seems to be paying any attention to me."

Recin nodded. "You fit in fine. There are few enough humans in the city that you might get some notice from them, but most Viashino can't tell one human from another if they're dressed alike."

When they reached the western plaza, several of the merchants had erected sun shades over their stands. Others had shut down to wait out the heat of the day. Recin took Talli to the center of the street and pointed out a tall building capped by a dome of dark stone.

"That's where we're going," he said.

"What is it?"

"A temple," said Recin. "There are several small ones scattered around and an even larger one down at the south end. But this one is the prettiest."

Talli peered at the building. "What kind of temple? I've never heard anything about the Viashino gods."

"Well, I said there were things I didn't know, and that's one of them. Viashino go in there and stand around. Sometimes they talk to one of the ones that work there—priests, I guess." He shook his head. "But what they're saying to each other is anybody's guess. They talk a different language in there, and I've never learned so much as a word of it. I don't even know what they call this place."

"What about humans?" the girl asked. "Will they get mad if we go in?"

Recin shook his head. "I go in there all the time; so do a lot of humans. It's always cool in there, and the carvings are really pretty. The Viashino don't even seem to notice we're there."

The doors to the temple were big enough to drive a loaded wagon through. As there usually were when Recin visited, a dozen or more Viashino leaned against the rails in the front room. They mumbled in their strange, sliding temple language, but didn't so much as turn their heads when Recin and Talli walked past. They went through a second smaller room, then entered a hallway of buff stone whose floor had been deeply worn by the passage of thousands of feet.

"Where is all this artwork you were talking about?" asked Talli.

Recin smiled. "Ten steps away."

They emerged into a room big enough to contain

both floors of Recin's family home twice over in all
directions. The room was lined with alternating bands
of dark and light wood that originated at the center of
the dome overhead. Every inch of the wood was covered in delicate, detailed carvings.

Talli drew an audible breath. "It's amazing."

Armies of thumb-sized humans marched against
hordes of menacing En'Jaga. Garan and Viashino
struggled on steep mountains. Beasts and monsters
danced around the smoldering ruins of towns. But surrounding these images of war and horror were even
more scenes of tranquillity and beauty. Rivers flowed
through gardens. Flights of casperjays flew above fields
of flowers.

"What can it all mean?" Talli said. She spun slowly
around as she took in the expanse of imagery.

"When you know, tell me," Recin replied. "I've been
trying to figure it out for years."

They stayed in the temple through most of the afternoon, leaving only when Recin reminded Talli that it
would soon be dark. Even after they had gone outside,
the human girl was still talking about the Viashino
carvings.

"I've never seen anything like it," she said. "We had
some stone carvings back at Farson, but this is so much
more. Whoever carved all those figures is a wonder."

"Viashino made all those figures," Recin said.
"There's a market not too far from here where craftsmen sell carvings and metal work. I can take you there
if you want to see."

Talli looked up at the purple sky. "It'll have to wait
for another day," she said. "I'm going to have to hurry
to get my things if I'm going to make it back to the
Splendent Hall before dark."

They stopped for a moment at a small stand and
Recin came up with the coin to purchase a cup of

sweet dried yuatara diced into tiny pieces. They passed the cup back and forth as they walked.

"I'll pay for the food as soon as we get back to where I left my money cache," Talli said between bites of the chewy fruit.

She looked at the buildings around them and frowned. "I don't think this is turning out quite as my father wanted. I haven't checked the accuracy of any of the maps, or looked over any government buildings."

"But you saw a Viashino home and a Viashino temple," said Recin. "Not to mention a lot of streets and houses. Getting a good idea of what the city is like is bound to help."

Talli stopped chewing for a moment. "I think my father would agree with you. He thinks—"

"Tallibeth Tarngold!" cried a voice from across the plaza.

Recin looked up to see a small dark woman come toward them with a brisk determined stride. Close behind her, two burly human soldiers pushed their way through the crowd.

"Karelon," Talli said. "What are you doing here?"

The woman stopped in front of them and frowned at the girl. "You've led us a long chase," she said. "Rael Gar told us where he had seen you with the Garan family, but by the time we'd gotten to their home, you were gone. We've been worried."

Recin remembered the woman from the night Tagard had come into the city. Then she had seemed cold, but now her high forehead was creased with lines of concern.

"I'm fine," said Talli. "Why were you looking for me?"

The woman took a deep breath. "Something's happened. We've got to get you back to the Splendent Hall."

"What's happened?"

"There's been an attack on your father's life," said the woman. "Even now, he lies wounded in his chambers."

CHAPTER
6

IN THE HEAT OF THE AFTERNOON, TALLI felt a wave of icy cold wash over her. "My father's not dead," she said, hoping that it was true, but fearing it was not.

"No," Karelon replied. "Tagard was barely wounded. But not because the attack wasn't serious. He wants you to come back to the Splendent Hall in case this assassin was only part of a plot to move on all of us."

Talli nodded. "I'll come, of course." She turned to Recin. "I'm going back to the hall. Can you get the things I left at your home and bring them to me there?"

The young Garan nodded. "I'll bring them. And I hope your father's all right."

Karelon turned to face Recin. "Is that so? Where are your loyalties, Garan?" She took a step forward. Her dark eyes narrowed as her gaze swept up and down over him. "Rael Gar says your family betrayed the Garan. Were you plotting to betray us, as well?"

Recin's eyes swirled at the insult to his family, but

when he spoke his voice was calm. "I was only doing what she asked."

"Were you?" The woman extended a slim finger and pressed it against Recin's chest. "You've spent a lot of years with the scaleheads. Do you think like a Garan or a Viashino?"

"Karelon," called Talli, "we should hurry."

The woman nodded. She pulled back her hand, then turned away from the young Garan and walked off down the street. Talli took a final glance at Recin, then followed Karelon.

The soldiers moved quickly through the crowded streets, but not quickly enough for Talli. She wanted to run back to the Splendent Hall and see for herself that her father was still alive and breathing. An image of her mother lying broken on the ground appeared in Talli's mind with such clarity that she gasped. Though Karelon had said her father's wounds were not severe, Talli would not believe that until she had seen it for herself.

As they strode down the main road back to the hall, she felt the crowds of Viashino looking at them from every side. Walking with Recin, she had almost grown used to being among the scaly people. And looking at the carvings inside the temple had made her think that there might be something more to the Viashino than she had been ready to admit. But now that her father was wounded, she saw them again for what they really were: the enemy. The killing animals that had murdered her mother.

They met another squadron of soldiers along the main street, and Karelon instructed them to let everyone know that Talli had been located. Outside the Splendent Hall the soldiers were lined up almost shoulder to shoulder. Familiar faces looked at Talli with interest, then with surprise as they recognized the face under the carefully wrapped head covering. She hurried up the ramp into the huge building and pushed her way through even more soldiers who choked the central corridor.

Outside her father's quarters, a shrouded figure lay on the floor. Around it were drips and smears of dark blood. Talli's heart leaped into her throat at the sight of the still form on the cold stones. She kneeled down and steeled herself to lift the edge of the blood-soaked cloth.

It was a Viashino. From his size, the attacker had been quite young, hardly more than a child. Its yellow eyes were open and dulled. Blood came from the nostrils at the end of its long snout and more blood turned the teeth in the open mouth a hideous shade of pink. He was skinny, this dead Viashino, so rawboned that he might have been starving.

Talli lifted the covering sheet farther and saw that the Viashino's clothing was poor and tattered. All in all, the creature looked more like some impoverished back-alley survivor than someone that would be involved in an attempt on the king's life. But on the stone beside the body there was a bright steel knife.

"Was this the only one?" Talli asked.

A woman soldier with a thin scar on her forehead stepped forward. "This is the only one we know of," she said. "We've searched the hall for others."

"We'll find out if anyone else was involved," said Karelon. "I'll take care of it personally."

Talli drew the sheet back over the still form. "The knife looks like the kind they use in the kitchens here. What about the servants? The cleaning staff? The cooks? Has anyone talked to them?"

"I . . ." the soldier started. The woman cast a nervous look at Karelon and her burly guards before turning back to Talli. "I don't know," she finished.

"Go to the kitchen and round all the workers up," Talli said. She stood and pointed down the long corridor. "Take them to that big circular room beside the wellhouse and keep them there until I get a chance to question them."

"Wait," Karelon shouted. "You can't do that."

Talli looked at the woman with surprise. "What's wrong?"

There was a moment of hesitation before the dark-haired woman replied. "Nothing," said Karelon. "Nothing. It's just that your father charged me with the security of this city. If you start interfering, he might be upset."

"Upset?" Talli frowned. Her father did try to lay out clear areas for each of his officers so there would be no conflict over duties, but surely this was a duty that would only benefit from additional attention. "I think he'll understand that this is something that might need more than one person to unravel."

Karelon's features hardened. "Don't you trust me to find the truth behind this attack?" There was a hard, cold edge in the woman's voice. It was not the first time that Talli had heard that tone, but she had never before been the one at which it was directed.

Through the long years of war, Karelon had been one of the few constants in Talli's life. Aside from her father, there was no one she held in such respect. With the dark-haired woman already arguing with Tagard, the last thing Talli wanted to do was to drive a wedge between herself and Karelon.

"I'm only offering my help," Talli said carefully. "I'm sorry if I overstepped."

The war leader nodded and the tightness around her mouth softened. "I understand, this attack on your father has to be upsetting for you. Come. We'll discuss it again after we've seen the king."

They started to walk away, but they were stopped by the soldier that Talli had spoken to. "What do I do?" the woman asked. "Stay here?"

"No," said Karelon. "Go ahead and gather the servants. No matter who does the questioning, it is something that should be done."

Talli had another thought. "What about Lisolo's quarters? Have the bey or any of his helpers left their area?"

The woman swallowed nervously. "I don't know."

"I think we should ask them, as well," Talli said to Karelon. "A Viashino committed this crime. The leader of the Viashino may well know why."

Karelon nodded, but a hint of irritation returned to her face.

"Have the bey's people brought in with the rest of them. Someone will be along shortly." The soldier nodded and hurried off down the hall. Karelon led Talli in another direction, away from the chambers where the humans had been staying.

"We thought it best to move Tagard to another area until we were sure that this attempt was not part of some larger attack," said the war leader. As they turned down first one hallway then another, Karelon waved her arms at all the doors and passageways. "We should raze this building and put up a proper keep," she said. "There are too many ways in and out. This Splendent Hall is an indefensible mess."

"You should suggest that to my father," said Talli.

"I already did," said the dark-haired woman. "He thinks this building is an important symbol, just like that damn lizard, Lisolo."

Talli nodded, but her mind was filled with a tumble of different feelings about the Viashino. Only that morning she had argued with her father that the scaly people should be punished. Then she had seen how they lived, and their art. Now a Viashino had attacked her father—just as one had killed her mother. She needed time to think, time to sift through her feelings.

Finally they reached a small wooden door surrounded by a dozen troopers in full field gear. Each of them lowered their head in respect as they approached, but whether that respect was for her or Karelon, Talli didn't know. She put her hand to the door and found her heart beating hard against her ribs. For a moment, she was sure that she would open the door to find her father lying just as dead as the skinny Viashino back in the hallway.

But when she opened the door, she found the king of all Tamingazin sitting at a small stone table, drinking blackthorn tea. Tagard looked up at her and smiled. "I see Karelon has brought you home in one piece," he said.

Talli's relief at seeing her father was momentarily dented by irritation. She had gone through the city all day unprotected. She was not some child that needed Karelon's protection to get home safely. Then another emotion overwhelmed Talli's irritation. She rushed to her father and hugged him tightly.

"I was afraid you were dead."

"Careful," said the king, wincing. He pushed himself free of her grip and turned back the edge of his cloak to reveal a swatch of coarse gray bandage smeared with some yellow poultice. The bandage was on his shoulder, but it marked the location of the wound only inches from his neck. Or his heart.

"My attacker was neither a good aim, nor particularly strong," said Tagard, "but his blade went deep."

"You are going to be all right?"

He nodded. "Certainly." He looked his daughter up and down, and a smile returned to his face. "Look at you. You seem to have become quite the native."

Talli had almost forgotten she was still wearing the short, light dress of the city women. She reached up quickly to remove the scarf that was wound around her head and let her blond hair fall across her shoulders. "I thought it was best that I attract as little attention as possible."

"Clever," said Tagard.

Karelon stepped into the room and closed the door behind her. "It's good to see you up," she said. "Has the physician left?"

"Yes," said Tagard. "But my defender is still here." He nodded to the bench at the side of the room.

"Defender?" Talli turned and found that there was someone else present. Seated in the corner of the room was the ambassador from Suderbod. The small, bearded man was wearing a bright yellow jacket and soft hat of pink streaked with red. Talli searched her overtaxed mind for the man's name.

"Ursal Daleel?" she said.

The man stood up quickly and nodded. "You've a fine memory, Princess."

Talli frowned in puzzlement at the unfamiliar term. "Princess?"

Daleel stood. "It's a title we use in my land for the daughter of a king. What do you say here?"

"The daughter of the king," Talli said with a shrug. "If I have a title, it's Councilor."

"The ambassador was with me when the attack was made," said Tagard, "and it's a good thing he was."

The Suder clapped his hands together and lowered his head. "I was only lucky enough to see what was happening. My help was purely incidental."

Tagard laughed. "Incidental or not, if you hadn't seen that young Viashino coming, he might have buried his blade in my heart, not my shoulder. I owe you a debt."

"Yes," said Karelon. "The whole valley should show its gratitude to Suderbod." She moved closer to the bearded man. "Surely there is something we can do for him in return."

Daleel bowed slightly. "Your hospitality is all that I ask."

Talli looked at the ambassador more closely. With his garish clothes, his floppy pink hat, and his over-tended beard, she had always dismissed him as useless. He did not look formidable in any way. But if he had been quick-witted enough to see the attack coming and brave enough to get between the king and a blade, then maybe there was more to the man than Talli had allowed.

"You have been asking to see me for days," said Tagard. "What was it you wanted?"

"It's only a small matter," said the Suder. He reached into his jacket and produced a rolled piece of gray parchment. He slipped off the ribbon binding it and spread the paper on the table before the king. "As you know, Suderbod is a place of many people and little tillable land. All we want is the deed to one small area in Tamingazin where we may raise crops to feed our hungry populace."

Tagard leaned over the paper and studied it closely. "You want to bring Suder farmers into Tamingazin? And Suder workers to harvest the crops?"

"Only a few hundred," said the ambassador. "At present, much of Suderbod's wealth goes for the import of food. I believe the inequity of farmland was one of your own people's complaints with the Viashino, so I'm sure you'll understand our desire to provide for ourselves."

"I think we'll have to consider this at more length," said the king.

"We would, of course, pay for this privilege," the

ambassador added quickly. The little man smiled broadly. "Suderbod may be poor in land, but our treasuries are far from empty."

"As I said, I'll consider it," said Tagard. He returned the ambassador's smile. "You do have my appreciation for your invaluable help today."

Talli stood quietly while the two men continued to talk. Now that she was back home, and knew her father was all right, she realized that she was both tired and hungry. Though she had often marched farther during the war, the trip around the city had been lengthy. The tension brought on by both Rael Gar's visit to Recin's home, and by the attack on her father, had made the day exhausting.

After a few minutes, Tagard was able to bring his talk with the Suder to some kind of conclusion and Karelon escorted the little man out the door. For the moment, Talli was alone with her father.

"You look like you're the one who was attacked," said Tagard.

"What's wrong?"

Talli shook her head. "Nothing. It's been a long day, and I was worried about you."

Her father laughed. "We fought a lot of battles over the years. You should know by now that it'll take more than one half-grown Viashino with a knife to do me in."

The door opened and Karelon returned. "The Suder wants to speak with you again in the morning," she said. "I told him that would depend on your health."

Tagard sighed. "I think I might well have a bad night," he said. "I could do with a few days to study this proposal before that man begins to pester me about it."

"I think there might be merit in what the Suder has to say," said Karelon. "Maybe you should meet with him tomorrow."

Talli looked at the door and frowned in thought. The Suder ambassador had been helpful to her father on at least two occasions, but there was something about the man she didn't like. Something that went far beyond his outlandish clothes.

"I don't trust the Suder," she said. "I think he has more on his mind than what he's said."

Karelon turned and gave Talli a flat stare. "I think we should put more of our trust in humans like ourselves and less in the scaleheads. Speaking of which, don't you have some servants to talk to?"

"Servants?" said Tagard. "What's this about servants?"

Talli was still looking at Karelon. She wondered what had caused the woman to suddenly agree to her help in the questioning. "I wanted to make sure that none of them were part of the attempt to kill you."

The king looked over at Karelon. "Don't you already have people checking on this?"

"Yes," said Karelon. "As I'm sure you'll remember, administration of the law was put under my authority. But your daughter volunteered to help me in this matter."

The king nodded slightly. "All right, talk to the servants. But after this, it's in Karelon's hands. I could throw a stone out the window and strike a Viashino that would like to see me dead. I have enough for you to do without your spending all your time looking for more."

With a final nod to her father, Talli left the room. As soon as she was down the hall and out of sight of the cluster of guards, she stopped, leaned against the wall, and drew a long ragged breath. Too many things were going on that she couldn't sort out. Rael Gar was out to extract some mysterious form of Garan justice on Recin's family for an even more mysterious crime.

Karelon's behavior was strange, and Talli had no idea why.

Through the years of war, Talli had dreamed of the day when it would end. Now that peace had come, it was turning out to be very confusing. A month before, she had been confident that everyone in her father's army was working toward the same goal. Now she wasn't sure that any of them were. As frightening as it had been to be undefended among the crowds of Viashino, Talli found herself wishing she could leave the Splendent Hall and all the people in it.

She closed her eyes and took another long breath. The war had not been settled in a week; no doubt the peace would also take time to reach its final form. She straightened her shoulders and headed for the well-house.

At least two dozen Viashino were waiting for her. Talli hadn't realized that there were so many servants in the Splendent Hall. They huddled together in a knot, their claws tapping the stone floor, while two human guards stood nearby.

Talli drew herself up straight and looked into the yellow eyes of the creatures. Any one of them might have played a part in the attempt on her father's life. "Bring one of the servants over here to me," she said to a guard.

The first Viashino they brought across was a tall, older female who worked on the loading docks below the hall. She answered Talli's questions, but admitted to no knowledge of the crime. Next, the guards selected a small, gray-green creature from the end of the line and pushed it toward Talli.

Halfway across the floor, the Viashino suddenly screamed and threw its clawed hands across its muzzle.

"You're going to kill us!" it cried. "You're going to

kill us all." It twisted its head to the side and translucent eyelids dulled its eyes.

"Did you have anything to do with the attack on King Tagard?" said Talli.

The Viashino didn't seem to hear her. "You're going to kill us all," it said again. Then it began to moan.

Talli gritted her teeth. "I'm not going to kill anyone," she said. "I'm just looking for information."

More of the Viashino in the room took up the moan. It took more than an hour to get them all calmed down enough to resume the questioning, and several more hours to talk to them all. By the time she finished with the last of them, it was very late and Talli was almost asleep on her feet as she headed back to her room. Even in the middle of the night, the corridors of the Splendent Hall were filled with activity. Soldiers came and went. Some of the servants she had just finished with rushed to complete their tasks.

Talli saw Rael Gar marching down the central hall, leading a handful of warriors off on some late errand. Her first thought was that the Garan leader was off to do something to Recin and his family. But the rest of the Garan were out on the border, and the men he was leading were all humans. If he really was concerned with enforcing some law of the Garan Agnate, she doubted he would take humans along to do it.

A dozen steps later, she passed the sorcerer, Aligarius, also running somewhere in the middle of the night. Though she called out a greeting, the old man passed by her without a word as he hurried down the hallway. She stared after the sorcerer, a little shocked by his appearance. Only a few days ago, she had noticed that Aligarius was gaining weight, but now he looked even more gaunt than when they had first met.

Talli took an oil lantern from a table and lit it from the greater torch at the corner of the hallway. Lamp in hand, she reached her own rooms and shut the door behind her gratefully.

The rooms she had taken had once belonged to one of Bey Lisolo's assistants, and they still bore the scent of the sweet perfume many wealthy Viashino wore. Other than the fading aroma, there was little left of the previous resident—Viashino furniture was poorly suited to humans.

She went through the empty front room to the bed-chamber, where she was both surprised and pleased to see her own clothes and short blade sitting on a table. Recin had been as good as his word.

She wished for a moment that the young Garan was there to talk to. He hadn't fought for her father's side in the war, and she supposed that he was as much an enemy as any Viashino in the city. But there was something about Recin that made conversation with him come easily. Maybe it was only that he was nearly the same age that she was. Or maybe it was that he was the only person she knew who didn't seem to have some hidden motive.

She found her nightdress among the few things she had stored in a traveling chest. Talli scowled as she closed the lid of the battered trunk. More than ten days in the city, and she was still living out of a box. There was not even any furniture in the room except for her bed and table, and even they were only pieces that had been dragged in from some storeroom.

Talli thought about the furniture she had left behind back in Farson Hold. It had been years since she had spent a night in her own bed. Perhaps after the spring rains had passed and things were more settled, a few of her things might be brought. In the meantime, she resolved that she would get Recin to show her where she could get some good furniture. She had lived out of a travel chest and sleeping roll long enough. Like it or not, it looked like Berimish was going to be her home for years to come.

She started to slip off the dress she had borrowed from Recin's mother and laughed. It was actually lighter than her nightdress. In the warmth of the room, it might be more comfortable to sleep in what she had worn during the day.

Though she was so exhausted she could barely stand, there was one more thing Talli had to do before sleep. She went back to the trunk in the corner and lifted the lid. From down among the pile of clothing and gear she drew out a necklace with a small twist of silver wire wound round a nubbin of glimmering stone. She took it over to the table and held it near the lamp, watching the rainbow reflections skitter around the room. The necklace had belonged to her mother. Keeping it was a violation of tradition—all of her mother's personal things should have been destroyed along with her body. Otherwise her spirit might be confused and not follow the path into the next life.

Still, Talli could not stand the idea of destroying the necklace. It was all she had left of her mother. Whenever she held it, her fading memories of her mother seemed sharper, and the saddest of days seemed a little brighter. And if the necklace kept her mother's spirit close at hand, Talli wasn't sure that was a bad thing.

She was still staring at the necklace when there was a knock at the door. She groaned, but quickly returned the necklace to her trunk and went to the door. Outside she was surprised to find her father and a pair of troopers.

"Do you feel up to talking for a few minutes?" asked Tagard.

"Yes," said Talli. "I would have come by to see you after I finished with the servants, but I thought that at this hour, you would be asleep—especially with your wound."

Her father patted the bandage at his shoulder. "This is only a reason to stay up. It shows that we have a lot more work ahead of us." He turned to the two men who stood at his back. "Wait here. I'll be out shortly."

Talli stepped aside as her father entered the room and closed the door. "Are you sure the physician didn't tell you to rest?"

"Physicians always say to rest," he replied dismissively.

"So, what did you decide about the Suderbod ambassador?" asked Talli. "Are you going to give them part of Tamingazin to farm?""

Tagard laughed. "Not while the two moons are still in the sky." He ran his hand over the evening stubble on his chin. "The Suder have always wanted this valley for their own. Their own land is in the middle of a swamp. Even with the magewall to keep them out, Lisolo tells me that they made noises about an invasion no more than a year ago. I don't think we should start letting them in by the hundreds."

Talli stared down the hall into the shadows. "Do you think the Suder had anything to do with the Viashino who tried to kill you?"

"I don't know," said her father. He sighed and shook his head. "But the thought had occurred to me. This Daleel Ursal was just a little *too* convenient in his timing. What did you learn by questioning the servants?"

"Not a lot," said Talli. "The dead Viashino was called Thesil. It seems he used to be a kitchen helper, but he was dismissed for stealing some days before we came to Berimish."

"As thin as he was, I can well imagine he stole some food," said the king.

Talli shook her head. "Not food—money. It seems

Thesil's job was to take food to the rooms of ambassadors, and he tried to lift some jewelry from an Acapistani. One thing everyone agrees on: they never saw him eat, not even when the workers ate together."

Tagard stroked his chin. "Did anything you learn tell you why this skinny young thief would want to kill me?"

"No. Nothing."

The king nodded. "Whatever his reasons, his actions are going to force me to make some changes in how we deal with the Viashino."

"I understand," said Talli. "You certainly can't put Lisolo on the council when his people are trying to kill you."

"That's where you're wrong." The king leaned back against the stone wall. "What we have to do now is speed things up. First thing in the morning, I'm calling a meeting of the council—and that includes Lisolo."

Talli wished she had a chair to sit down in. "But why?" she asked.

"Word of what happened today is all over the city by now," he said. "Some people will be angry, some embarrassed. But very few of them will blame the young Viashino. They'll be angry that we're still here, and embarrassed that he had the bravery to do what the rest of them haven't. We'll be lucky if the people of this city don't rise up and kill us all in the next day or two."

"Kill us?" Talli said. "Over this? It's not like you were the one who attacked him."

Tagard nodded. "That may be, but already two patrols have been attacked and injured. I've had to double the number of soldiers in each patrol." He put his hand over his bandaged shoulder and winced. "We took this city without shedding blood, and they've not forgiven either us or themselves."

"What can we do? Will putting Lisolo on the council be enough?"

"I think it will help," he said. "They'll be less likely to attack us if they think that their own king is with us. But I have something else in mind."

"What?"

"We're going to have a ceremony. Tomorrow at mid-day, Lisolo himself is going to proclaim me bey of Berimish as well as king of all Tamingazin." Tagard made an elaborate bow and smiled at his daughter. "We'll put on a good show. It should help link me and Lisolo together in the minds of everyone and take their thoughts away from mischief."

"What about Lisolo?" asked Talli. "Why should he go along with this? And what will Rael Gar and Karelon think?"

"Lisolo may be a Viashino, but he's not uncaring. He no more wants to see this town go up in flames than we do. As for the others . . ." Her father reached out and pushed a strand of hair away from Talli's face. "They are against me on this. But I think they'll come around. What I want to know is, do I have your support?"

Talli reached up and took her father's hand. "I don't like the Viashino, but you're the one who brought us through the war. If you don't have the answers, then who does? Besides, you *are* my father. You can always count on me."

Tagard's smile grew broader. "That's good. You've got more of a following among the troops than you might think. They haven't forgotten how you led the raids or your bravery in battle. Your support will mean a lot." He stood and looked at his daughter for a long moment, then nodded. "Now it would be best if we both got some sleep. Long ceremonies have a way of exhausting the most battle-ready soldier."

Talli walked with him to the front of the chamber and put out a hand to open the door. But before she pulled the handle, another thought came to her mind. "Father, I know that you and Karelon don't agree about Lisolo and the Viashino, but don't let it stand between you in other ways."

Tagard put a hand on his daughter's shoulder. "Talli, I know how much you've wanted this, but I'm not about to marry Karelon. I've already told her as much."

"Why not?" Talli said. One part of her mind was insisting that she had said too much, but she was too tired to listen. "You shouldn't be alone. And I need . . . "

"Ahh, Tallibeth." The king wrapped his arms around his daughter and pulled her in a tight hug. "It's not the right time," he said. "Not now, when there's so much to do. Later, when this land is truly at peace, then maybe I can think about things like marriage."

Talli swallowed her sadness and pulled free of his grip. There were years ahead and plenty of time for her father to change his mind. With one hand, she opened the door. With the other, she wiped the embarrassing wetness from her cheek.

"Good night, Father."

He started out the door, then stopped and turned back. "I was happy to see you in local clothing today. Do you think you could come up with something appropriate for the ceremony?"

Talli winced. "Do I have to?"

"I think it would help. When we get through this, I'd like to talk about what you learned on your visit out among the people."

"All right," she said. "I'll see if Recin knows where I can get something fancier to wear for tomorrow."

"Recin? Not the Garan boy."

"Yes. He's the guide I got to show me around Berimish," said Talli. "He lives at the north end of

town with his mother and aunt." She fingered the
sleeve of the soft gown. "I borrowed this from them."

Her father stepped back into the room and shut the
door. "Does Rael Gar know that you've seen them?"

"He was there when I was," she replied. "I was going
to talk to you about it later. Why is this so important?"

Tagard sighed and put his hand against his forehead.
"These city Garan are considered traitors by the rest of
the agnate. Rael Gar came to me yesterday to discuss
them. He wants to bring them to trial here and punish
them for some crime they committed years ago."

"I never heard of a Garan punishment short of
death," said Talli.

"Without a doubt," admitted the king, "that's the
sentence he's after. For reasons I'm not sure I understand, Rael Gar hates these people, especially the
woman called Janin. If we leave it to him, I think he'll
see that they're killed, then he'll go out, burn their
house, and salt the ground where they walked."

"What is it they did that was so bad?"

"I'm not sure. It seems that Janin used to be the gar."

"She was the leader of the Garan?" Talli asked with
surprise.

"So it seems, until she committed some crime that
the Garan consider unforgivable." Tagard shook his
head. "The best thing would be for you to stay away
from these Garan. Our relationship with Rael Gar is
strained enough."

"If he wants to try them for a crime against the
Garan," said Talli, "shouldn't he take them to the
Garan Agnate to do it? Why should we be involved?"

"He should take them to the agnate," said Tagard.
"However, Rael Gar wants this matter over quickly,
and I've already agreed to go along with him on this."

"You can't," said Talli. "I extended my protection to
them."

Tagard scowled. "You shouldn't have done that."

"I gave my word, we have—"

"No. Not this time," said her father. "The Garan troops are defending the borders of Tamingazin this very moment. If we have to move human troops out of Berimish and the villages to take over for them, we won't be able to hold the city."

Talli blinked. "You really think Rael Gar would leave the alliance over this?"

"I don't just think so. Rael Gar told me that himself." Tagard shook his head sadly. "I don't like it, but these city Garan are his price for continued Garan help."

"So we let Rael Gar kill them?" said Talli. She went to her father and stood looking up into his shadowed face. "Recin was very helpful to me, and so was his family. What if Rael Gar is lying about this great crime?"

"He may be. But this is part of the price we pay for peace."

Talli closed her eyes. She was too tired to fight with her father, too tired to even think straight. "Can I at least go talk to Recin and warn him?" she asked. "Maybe his family can manage to get out of town."

"All right," Tagard said reluctantly. "But be quick about it, and try not to irritate Rael Gar more than you have to." He turned and went to the door for a second time.

"Father?"

Tagard hesitated with his hand on the latch. "Yes?"

"If we start giving up lives for peace, then how is it better than war?"

The king sighed. "I don't know," he said. "I don't think we've really found peace yet." With that he slipped out and closed the door.

Talli went back to her bedroom and sat down on the

edge of the bed. Her father was not going to marry Karelon. At least not now. Recin's family was to be killed, and it seemed there was nothing she could do.

"I can warn them," she said to herself. "If they know that my father isn't going to protect them, maybe they can get away from Rael Gar in time."

She slid out of the pale orange gown that belonged to Janin and carefully folded it. Then she put on her heavy nightdress and lay down to a brief, troubled sleep.

Interlude

STONE PEOPLE

I heard of Tagard long before he started his raids on the Viashino towns.

There are hundreds of humans in Berimish, all of whom are sworn to Bey Lisolo, just as are the Viashino. But, as is usual, things are not as simple as they might first appear.

In the northern part of Berimish, where most of the humans live, there is an expression that I think you will like—

Laws are laws, but the alleys are dark.

The city dwellers may make a great noise of loving their Viashino neighbors, but like humans everywhere, they chaffed at the idea of taking a position lower than any other race. Right up until the city fell, you could catch a man of Berimish on the street, and he would loudly proclaim that Lisolo was bey. But catch the same man in his cups, and Tagard's name was on his lips. More than a little illicit trading went on between the city humans and their wilder cousins in the hills.

Ever since the human holds united under his banner, Tagard has been the darling of the humans in this city. When the city fell to his forces, they were as proud as if they had done it for themselves.

It was easy to dismiss Tagard and the humans of the Tamingazin hills. I was as guilty as anyone in underestimating them. With their heavy clothes and heavy swords, they displayed all the grace and dignity of En'Jaga. Their "holds" are nothing but jumbled piles of old stones, and their farmlands are so close to played out, it is a wonder they can feed themselves.

They feel themselves superior, but they take neither action nor training to prove it. I have not seen one human here, inside the city or out, with the discipline to hold the lowest post in Suderbod.

But what this Tagard has done bears watching. If his government fails, we may find opportunities in his wake. And if he succeeds, all the better.

—From a dispatch by Ursal Daleel, Ambassador to the Valley of Tamingazin from the Court or Hemarch Solin, Conqueror of Suderbod.

CHAPTER
7

THE MORNING DELIVERIES BEGAN LONG before dawn. First Recin carried long loaves of warm crusty bread to the inns near the docks while a fine rain pattered along the empty streets and softly hissed into the river. Then he hurried back to the bakery just as Getin was removing racks of highly spiced flat bread from the big oven. Only after the sacks of the aromatic bread were in the hands of vendors in the southern plaza did the first glow of morning appear in the eastern sky.

He paused by the stone pool and looked across the waters to the Splendent Hall. The day was going to be hot. Already the thin rain clouds were clearing and there was steam rising from the marsh on the other side of the city walls. The rising sun peeked through the clouds to color the whitewashed walls of the hall— all colors from a bright festive yellow to a brooding bloodred.

The colors seemed to match the mood of the city. Not long after Talli had gone with the other humans,

Recin had started hearing rumors about the attack on the king. From some he heard there had been one Viashino involved, from others that a whole band of rebels had stormed the palace. He heard that the king was dead. He heard that the king was untouched. One thing that was the same from rumor to rumor was that it was always some noble Viashino against the invading human king.

By the time Recin had made it back home, there were already fights breaking out between humans and Viashino who had lived side by side all their lives. Patrolling soldiers were being pelted by stones and menaced by growing crowds. Some of the Viashino city guard appeared in the streets in their old uniforms and called for support.

Janin had ordered boards put in place of the bakery's cloth door and the storm slats over the windows closed. They dimmed the lights and stayed downstairs where they could run if they had to. The first half of the night had been punctuated by shouts and the sound of running feet.

Then, near the middle of night, a messenger had gone through the streets, proclaiming Lisolo's appointment to the ruling council and Tagard's impending coronation as bey. The nature of the shouting gradually changed, and uneasy peace took over.

That peace still held, but Recin could feel the tension everywhere he went that morning. Half the merchants he spoke to were eager to celebrate, hoping that the coronation would generate more business, the other half were worried that their stores and stands might be burned to the ground at any moment. Recin did not know which of them was right.

As he watched sunlight brighten the walls of the Splendent Hall, he thought of Talli. Even during the most frightening hours of the night, his thoughts had

slipped toward the blond girl. Recin's mother had
often warned him against getting involved with the
human girls in Berimish. With no other Garan around,
she knew he would be tempted. Matings, even mar-
riages, between Garan and human were not unknown.
But according to his mother, they were doomed to be
bitter and childless. Recin had not worried much
about this in the past. Now it was at the front of his
thoughts.

"She's beyond you," he said aloud. "She's the daughter of a king, and you're the son of a baker. She's a
human; you're Garan." His head fully agreed with the
statement, but it did little to convince his heart.

He had not been able to see Talli when he had
returned her clothing. With the ceremony coming up
and the trouble in the city, he doubted that Talli would
be coming to see him. He wanted to see her, but he
would have to find patience. Somehow.

A breeze blew in from the west, fretting the surface
of the pool. Recin looked across the water, put a hand
to his mouth, and stifled a yawn. Tension and desire
were both strong forces, but a sleepless night still took
its toll. He stretched and remembered that breakfast
would be waiting back at the bakery—along with more
chores. His dreams of Talli would have to wait.

But as he started to turn away, a slim figure topped
by blond hair appeared from one of the hall's many
doors and started up the street at a rapid clip. Recin
sped around the pool and ran hard to catch up with
her. She was wearing her dark mountain woolens,
and bits of bronze decoration bounced on her shoulders as she strode briskly down the street. Recin had
to keep up a fast pace just to catch up to her. Too
breathless to shout, he reached out and touched her
on the arm.

Talli's reaction was startling. With incredible swiftness,

she spun around, dropped the bundle she was carrying, and drew the short sword from her belt. There was a fire in her eyes that made Recin's heart stop in his chest.

Then Talli blinked, and her face softened. "I thought you might be Rael Gar," she said. Her short sword went back into its leather scabbard with a soft hiss.

"No," said Recin. He struggled to draw in enough air to combat both his run and his fear. "Is Rael Gar after you?" he managed. "Would he really try to hurt you?"

She shook her head and bent to pick up her dropped bundle. "I don't think he would hurt me—he knows he would never get away with that—but he might try to scare me, and I wanted to do the same for him."

"Well, it scared me enough." Recin put a hand against his chest and rolled his eyes. "I think my heart stopped beating."

"It might soon enough," said Talli. "What Rael Gar's really after is you. You and all your family."

"I know he's mad at us, but my mother told me not to worry about him," said Recin. "She says there's nothing he can do to us here and that he has to wait for midsummer day before he can go to the agnate."

"She's wrong," said Talli. "He wants to put you on trial right here in Berimish." Her blue eyes looked away. "He wants to kill you all."

It took Recin a moment to really understand her words. Even before he had known the warrior's name, Rael Gar had haunted Recin's dreams. Now the killer from his dreams had come back, and he wasn't going to stop until the whole family was destroyed.

"We have to tell my mother," he said slowly. "She'll know what to do."

"I hope so," said Talli. "I've stayed up half the night, and I can't think of anything."

The two of them turned together and headed down the street at a rapid pace. Most of the shops they passed were only beginning to open for the day's business. There were few people on the street of any sort, but those Viashino they went by paid far more attention to Talli than they had just the day before. Some of them only stared, but others made gestures of open anger. Talli didn't seem to be aware of the meaning of the Viashino's lowered necks and bobbing heads, but Recin understood them well enough and it made him nervous. He was grateful when he reached the bakery and slipped inside.

Aunt Getin came out of the kitchen at the sound of the front door. "It's about time you got back," she said. "I've got two trays of . . ." Her golden eyes turned to Talli and she stopped in midsentence.

"Where is Mother?" asked Recin.

The colors that rippled through Getin's eyes showed glimmers of both anger and frustration. "I listened to you," she said to Talli. "I thought your people meant what you said, but this city is ready to swallow its own tail."

"My father is trying," the human girl replied. "It's not his fault that someone tried to kill him."

Recin stepped between them. "We've got a bigger problem to worry about. Where's Mother?"

"Back here," called a voice from the kitchen. Janin stepped into the room, wiping her hands on a rag. "Its good to see you again so soon," she said calmly, "but I hope this visit won't be as eventful as your last."

"I'm afraid I can't promise that," said Talli.

"Rael Gar is coming," said Recin.

His mother nodded. "I told you he would. But we're no longer part of the agnate, the gar has no hold over us."

Talli shook her head. "That's not what Rael Gar

thinks. He's planning on putting you on trial and having you executed."

"Well, he can plan all he wants, but your protection—"

"Is worthless," said Talli. She swallowed and looked down at the floor. "I'm sorry, but my father is too dependent on the help of the Garan. Right now the only thing guarding the inside of the magewall from invaders is Rael Gar's forces. He won't do anything that might cause Rael Gar to leave the alliance."

Recin waited for his mother to reply, but she only stood in silence. "What do we do?" he asked. "Can we leave?"

"And go where?" asked Getin. "All we own is in these walls."

Janin held up her hands. "I don't know yet. We'll have to think."

"But what if he comes today?" asked Recin.

"He won't," said his mother. "He wants to have a trial, and he'll want to do it himself. That means he'll have to wait until after Tagard's ceremony is past."

Talli raised her head and brushed her thick hair back from her face. "I'm sorry," she repeated. "I didn't know what to do except tell you."

"That's better than not telling us," Janin replied.

"Rael Gar has helped my father for years," said the human girl. "He's always seemed so calm. Almost as if he didn't get upset or angry about anything."

"Humans often think that the Garan don't have any emotions," said Janin. "But the emotions are still there, no matter how calm the face."

"He doesn't stay calm when he talks about you," said Talli. "Why is he so angry? What happened to make him so mad?"

Recin watched his mother closely. Though he knew the outlines of the story, his mother had always been reluctant to share any details.

"It was a long time ago," said Janin. She turned away from them and walked slowly to the single window. "I was gar," she said softly, "the leader of the Garan Agnate, and my husband, Ranas, was tak. It was winter, and bitter in the mountains. Winds rolled down from Skollten, bearing snow and hard sleet. The hunt brought back less food each day. The old ones were starving, and the children were freezing in their bedrolls." She paused for a moment, and though it was a steamy warm morning, she hugged her arms around herself and shivered as if she were still in those snowy mountains.

"I led the Garan into the western passes," she continued, "looking for food and protection from the weather." Janin hesitated again and gave a long sigh. "It was a mistake. A tribe of En'Jaga had come through the magewall and were there before us."

Getin hurried across the room. "You don't have to tell it. Not now."

When his mother turned, Recin saw that her eyes were silver with remembered pain. "I think I should tell it," she said. "Maybe I should have told it long ago."

Recin was stung by the emotion in his mother's eyes. He wanted more than anything for her to go on, but not at the cost of seeing her in pain.

"You don't have to," he said. "I don't need to know."

His mother looked at him and nodded slightly. "Wait until you've heard it all, and then tell me."

She reached behind her head and loosed the tie that kept the brown hair back from her face while she was in the kitchen. The dark curls framed her face and made the distinctive Garan shape of her cheeks and eyes more noticeable. Again, she turned away from the others in the room, pacing slowly across the floor as she told her story.

"There were at least two hundred of the En'Jaga. If there had been fewer, we would have taken them, but two hundred . . . Hands and feet can only do so much against the armored hide of an En'Jaga. That many surpassed the ability of even the whole agnate to handle." She shook her head and Recin saw her hands move into the stiff, lethal position they had taken when she faced Rael Gar. "Every time we clashed, we lost three or four Garan for every En'Jaga that fell. There was a storm in the heights, we couldn't go back. We tried to move to the south, but the En'Jaga blocked our way."

Aunt Getin suddenly slapped her hand against the counter. She stepped past the racks of baked goods and ran into the kitchen. From a distance, Recin heard a sound that might have been a sob.

"What did you do?" he asked softly.

His mother returned to the window and looked out onto the alley. "I did nothing," she said. "It was your father who acted. Each night he slipped away. I thought he was going on a night hunt, but several times he returned without food. Ranas Tak was a wonderful hunter. For him to fail in a single hunt was rare. This time he failed three days in a row. I knew that something was wrong with him, but I did not know how wrong until he left one evening and didn't return." She stopped and was silent for long seconds.

"What happened?" Talli asked at last. "Did he come back?"

"Oh, he came back. He wouldn't tell me where he had been or what he had been doing. It was the first time in our marriage—the first time in our lives—he had kept a secret from me. Soon after his return, the En'Jaga began to leave." Janin turned toward them, but her eyes were still focused on scenes that were miles and years away. "We didn't know why at first. All I knew was that the En'Jaga were retreating to the valley, and we could bind our wounds. I thought they had merely moved on, but Rael Tak found out otherwise. He found the bodies, and he found Ranas's footprints with them."

"Your husband, Recin's father, was killing the En'Jaga?" Talli said. "But how did he do that?"

"I tried to find out, but he wouldn't talk to me. He denied having anything to do with the En'Jaga's death." Janin's gaze came back to the present and her dark eyes turned to Recin.

"But Rael Tak followed him one night and told me what he saw. He saw Ranas use a Viashino crossbow to kill."

Talli drew a sharp breath. "He used a bow?" she said. "A weapon?"

Janin nodded.

"But how did he die?" Recin asked. It was the one part of the story he had never understood. "Did the En'Jaga attack again?"

His mother shook her head slowly. "He used a weapon."

Recin shrugged. "I know that Garan aren't supposed to use weapons, you've told me that much, but he only did it to save the people. No one would . . ." He saw the silver glint in his mother's eyes and his words trailed off.

"Kill him?" She nodded. "That is exactly what the law calls for. Any Garan who uses a weapon—whether in hunt or in battle—must be killed. It has been the law since we came to this valley from the mountains of Skollten."

"But you were gar," said Recin.

"Rael Tak caught your father using the bow and fought him. He came back to our camp, and Getin and I followed him into the night. By the time we reached

Ranas, your father was unconscious, almost dead," said Janin. "Rael Tak confronted me right then, ordered me to carry out my duty and kill Ranas. I refused." She looked down, and her hair closed in around her face. "I knew my duty, but I insisted that it was a matter for the whole convocation to decide. While Getin and I tended Ranas, Rael Tak ran back to the camp and consulted with the others. He returned with a decision of death, but by then it was too late— Ranas was dead already."

Acid burned at the back of Recin's throat. He could picture everything his mother described far too well. All his life he had wanted to hear this story, and now that he had, he wished he hadn't.

"Even though I was only days away from delivering my child, I should have been next. I had neglected my duty as the gar and the convocation had ruled that I had to pay with my life.

"But I couldn't let my child die. Getin, no more than a child herself, was with me. She helped me flee down the mountain. It took us days to get through the forest while avoiding both Garan and En'Jaga. Finally we reached the valley, and then we came here."

She looked at her son and spread her hands. "That's how we came here. And that's why Rael Gar is still after us."

Recin didn't know what to say. It was one thing to know that your father had been killed. It was a very different thing to know that he had been beaten and left to die in the snow. He felt that he ought to go to her, to comfort her somehow. But her pain was rooted so far in the past that it was out of his reach.

"That's not all," Talli said suddenly.

Recin's mother turned to her. "Not all? It's all I have to tell."

Talli frowned and shook her head. "That's not what

I mean. I'm not even sure what I do mean, but I don't think that Rael Gar is after you just because you broke some piece of Garan tradition."

"Why else would he be after us?" asked Recin.

"I don't know," the human girl admitted. Her forehead creased in thought. "I've been around him ever since the Garan joined forces with my father—more than two years—but I can't say I understand him. I only know I don't trust him."

There was a commotion outside as a wagon navigated the narrow alley. Close behind it marched a maniple of human soldiers dressed in their finest.

Talli went to the window and frowned out at the street. "I have to go," she said. "The ceremony to name my father bey is in only a few hours, and I promised I would hurry back."

"You've warned us," said Janin. "That's more than you owed us."

"What will you do now?"

"As I said," said Recin's mother, "we'll think, and talk. Rael Gar won't be up to anything today, and I'm not ready to run just yet."

Recin walked over to stand near the blond girl. "I'll walk with you back to the hall, if you want. There are still a lot of upset Viashino in the city."

She shook her head. "You stay here. I'd rather risk running into a Viashino than take the chance of delivering you to Rael Gar." She turned and looked from Recin to his mother. "If you're still here after the ceremony, I'll come and see you. If not, then good luck." She turned and walked quickly from the bakery.

"She's a remarkable girl," said Janin. "If her father is anything like her, it's no wonder he's got the whole valley following him."

"But she can't protect us. What are we going to do?" Recin asked. "Are we going to run?"

"I don't know." His mother ran her hand across the flour-dusted wood of the counter. "There was a time when I owned nothing and wandered from place to place without a thought. But we've built a home here." She looked around at the small room. "If we leave, I'll miss it."

Getin called from the kitchen, and Recin's mother went to help her. Recin was left standing in the front room, wondering what it would mean if they did leave Berimish.

Except for occasional berry-picking trips into the edge of the Great Marsh, he had never gone beyond the safety of the city's stone walls. He knew that other Garan lived in the chill mountains at the edge of the valley, and he had thought about what it would be like to live there. But he had no real desire to try it. He was Garan by blood, but he had spent his life inside, out of the weather, and with a bed to sleep on.

He didn't suppose he had to worry about the harsh mountains. If they did run, the last place they would go would be to the other Garan. Maybe they would go south to the soggy swamps of the Suder. Or even farther to the jungles of Acapistan, where he had been told that summer lasted all year. Or to the islands where humans fished and sailed their boats over blue waters. It all sounded exotic and interesting, but to Recin none of it sounded as good as the idea of staying in Berimish.

A group of three Viashino hurried by outside. Through the window Recin heard the familiar voice of his friend Heasos talking about Tagard and the ceremony. A moment later, a yellow-gray head and lengthy neck appeared in the doorway.

"Hey, Garan," said the Viashino. "Coming to see the hill human get the torc?"

"I don't know," said Recin. He tried to shake his

thoughts of Rael Gar and smiled for his friend. "What's that you've got on?"

Heasos stepped the rest of the way into the shop. He was wearing a robe of deep blue with red trim. "They said we could wear our city guard uniforms to the ceremony," he said. "Lisolo's honor guard even got their weapons back."

"And after?"

An S-shaped ripple ran through Heasos's neck—a gesture of uncertainty. "If Lisolo is really part of the council, then Viashino are as much a part of the alliance as humans or Garan. Why shouldn't we have the same rights to carry weapons?"

"Do you really think he'll keep his word?"

"You're the one who's seen him," said Heasos. "What do you think?"

Recin frowned. Tagard had not stepped in to keep Rael Gar away from his family, but he could not forget his one meeting with the man on the night Berimish had fallen. "I think he'll keep his word."

Janin appeared from the kitchen, and Heasos raised his chin in greeting. "Morning, Mother of Recin," he said. Having no knowledge of his own mother, Heasos seemed endlessly fascinated that Recin actually lived under the same roof with Janin.

"You're looking very fine this morning, Heasos," Janin said. "Are you going to the ceremony?"

"Yes," said the young Viashino. "My patrol has a spot near the front of the line. We should get a good view when Lisolo slides the torc onto this human." He opened his mouth in a sharp-toothed grin. "We're betting it'll slide all the way to his feet."

Recin laughed with his friend, but his mother walked across the room and looked out at the increasing string of Viashino and humans on their way to the ceremony.

"Why don't you go with him?" she said.

"To the ceremony?" Recin looked at her with surprise. "But shouldn't I stay here so we can talk?"

Janin shook her head. "We'll talk later. Right now, I want you to go with Heasos. If you leave now, you'll be able to find a place where you can see what's happening."

"We need to hurry," said Heasos. "My patrol will be getting into position."

Recin was reluctant to go, but he had never had any luck avoiding what his mother wanted him to do. "All right, let's go."

Heasos nodded again to Janin, then stepped through the door. Recin started to follow, but his mother moved across the room with surprising speed and took his arm. "You're not going there just to watch Lisolo and Tagard," she said. "I want you to keep an eye on Rael Gar. If he leaves, you come back here. Fast. He'll wait till after this ceremony, but he hungers to get us out of the way."

"Right," Recin said with a nod. He started to move again, but Janin's grip was still tight.

"And watch out for your friend Tallibeth," she said. "If Rael Gar is up to something, and she knows it, then she's in danger."

"But how will Rael Gar know?" asked Recin. "Talli's not going to tell him that she suspects him."

"Rael will know," said his mother. "Somehow, he always does."

She loosed her grip on Recin's arm, and he hurried out into the streets.

CHAPTER

8

TALLI LOOKED INTO THE SHEET OF POLISHED steel and frowned. She had forgotten about her father's request to wear Berimish-style clothing to the ceremony, and she had forgotten to ask Recin about where she could find such clothing. Her father had not forgotten.

Now she was stuck wearing what the servants at the Splendent Hall were able to dig out of some dusty storeroom. The clothing turned out to be a gown of pale green that stretched almost to Talli's ankles. It wasn't how it covered her legs that she minded—after wearing the shorter casual clothing, she was glad of that much—it was the parts it *didn't* cover that bothered her.

"Why do they try to keep humans half-naked in this city?" she grumbled, trying to pull the top of the gown at least halfway to her shoulders.

"It's the heat," said the Viashino who had brought the gown. "Humans get too hot here."

"That's what everyone keeps saying," said Talli. She tugged again on the gown. "I think I'd rather be hot."

The Viashino made a hissing laugh and jabbed a pin into a loose fold. "We need to make a few changes if this is going to fit right."

Talli groaned, but nodded her agreement. The Viashino began moving around her, making subtle adjustments to the gown. She doubted that anything could make it cover more of her exposed skin.

The Viashino was an older creature, with the network of yellow-green lines along its head and neck that identified it as female. Talli was not sure if that comforted her. She had never been so close to any Viashino for so long. Despite what she had seen of their city, and her experience with the servants the night before, it still made her nervous.

There was a knock. Before she had a chance to say yes or no, the door swung open and Tagard came in. "It's time," he said. "We need to get out there."

Talli scowled at her reflection for a moment longer. "All right," she said. "But I feel ridiculous."

Her father smiled at her. "You look fine. I'm sure the people here will appreciate the effort you've made."

"I hope so," Talli said, with a final tug at the top of the gown. She followed her father out of the room, walking carefully to avoid stepping on the hem of the long dress.

Tagard was dressed in the same polished armor he had worn when he had climbed to the institute to meet Aligarius. Talli remembered complaining when her father had had the armor made. Brass plate might as well have been paper when facing iron weapons, and the ceremonial plate was far too thin to stop the weakest blow. Tagard had argued that this was armor for show, not fighting. In battle he wore the same padded iron cap and jacket of steel leaves as every other human in the army. But when the contest was one of words, appearances counted. Talli had to admit that the polished brass breastplate with its black cloth sleeves was well suited to him.

Rael Gar and Karelon were waiting together a few steps down the hall. Talli stared into the Garan's impassive face, waiting for him to make some comment about the incident at Recin's bakery, but Rael Gar didn't give any sign that he even remembered.

Karelon's face was not nearly so expressionless. At her first sight of the king and his daughter, the dark-haired woman raised an eyebrow in surprise. "Where did you find this clothing?" she asked Talli.

Talli fingered the green gown. "The servants found it somewhere."

"I thought it would be appropriate for her to dress in the style of Berimish," said Tagard. "If this is going to be our home, we should be open to its ways."

"Yes," said Karelon. "Of course." Despite her words, the expression on her face made it clear she didn't agree with Tagard's idea. Talli desperately wished she had something, anything, to cover the scanty gown.

"Is everything in place outside?" asked Tagard.

"I've constructed the platform for the ceremony," said Karelon. "I had to move it to the eastern edge of the ramp to provide spectators a better view."

There was a mumbling among the guards down the hall. Talli turned and saw the humans and Garan moving aside as the looming form of Lisolo approached. Unlike humans, Viashino grew all their lives, and Lisolo was a very old Viashino. His red-spotted throat, with its ruff of enlarged scales, stretched high above the heads of the humans, and his long head almost scraped the ceiling. None of the Viashino Talli had passed in the streets had been even close to the imposing size of their bey. Following in his wake were a trio of smaller Viashino, looking much like young water-bills trailing after their mother.

The Viashino leader stopped near Tagard and lowered his head. Talli had learned enough of Viashino gestures to know that this was usually a sign of anger. But Lisolo did it slowly and gracefully, like a human performing an elaborate bow. He raised his head and formed his neck into a graceful S-curve.

"King Tagard," said the Viashino, his voice as deep as water running through a dark cave. The smaller Viashino composed themselves around their giant leader.

"Lisolo," Tagard said simply. "Are you ready to take your place on the council?"

Lisolo nodded. "I am." He turned his head to the side and Talli shivered as his deep gold eyes fastened on her for a moment. "As we have agreed."

"Good," said Tagard. "Then it's time for us to get out there and show the people of this city that we are united."

Talli took a breath of relief as Lisolo directed his attention back to the king and nodded in agreement. Over his robed back, she could see the heads of Karelon and Rael Gar as they stood on the other side of the hall staring at the Viashino. Karelon's face was twisted in disgust. None of Tagard's efforts had done anything to lessen Karelon's hatred of the Viashino in general and Lisolo in particular.

"It's nearly midday," said Tagard. "We only need Aligarius, then we can begin."

"The wizard has been undependable the last few days," said Rael Gar. "I've already sent a soldier to bring him."

A moment later, Aligarius came staggering along the hallway with a soldier on either side. He looked even worse than when Talli had seen him last. Deep grooves cut across his pallid forehead, and his eyes were sunken and dry. He stood in front of Tagard, staring straight ahead as if he did not even see the people around him.

Talli reached out and touched the old man lightly on the arm. "Are you feeling well?" she asked.

Aligarius turned to her and blinked. "Yes. I'm fine," he said. "Really quite fine." He smiled slightly, and Talli returned the smile. But she was still worried about the old man. The sorcerer was an important symbol of Tagard's power. If Aligarius was seen to be ill, it might give more courage to those who wanted to throw the new king out of Berimish.

"Let's get out there," Tagard said. "The people have been waiting for almost an hour now. As hard as the sun is here, half of them will pass out if we wait any longer."

"Hold there," said Aligarius. "I have something for you." The sorcerer fished in the folds of his robe and came out with a small charm on a length of woven cord. He started to hand the item to Tagard, then he pulled it back.

Tagard looked at Aligarius with a puzzled expression. "Did you want me to wear that?" he asked.

"Yes," said the sorcerer. "You need to wear this." He extended his hand again. "This will help."

The king took the talisman from the wizard and quickly slipped it over his head. "Thank you." A tiny bit of red feather and black-veined copper hung against the front of Tagard's armor.

He turned back to the soldiers at the top of the ramp. "All right," he said. "Let's go."

Tagard signaled to the men outside, and Talli heard the sound of a hundred aldehorns proclaiming their deep raspy notes into the warm Berimish air. As the first tones faded, another hundred men began beating out a steady rhythm with polished sticks of dark heavy wood. It was a nostalgic sound, reminding Talli of the first days of the war, of the stone walls of Farson Hold, and of her mother standing at her father's side.

Tagard looked over at her and gave his daughter a quick smile.

"You lead the way," he said.

Talli nodded. As she started down the hallway, she found that she was suddenly more nervous than she would have believed. Facing the crowd outside seemed almost as bad as the idea of climbing the narrow ledge to the Institute of Arcane Study. The sunshine was so bright that she could scarcely see beyond the end of the hall. When she finally emerged into the sunlight, there was a cheer so loud that it left her disoriented. She held her hands up to shade her eyes and squinted at the gathered crowds.

Those closest to the Splendent Hall were mostly the humans who had marched under Tagard's banner. But there were also several groups of Viashino in the front rows. These were dressed in dark clothing that was different from what most of the Viashino wore in the city; she immediately took it to be some kind of uniform. Behind those front ranks were gathered thousands of Viashino and humans, so many that Talli thought the rest of Berimish must have been empty. To find a place from which they could see, people were ranked along the roofs of buildings across the street and even stood in the waters of the pool.

A platform for the ceremony had been hastily constructed at the end of the ramp, with a cluster of chairs and a resting rail for Lisolo. The cheers died down as Talli found her place on the platform and settled into one of the chairs, only to start up with renewed energy.

She looked over her shoulder and saw Rael Gar stepping into the sunlight. The Garan walked down the ramp quickly and didn't so much as look left or right. Rael Gar had insisted that all Garan be stationed outside the city, so there were none of his own people to cheer, though Talli was not sure they would have broken their restraint for such a thing. The human forces gave him a greeting loud enough to make up for the absence of other Garan. Rael Gar reached the platform and took his seat.

A moment later, the cheers rose again as Karelon stepped into the light. Where Talli wore her light Berimish gown and Tagard was dressed in his elaborate armor, Karelon wore the heavy battle armor and dark woolens from her home hold. A blistered, worn cloak trailed out behind her, flapping in the warm air. She held one hand in a dark leather glove high in the air, giving the signal for the troops to advance. The effect of her appearance was obvious. Soldiers that had fought with her in dozens of battles broke into wild cheering and waved their swords above their heads.

Aligarius was next. He came down the ramp rapidly and was greeted by cheers that were not nearly as enthusiastic as the ones that had come before. From the Viashino in the crowd came scattered low whistling clicks. Talli didn't need anyone to tell her that this noise was not a sound of approval.

As soon as Aligarius dropped into his chair, there was cheering of a very different sort. This time the soldiers were almost silent, but the crowd behind them roared. Lisolo had emerged into the light. The great Viashino made his way down the ramp slowly, making slight gestures with his head and neck that might have had subtle meaning to the Viashino crowd, but had no meaning to Talli. In his clawed hands, he held a bundle wrapped in soft blue cloth. The timbers of the platform groaned under his feet as he walked to his railing and leaned his weight to the side.

The cheers gradually quieted, and all eyes turned to the top of the ramp. Unlike the others, Tagard did not immediately appear as soon as Lisolo had taken his place. There was a shuffling of feet among the soldiers and growing whisper among the Viashino as they waited for the new king to appear.

Talli smiled to herself. Trust her father to add every moment of drama to what was sure to be a dry ceremony on a hot day.

Suddenly Tagard stepped out of the shade of the Splendent Hall and into the harsh sunlight. Golden reflections showered off his polished armor and flashed across his hair. Talli and the others rose from their chairs. A cheer rose from the soldiers, from the Viashino troopers, and finally from all the crowd. Talli was shouting for all she was worth, but her own noise was lost in the deafening tumult.

Tagard came down the ramp almost at a run and leaped into the center of the platform. As he raised his arms over his head and smiled at the crowd, the cheers increased until Talli wondered if the very walls of the city might crumble at the sound. Tagard took his time quieting the crowd, making sure that he turned to look and wave at all sides. When the cheers had finally died down, Tagard went and placed a hand on Lisolo's scaly shoulder—which only started the crowd roaring all over again.

Finally, the cheers dropped to a scattered few, and Tagard walked to the edge of the platform. "People of Tamingazin," he called. "All of you know all of us, and I won't make you stand in this heat while I regale you with the story of how we came to be here."

This statement alone was enough to bring another round of cheering, especially from the humans in the crowd who couldn't take the heat as easily as the Viashino. Talli glanced over at Karelon and saw that sweat was pouring down her face and soaking her dark wool clothing. Talli had to fight back a grin at the woman's discomfort. Karelon had been very smart in knowing how to draw the loyalty of her troops, but in the valley sunshine, dressing in the dark mountain armor had to be like wearing a brick oven.

Tagard waited for the crowd to be quiet, then spoke again. "Today we're here to show that what we said we would do, we have done. Tamingazin is home to human, Garan elf, and Viashino. And so is our council." He stepped to the front of the platform and the smile slipped from his face. "But one person will lead this council. Only one will be your king and bey."

He paused then, and stood with his eyes closed for so long that Talli began to worry something was really wrong. When he finally opened his eyes and looked up, there was an expression of grim determination on his face.

"I am not here to proclaim myself king of Tamingazin," he said.

The crowd exploded with questions and shouts. On the platform, Karelon jerked forward so hard that she tottered at the edge of the chair, and Talli felt her heart flutter in her chest. Surely, after all that they had been through, her father was not going to give it all away.

"I will not proclaim myself king," Tagard continued. "If I am to be king, *you* are the ones who must name me king."

He turned to Lisolo and nodded. The Viashino unfolded the blue cloth to reveal the torc that every Viashino leader of Berimish had worn for as long as there had been a Berimish. It was the first time Talli had seen it in the light, and she was fascinated by the rows of tiny characters that had been carved into the dark stones and bands of polished metal. Like those in the temple Recin had taken her to, none of the characters was easily understood, but there was a power to them—a raw, emotional force that said this object was more than just a hoop of metal and stone.

Tagard took the torc from Lisolo's hands and raised it up for all to see. "All your lives you've lived with kings or beys that were chosen by someone else. Now you will choose your own." He held the torc high overhead. "Who will be your king?" he shouted.

There was a moment of unsettled rumbling, then one group of soldiers near the front shouted "Tagard!" The name was picked up and repeated by others, soon hundreds of throats were crying Tagard's name over and over. And it didn't stop with the humans. The Viashino picked up the cry. Soon the cry was so loud that it made the previous cheering seem like a whisper in the dark.

Without another word, Tagard handed the torc back to Lisolo. It was the Viashino leader who actually lifted the dark circlet and lowered it over Tagard's head. The ring, designed to fit the massive neck of an adult Viashino, was far too big for a human. But even resting on the shoulders of Tagard's bronze armor, it somehow looked right.

"Humans and Garan!" the Viashino shouted in his cave-deep voice. "Here is your king! Viashino! Here is your bey!"

In the shouting that followed, Talli found that tears were running down her cheeks. It seemed impossible that there had been conflict and rebellion in Berimish only hours before. Her father had been right: humans, Viashino, and Garan—all together. She felt an emotion that was so strong darkness pressed in at the edges of her vision.

She looked from her father down to the jubilant crowd, then back at her father. What she saw there was so puzzling that at first her mind refused to accept it. An iron spike seemed to have grown from the back of Tagard's bright armor. Talli frowned. She didn't remember there being any decoration like that on the ceremonial armor, and it certainly didn't look like part of the torc.

Then another of the iron spikes sprouted next to the first one, and Talli realized what they were. Crossbow bolts.

She jumped out of her chair and reached her father just in time to keep him from toppling off the platform. His blue eyes were closed, and his face was twisted by shock and pain.

Talli drew her father back and fell to her knees on the rough wooden planks. One of the bolts had hit with enough force that the point had gone through Tagard's back and emerged from the shining metal of the breastplate, where it pressed against the charm that Aligarius had given him. Blood poured out around the shafts, impossibly red and bright in the tropical sun.

Talli was barely aware of the others moving and shouting around her. Distantly she heard the sound of the crowd change from cries of joy to screams of terror and outrage. Soldiers climbed onto the platform, and with their help Talli carried her father back up the ramp into the Splendent Hall. Talli tried to keep her hands pressed around the shafts of the bolts as they walked, but Tagard's blood continued to pour out in pulsing waves, spilling across Talli's fingers and splashing on the white stone of the ramp.

"The physician!" she cried as they carried the fallen king. "Get the physician! And bring Aligarius, he may have magic that can help." One of the soldiers ran off to carry out her orders.

They didn't try to reach the king's chambers, but laid Tagard down on the floor of the hallway, just out of the sun. It was Talli that brushed the bloodstained charm out of the way, put her fingers around the iron shafts of the bolts, and pulled them free. The first one came out easily, bringing a dark welling of blood that filled the inside of the armor and dripped out around Tagard's arms and neck. The one that had penetrated the king's chest took more effort, and in the end she had to push it through and pull it out from the back.

While she worked, the soldiers stood around with their padded helmets under their arms, shuffling their feet and looking as if they had been struck senseless.

"Help me get this armor off," she shouted at them. "We've got to stop the bleeding."

The leather straps that held the back and chest plates together were slick with blood, and Talli's fingers felt as useless as stumps. When the straps were finally free, blood sloshed from the opened armor in such quantities that even the soldiers cried out. It flowed across the floor of the Splendent Hall, and splashed against the feet of those nearby.

The trooper who had gone to follow Talli's instructions came running back up the ramp. "The Viashino physician is coming," she said. "But I can't find anyone that knows where Aligarius went."

Talli clamped her hands over the wound on her father's chest, trying to staunch the flow. Bubbles of blood and air leaked between her fingers. Blood plastered her borrowed gown against her body. She could feel the wetness through the thin material. There was blood on her arms. On her legs. In her hair. On the stones of the floor. On the dark stone of the king's torc.

Tagard's eyes snapped open. "Talli," he said. There was a soft liquid whistle in his voice. His fingers came up and tangled in his daughter's blond hair. "Don't let them take it apart. Don't let them go back."

"Be quiet," said Talli. "The physician is coming."

The king shook his head. "Don't let them take it apart," he repeated. "That's all that matters."

"Father . . . "

"Promise me," said Tagard.

Talli nodded and a mixture of her own tears and her father's blood splashed on the floor. "We'll do what you wanted," she said. "All of us together."

Tagard nodded. For a moment, it seemed he was going to sit up. Then he sighed, and his head fell back on the stones.

It seemed that hours passed before the Viashino physician appeared, though it had to be only minutes. Talli pulled her hand away from her father's wounds and stood aside as the Viashino bent and examined the damage.

"Bad," said the physician. He hissed through his sharp teeth. "Very bad."

"Save him," Talli said.

The physician bent to his task. For the first time, Talli looked down the ramp to where she had been standing a moment before. A trail of drying blood led down the ramp to the platform. The plaza that had been packed with cheering people was suddenly all but empty. An overturned cart lay on the ground and a few bits of cloth or paper littered the pavement. On the platform were only empty chairs. Rael Gar and Karelon were gone. A line of soldiers stood at the door, blocking admission to the Splendent Hall. Except for those soldiers, there was not a soul in sight.

In the silence of the hallway, Talli gradually became aware of the whistling of her father's breath. It was a ragged, frightening sound, and with every second it seemed to rise in pitch. The physician stood and shook his long neck.

"The bolt has passed through his lungs," said the Viashino. "And the sack that holds his heart has been cut."

Talli felt her own heart stop. "What does that mean?"

The physician looked down. "It means he will die," he said. "I'm sorry."

Talli wanted to believe that the physician was wrong. He was a Viashino, maybe he was not really trying to help. But the sound of her father's breathing was enough to prove the truth of the creature's words.

Tagard's breathing stopped for a moment and Talli dropped to his side. "Father," she said.

The king moaned and took another whistling breath. His lips moved, but his eyes did not open. The whistle in his breathing grew higher and higher until Talli could hear nothing but the bubble of blood escaping his chest.

And then there was nothing but silence.

She bent over her father, ignoring the flow of crimson, and pressed her face against his tight blond curls. She was still there when she heard the sound of footsteps approaching along the corridor.

"Is he dead?" said a voice.

"Yes," said a deeper voice. Lisolo's voice.

Talli looked up and saw the large Viashino looming a few steps away. She wondered how long he had been there. Near Lisolo stood Karelon and a knot of her soldiers.

"Where have you been?" asked Talli.

Karelon looked at her with a surprisingly harsh expression. "I've been taking care of the city. Someone had to act, or there would have been chaos."

"You're right." Talli touched her father's cheek, then stood.

The Viashino doctor stepped forward and pulled a sheet of coarse cloth over Tagard's body. Talli had a sharp memory of the Viashino who had tried to kill her father only the day before. Then it had been only fear, but now it really was her father's body stretched out on the cold, bloodstained stones.

She pushed her tangled hair away from her face and tried to look as dignified as she could in her blood-drenched clothing. In the shadows of the hallway, the gown was cold and sticky. "I'm sure my father would have wanted you to do just that," she said.

"Yes," said the dark-haired woman. "I'm sure."

Talli took a deep breath. "We'll have to have a meeting of the council. We have to decide what to do next."

"Maybe we should start by finding out who did this," said Karelon.

"Yes," agreed Talli. "I should have thought of that."

Karelon smiled, but it was not an expression that anyone would have mistaken for happiness. "We've already caught the killer," she said. She signaled to the soldiers at her side, and a struggling form was pushed down the hallway. The figure sprawled at Talli's feet, his hands in Tagard's spilled blood.

"I believe you already know this one," said Karelon.

Talli looked down . . . into the face of Recin.

Interlude

REND MY FLESH

It is night as I write this—a cloudy, winter night, with not so much as the lesser moon in to break the darkness—and my thoughts are as black as the sky.

Less than a year has passed since your mother left us. The bitter fight with Vindicant Hold has left little time for musing, and during the day matters of our own hold leave me little time to grieve. It is at night, especially on cold empty nights like this, that I miss the warmth of her next to me and the comfort of her voice at my ear. These are the times when thoughts of doubt and death creep close. I hope that, at your young age, you are less troubled by such speculations.

By rights I should have written this letter on the very day that your mother fell. If more bad luck had come to our family in the past year, you would have been left without the confirmation of my inheritance.

You are still in your childhood, but there can be no doubt that all my pride rests with you. All our lands, our animals, and our place at the hold table are yours at my death. I cannot settle the leadership of the hold on your shoulders—that is a position you must earn for yourself. But if you want this, I believe you will have it. You have your mother's strength of will. Your inheritance will stretch as far as your own ambitions.

I task you with my body in death, because I know you will see that my wishes are carried out. Most of the hold has taken to burning, but your mother did not believe in this, and neither do I. Rend my flesh in the traditional way so that no spirit can ride me after death, and my own soul might be freed. Make the cuts deep and be sure to break my legs.

If I am close to Farson when I die, lay me out for the

mountain cats. If elsewhere, then either field or forest will do. Any bones you find later, be sure that they are shattered and spread.

Writing about my own death is not easy. I would say that I hope you never have to follow these instructions, but I do not believe I can face the alternative. It is only proper that the parent should precede the child. Though your mother is dead, our union lives in you. If you should reach your end before me, it would be more than I can stand.

One of the scouts along the western wall is calling my name, and I must be brief. Now that I have faced this task once, I hope it will be easier in the future. Next time I will tell more of my hopes for you.

> —*Letter from Tagard Tarngold to his daughter Tallibeth. Six years out of date at the time of Tagard's death. No other letters were found.*

CHAPTER
9

WHEN RECIN FOLLOWED HEASOS TO THE ceremony, he quickly found that the positions nearest the platform were already well packed by those who had come earlier. It was less than a month till the celebration of the Eight Days, the largest Viashino holiday of the year. Many of those in the crowd were wearing the bright clothes and shining jewelry usually reserved for the holiday. It was hard to spot a square foot of open ground within a hundred strides of the Splendent Hall.

"I see some of the guard up next to the ramp," said Heasos. "I should probably go up there with them."

Recin nodded. "Looks like I'll have to watch from back here."

"You'll never see over all these bigger folk, little Garan." Heasos pointed at the building to their left. "Maybe you should follow them."

Recin looked in the direction of his friend's pointing claw and saw several Viashino climbing a rope to the roof. "That looks like a good idea," he said. "See you after the ceremony?"

"Of course," said Heasos. "As long as that means we'll go back to your mother's shop and get something to eat."

With a brief wave, the two friends parted. Recin went quickly to the rope and waited his turn to climb to the roof. Many people had already thought of this escape from the crowded plaza. Hundreds of Viashino and a handful of humans lined nearby roofs, staring at the crowds below and talking about the upcoming ceremony.

"Are you one of them?" a young Viashino asked soon after Recin reached the top of the rope.

"No," he said. "I've lived here all my life."

"Oh," said the Viashino, obviously disappointed.

Recin walked along the edge of the roof and jumped the narrow gap to the roof of the next building. This building was a three-story affair, and the area to stand on the second floor was little more than a wide ledge. It was less crowded than the shorter structures on either side, and Recin managed to step around a few Viashino and find a place to sit down.

It was amazing how much the feeling in Berimish had changed in only a few hours. In the middle of the night, rioting and rebellion seemed only moments away. Now there was a holiday feeling in the air. In the street below, a human pushed a handcart loaded with fruits and salted rolls. He was doing a good business, and Recin was sorry he hadn't thought to do the same thing. The next time Tagard called for some kind of meeting, he would be ready.

Then Recin remembered that there would be no next time, at least not for him and his family. Rael Gar was coming to take them all to trial, and if they were to survive it meant they would soon be leaving Berimish. The smile dropped from his face. This might be a day for the rest of the city to celebrate a new beginning, but for Recin it was the beginning of the end.

He looked down at the street below. It was easy to spot the human troops in their dark heavy clothing. In the midst of the brightly dressed Viashino, the humans looked like stones scattered in a bed of flowers. As far as Recin could tell, Rael Gar was not among them. He had a momentary flash of fear. Maybe Rael Gar was at his house right now, taking away Recin's mother and aunt. But the gar would surely be there for the ceremony. It was only afterward that Recin would have to worry.

"Recin!"

He turned and saw a chubby Viashino in a robe of eye-searing yellow working his way along the ledge. "Isalus," he said, recognizing the pattern of dark spots down the side of the Viashino's muzzle. "Who's watching your stall?"

The spotted Viashino gave him a needle-toothed grin. "No need. Everyone in the city is here. No one is left to buy stuffed rolls from poor Isalus." He twisted halfway around and crouched down with one leg dangling in the air and his stiff tail stretching away down the ledge.

The food vendor was not one of Recin's favorite people. Isalus had to be the most talkative Viashino in the city. Just taking a delivery to his stall could turn into a long boring ordeal, as the vendor related every piece of gossip that had reached his recessed ears. Recin was always careful to make Isalus his last delivery in the morning so he wouldn't be late getting to everyone else.

"Not the easiest place to get to," said the vendor. He stretched out his neck and looked down. "I don't like high places."

"Then why are you up here?"

"Too short," said Isalus. "Just like you."

A piece of weathered masonry smacked into the

ledge between them, sending a shower of dust and
plaster chips across Recin's legs. Recin leaned against
the wall and craned his neck to look up. For a moment,
he had a glimpse of a black figure silhouetted against
the bright sky. Then the figure leaned away from the
edge of the upper floor and disappeared.

"That looks like a human up there," Recin said
softly. "Or maybe a Garan."

"Whoever it is," said Isalus, "I wish he would be
more careful. It's frightening enough hanging in the air
without people dropping rocks on me."

Recin continued to stare at the place where he had
seen the dark figure. "What's on the third floor?" he
asked. "Maybe that would be a better place to sit."

Isalus gave a sharp Viashino laugh. "I already tried,"
he said. "But this building belongs to some important
human. He doesn't want anyone stomping around on
the roof."

"Well, someone's up there."

A wailing note sounded through the plaza. Recin
looked over the heads of the crowd and saw human
soldiers blowing into some strange wooden instrument.
More humans began to bang long sticks together,
adding a sharp rhythm to the hill music.

"A frightening sound," Isalus said over the noise of
the sticks and pipes. "I never thought I'd hear this wild
music being played in the center of Berimish."

The soldiers across the street suddenly shouted. A
slim figure dressed in green stepped into the sunlight at
the top of the ramp. A mass of flaxen curls gleamed in
the sun. Talli.

Isalus stretched his neck out in a great show of interest. "It's the girl child," he said. "In the market they say
she's lovely."

"She is," said Recin. He shaded the sun from his
eyes and watched as Talli walked down the ramp and

took a seat on the platform. Her bare shoulders and streaming loose hair were achingly beautiful.

"The woodworkers are already making statues of her," said Isalus. He tilted his head and peered down at Talli. "Maybe I'll get one myself."

Recin wondered how Talli would take the knowledge that the Viashino craftsmen were turning out little statues of her. Considering how she felt about the figurines in Heasos's apartment, he doubted she would be too flattered.

Soon after Talli had reached her chair, Rael Gar appeared at the top of the ramp. It was good to know where the warrior was, but a coldness fell over Recin as he watched the Garan leader walk down the ramp to the cheers of the soldiers. His family was going to have to run for their lives, while a murderer was being cheered. There had to be some way to put things right—though Recin couldn't begin to think of what it might be.

A woman in armor almost as dark as her hair was next. Recin recognized her as the one who had threatened to kill a Viashino on the night the human army reached the city. And she was the same woman who had called him a traitor. If he had heard the woman's name, he didn't remember it.

"They're not making any statues of this one," said Isalus.

"Why not? She seems pretty enough."

"Not where it counts," said the vendor. "Tagard's given her the city guard, and the word is she has no love for any Viashino."

After the dark woman came the sorcerer, Aligarius. Recin stayed silent, but Isalus joined the other Viashino in whistling their disapproval. It had become accepted wisdom in the city that impregnable Berimish would never have fallen if not for the trickery of this little bearded man from the institute.

The whistling quickly turned to boisterous cheers as Lisolo stepped into the sunlight. Recin felt his throat tighten at the sight of the old bey. Lisolo had been ruler of the city since before he was born. There was a great comfort in the imposing bulk and deliberate motions of the great Viashino.

There was a long pause after Lisolo reached the platform, and Recin could feel the tension rising in the crowd. Then Talli's father appeared, loping down the ramp at a near run, jumping onto the platform and raising his hands to accept the accolades of the gathered population. There was something about the man in his shining yellow armor, something that seemed to appeal to both human and Viashino. The Viashino artists rarely sculpted human males, but Recin suspected that carvings of Tagard would soon be available in every market.

When Tagard began to speak, his voice seized the attention of every mind in the plaza, and his shining figure was the focus of every eye. When Lisolo uncovered the torc of the king, there was a gasp from every Viashino on the ledge. When Lisolo placed the symbol of office around the neck of the human king, a fire of emotion licked across the crowd. Even with all that he was facing, Recin could not stop himself from joining in the eruption of joyous shouting.

Over all of it, he heard the sound.

It was a clean, high sound—almost a shriek. Recin looked away from the platform and twisted his neck to look overhead. This time he clearly saw the dark sleeves of what appeared to be traditional Garan clothing. And this time he saw something else: the pale, bent form of a Viashino crossbow.

The shriek came again as the bow discharged its bolt.

Recin turned quickly and saw Tagard stumble. He

saw Talli catch her father and pull him back from the edge of the platform. He saw the bright red blood as it smeared over the human girl's gown.

"No!" he cried. In a moment Recin had scrambled to his feet. Without stopping to think of the pain he might cause, he placed one booted foot directly on top of Isalus's snout and another at the broad base of the Viashino's long neck. From there he sprang upward and just managed to wrap his fingers around the rough edge of the wall above. He vaguely heard Isalus shouting below and felt clawed hands grab at his legs. A few strong kicks freed him from the vendor's grip, and with a single long effort, he pulled his chest up, over, and onto the third floor.

He was just in time to see a black form leap from the far side of the roof to that of the next building. Recin swung his legs over the edge. As he stood the cheers in the plaza turned to screams and cries of despair. He was across the roof in three fast steps, and then he was flying over the gap to the neighboring roof.

The figure in black was already at the far edge, and before Recin could get to his feet, the stranger had made another leap. Recin went racing up to the edge, then skidded to a halt. The margin between this rooftop and the next was not merely the space for ropes or climbing poles, it was an alley choked with Viashino fighting to get away from the plaza.

Recin looked down at the three-story fall, then at the distance ahead. The dark figure was standing at the far side of the building, but he had not yet jumped again. Recin took the steps back, ran forward, gritted his teeth, and jumped.

The distance seemed twice as far once he was in the air, and he was suddenly absolutely sure that he wasn't going to make it, but he cleared it by more than the length of a stride. Recin went to his knees as he landed, tearing the skin away from both legs. It took a moment for his heart to stop pounding against his ribs. He took a deep breath and started to stand. That's when the heavy stock of a Viashino crossbow cracked into the side of his head.

He covered his head just in time to take the next blow on his arms. As he rolled to the side, another struck him on the hip. Recin grunted in pain. For a moment the image of his mother coming into her fighting stance flashed in his mind. Recin had never studied the martial skills. If his black-suited opponent really was a Garan warrior, then to challenge him in hand-to-hand combat would be suicide. But to lie there and take blow after blow didn't seem like the best idea. He rolled again, trying to put some distance between himself and his attacker.

The figure in black came after him and raised the crossbow for another blow. Recin lashed out with one foot. There was a satisfying grunt of pain as his foot smashed into the dark figure's leg. The attacker stepped forward again, and again Recin landed a sharp kick. This time the dark figure stumbled and went to one knee.

Recin hurried to his feet, anxious to keep his advantage. As he stepped forward, the dark form looked up. Within the black hood that covered the attacker's head, eyes glittered in the sun. Green eyes.

"You're no Garan," Recin said. He kicked out at the hidden face.

The dark man caught his foot and jerked him forward. Recin lost his footing and landed on his back. The breath was driven from his lungs in one painful burst, and he was left gasping on the hot stone roof.

"No, I'm no Garan," said the man in black. "And neither are you."

The crossbow came whistling down faster than

Recin could move to block it. It cracked against his skull with a force that he felt all the way to his toes. Red fog spread across his vision, and darkness came close behind.

He awoke with a groan. For a moment, he thought he was back on the ledge of the city wall, with Heasos and the guards, and that everything that had happened since the magical fireball swarmed over Berimish had been part of some elaborate dream. But when he opened his eyes, the sun was blazing overhead and the city walls were blocks away.

It took several seconds for his stomach and head to stop swimming and let Recin roll to his knees. When he did, he was surprised to find the crossbow lying on the roof beside him. Still reeling from the blow, he reached down and picked up the heavy weapon.

"Put down the crossbow."

Recin looked up and saw a pair of human troopers struggling to get on top of the roof. "Where is he?" asked Recin. He looked around at the neighboring rooftops, but there was no sign of the man in black. "Did you see him?"

The first trooper to reach the roof pulled out his short sword. "Put down the crossbow. Now."

The bow slipped from Recin's fingers and clattered on the roof. "Did you see him?" he repeated.

"See who?" said the second trooper.

"There was a man, at least I think it was a man," said Recin. "He was wearing Garan clothing."

"I see a Garan," said a voice from across the roof. Another head had appeared at the edge of the building. This time, it was one that Recin recognized as one of the figures who had joined Tagard and Talli on the platform. Despite her size and the weight of the iron armor that she wore, the woman came up the rope much more easily than the armored troopers. She jumped up onto the roof and crossed quickly to where Recin stood swaying on his feet.

"There was a man here," Recin repeated. "He had this crossbow . . . "

The woman's fist struck the side of Recin's already whirling head. He staggered back, and his foot came down on nothing. The woman's hand shot out again. She grabbed the front of Recin's shirt, pulled him away from the edge of the roof, and flung him to the rooftop. "Tie this assassin," she said to the troopers. "We'll take him back to the Splendent Hall for execution."

"I didn't . . . "

A kick from the woman's heavy boot smashed against Recin's ribs and cut off his words.

"Be quiet," said the woman, "or we might decide to carry out your execution right here."

Recin was too hurt to argue. Between the bruises he had received in the chase and fight with the man in black, and those he had gotten from the woman, he ached from head to toe. The two troopers turned him over and wound his wrists with rough leather cords. Then all three of the humans lowered him on a rope to more troopers waiting in the street below. As soon as the armored woman reached the ground, the group started shoving Recin toward the Glorious Hall.

Berimish was strangely, ominously quiet. Groups of soldiers hurried past, but otherwise the streets were empty. Those buildings which had wooden doors had shut them, and both doors and windows were covered with cloth drapes. Carts and stalls stood abandoned at the edge of the street, and in the plaza where the ceremony had been held, bits of tattered paper and broken wood were all that showed where the platform had been.

"What happened?" asked Recin.

In response to his question, one of the soldiers drove

the haft of a spear into Recin's stomach. "Quiet," the human said. "You'll talk only when you're asked to."

Inside the Splendent Hall, a great cluster of men, Garan, and even a few Viashino were gathered at the end of one corridor.

When they saw Recin being dragged in, some of the humans lunged forward. "Let me kill him," snarled a young trooper with a lean, sunburned face.

An old soldier shoved past him. "I've followed Tagard for twenty years, let me be the one that feeds this bastard to the worms."

"Hold back," said the armored woman. "You'll all get a chance at a piece of this one." She put a hand in Recin's dark hair and turned him roughly around to face her. "But I get him first."

The woman let the soldier go and continued pushing Recin along the hallway. As they neared a place where diffuse sunlight leaked in to brighten the dark stones of the hall, the woman signaled the others to stop and stepped ahead of the group.

"Is he dead?" she called.

A huge form moved in the shadows, and Recin realized that Lisolo was only a few steps away. "Yes," said the Viashino leader. His voice, always deep, was blacker than any night.

The woman moved past Lisolo, and the guards pushed Recin forward. In a few more steps, he saw Talli sitting on the stone floor beside the dead and bloody body of her father. Recin had never seen so much blood in his life. It was splashed over the stones and lay in puddles in the floor. He would not have thought one human contained so much blood.

Talli looked up, and her gaze settled on the armored woman. "Where have you been?" she asked.

Recin barely heard the woman's reply. He could not take his eyes from the dead form of Tagard and from

Talli's blood-soaked arms. As soon as he had realized what was happening, he had known Tagard was the target, but even when he had chased the dark figure across the rooftops, he had not really considered that the new king could be dead. He had never heard of such a thing.

Suddenly Karelon grabbed him and shoved him forward. One of Recin's feet slipped in a pool of cooling blood. He fell painfully to his hands and already battered knees.

"I believe you already know this one," said Karelon.

Talli stood and looked down at him. Her gown was molded against her skin. She looked like a statue carved from some bloodred stone. The expression that gathered on her face was even darker than the spilled blood. "Did you do it?" she said, her voice as cold as the mountains she'd come from.

Recin shook his head. "No. I was . . . "

The armored woman drove her boot into his ribs. "We found him with a crossbow in his hands," she said. "I, myself, saw him on the roof of the building where the bolts originated. Others saw him leaping from building to building as he tried to escape."

"I was chasing the killer," Recin said. He spoke quickly, hoping to get his story out before the woman struck him again. "I heard the bolts being fired and chased the man who fired them. But he hit me, and the next thing I knew, the soldiers were there."

The woman snorted in disgust. "You heard the bolts being fired, with all the noise of the ceremony? Somehow, I find that hard to believe."

From the look on Talli's face, Recin could see that she was not inclined to believe him, either. "They were fired from the roof right over my head," he said. "As soon as I heard them, I climbed up and went after the man who fired them."

The armored woman started to say something, but Talli spoke first. "You said man. Did you see this person that fired on my father?"

"It was a human," said Recin. "He was dressed like a Garan—in the black ithi—but he didn't fight like a Garan."

Talli's gaze traveled over Recin's face. When she spoke, her words were cold and flat. "There are some Garan who don't follow tradition."

Recin felt a jab of mingled anger and embarrassment. "It was a human," he repeated.

"When we got there, only this Garan was present," said the armored woman. She leaned down and stared at Recin from only inches away. "Why didn't we see this man in black?"

"I don't know. He hit me with the crossbow and knocked me out. He got away before I came around. Maybe he left before you came."

A smile came to the woman's lips, but it was not a comforting expression. "There was a bolt already loaded into the bow when we found it. If you were fighting with someone, why didn't he just shoot you? Surely a bowman capable of shooting so accurately across the width of the plaza should have had no trouble killing a Garan that was so close."

Recin shook his head. "I don't know."

"You don't know how they got away. You don't know why you lived. I think you don't know because there was no one else on the roof." The woman turned to Talli. "This is your father's killer. We should execute him now, so that people will see that justice comes quickly to those that would act against the ruler."

Execute. The word rang in Recin's head like the blows he had taken at the hands of the killer. They didn't believe him, and now he would be executed.

Talli's lips were pressed into a thin white line. "Not

yet," she said. She peered down the hallway. "Lisolo, do you have a place in the Splendent Hall to keep prisoners?"

The great Viashino stepped out of the shadows. "Yes," he said. "A portion of the River Nish runs underground here, and there is a dock below the western storage rooms where ships can come to the hall. We keep people on the docks when it is necessary."

"Garan can swim," said the woman. "What's to keeping from escaping?"

"No one can swim in our river," said Lisolo. "At least, no one can swim there and live."

"Take him to this dock," Talli said to one of the soldiers beside her. "And be sure to keep a guard on him."

As the man started forward Recin had a sudden thought. "Isalus!" he shouted.

"What?"

"Isalus." The trooper took his arm in an iron grip and Recin winced. "He was with me during the ceremony. He'll tell you I didn't do it."

"Who is this Isalus?" asked Talli.

"He's a vendor from the south end marketplace," said Recin. "He lives down there, too. Everyone knows Isalus. Just find him and he'll tell you that I tried to save the king, not to kill him."

"South end?" said the armored woman. "He's a Viashino." A look of pure contempt settled on her narrow features. "You get on very well with the Viashino, don't you?"

"Find this Isalus," said Talli firmly.

The woman whirled around. "What good will it do to find a Viashino to vouch for him? He probably killed Tagard as part of some plot to put Lisolo back on the throne."

"Find Isalus, and we'll see." Talli went back to her

father's body and placed her hand lightly against the covering of sopping cloth. As she did, the trooper gave a rough jerk on Recin's arm and started leading him away down the corridor. "Find Rael Gar and Aligarius and bring them to the council chamber," he heard Talli say. "We need to have a meeting."

The armored woman's reply was muffled, but Recin could tell from the sound of her voice that she was angry. He strained against the grip of the guard as he tried to turn around so he could hear better.

"That's it," said one of the troopers. "Try and escape." He slid his short sword halfway from its leather scabbard. "It'll do my reputation a lot of good to be the one as kills Tagard's assassin."

"I didn't kill him," Recin mumbled.

"It'll be up to the new ruler to decide that," said the human. "Personally, I'd as soon see a Garan hang as a Viashino. Neither one of them's a real person." He gave Recin's arm a viscous jerk and pulled him down a dank, steep ramp toward the sound of lapping water.

CHAPTER
10

ALIGARIUS TIMNI HAD NEVER BEEN ON A ship before in his life. If he had anything to say about it, he would never be on one again. The Suder trading ship, Harra, had yet to leave the waters of the River Nish, and already the sorcerer had seen his evening meal go into the roiling water.

Ursal Daleel, most recently ambassador to Tamingazin from the Court of Hemarch Solin, patted the old man on the back and smiled. "Don't worry, my friend," he said. "Our journey will be short. Within the hour, we will pass through the magewall and reach the waters of the gulf. From there it is a matter of only a few days to Grand Sudalen and Solin's palace."

"A few days?" said Aligarius. He would surely be dead by then. No one could feel so thoroughly miserable as he did for a period of days and hope to live.

He looked to his left at the rolling hills of Tamingazin. The institute was somewhere in that direction, now invisible in the haze of the afternoon. Aligarius had lived there more than a century, but he never expected to return. He glanced to his right and saw only thick trees overhanging the river and dark sloughs that fed water into the heart of the Great Marsh. He certainly hoped that Suderbod would be more pleasant. This land beyond the river looked like Aligarius felt.

Daleel picked up one of several small wooden boxes from the deck and cracked open its delicately engraved lid. A cylinder of indigo stone glittered in the afternoon sun. At the sight of it, a fear seized Aligarius that was far stronger than his seasickness.

"Be careful," he pleaded. "If you drop it into the river, we will never find it."

"Would that be so bad?" asked the Suder. "Perhaps then the problem that it causes us would end." Daleel lifted the cylinder from the soft fur lining of the box and turned it over in his hand. "I still find it hard to believe that this bit of rock has protected Tamingazin for all these years."

The sorcerer could not take his eyes from the shining stone. He could believe that he had a part in Tagard's death, but that he had gone to the institute and removed this treasure and others from their resting place—that was almost beyond comprehension. "The magewall took the combined efforts of two hundred members of the institute working together for more than seven years," he said. "No accident can banish an exertion like that."

The Suder gave him an appraising look. "Yet you claim you can do away with this great spell in only a day."

Aligarius pulled the object from the ambassador's hands and carefully placed it back in its padded box. "No, doing away with it is far beyond my power."

Instantly, Daleel's face was creased in rage. "You said—"

"I know what I said," interjected the sorcerer. He held up a hand before the ambassador could continue. "Don't worry, we don't need to end the spell, just alter its form. This spindle doesn't generate the magewall; the wall is self-sustaining, drawing its force from the ground below. The spindle merely directs the wall, holds it in place. While I can't dismiss the magewall, with this tool I can move it, compress it, change it so that it no longer encircles the valley."

"And then our forces will be able to move into Tamingazin without resistance?" asked Daleel.

"Without resistance from the magewall." Aligarius closed the box and returned it to its place beside the others. "I can't speak for what resistance you might get from Tagard's army."

All anger disappeared from the Suder's face and he laughed heartily. "Tagard is dead," he said. He clapped the sorcerer on the shoulder and smiled. "And we have you to thank for it."

At the Suder's words, Aligarius felt as if his guts were full of squirming, biting rostiworms. Tagard had trusted him, and he had repaid the man's trust with betrayal. Of course, the death was really Tagard's fault. If the king had recognized all that Aligarius had done for him and given him the respect a master sorcerer deserved, it would not have been necessary for Tagard to die. "The others aren't dead," he said, "and the army is still there."

"I have made . . . additional arrangements," said Daleel. He shrugged. "By the time we return, there will be no army to speak of. I don't think there is any need to worry."

There was a shout from the bow of the ship, and a pair of Viashino went rushing past. Aligarius looked over the railing and saw that the silty green flow of the River Nish had at last reached the wide turquoise expanse of the southern gulf. A moment later, there was a flare of yellow light as the jutting prow of the ship thrust into the magewall. Snakes and ropes of cold white fire surged across the planking of the deck. One by one, the Viashino at the front of the ship were caught up in the magewall's invisible grip.

Though he knew what the force was, Aligarius still shrank back from the approaching fire.

Daleel shook his head. "No matter how many times . . ." he began. Then the fire was on them.

For Aligarius it was as if he had suddenly fallen into a lake of liquid glass. The breath froze in his lungs. Even his heart ceased to beat in his chest. The very air took on an amber tint. His thoughts slowed to the pace of a tree growing on hard ground. He felt his heart make one sluggish, ragged beat. After what seemed like an hour, it made another. The Viashino at the front of the boat suddenly blurred and began to move at an impossible speed.

". . . I still hate it," finished Daleel.

Aligarius staggered on his feet as the pressure of the magewall lifted. The Viashino at the front of the boat returned to a normal speed. For a moment, the ship held almost unmoving in the water, pinned by the magewall still gripping it at the stern. Then they were free and drifting away from the Tamingazin coast.

"It'll be quite a relief to have that thing out of the way," said the Suder.

"Yes," agreed Aligarius. "It will."

Cranks spun, ropes went whistling through rings of tarnished brass, and broad sheets of heavy cloth were spread across the deck. With creaking slowness, a tall mast rose into the air.

Even before it was fully upright, Viashino swarmed into the rigging to begin hanging the great sails.

"Have you been on the sea before?" asked Daleel.

Aligarius shook his head. "No. At least, not in a very long time—and never in a ship."

"Perhaps when we get to the court, Hemarch Solin will take you for a voyage in his personal barge." Daleel held his fingers out with only a small space between them. "It makes this craft we are riding on look like a bit of cork drifting in the sea."

"I think I've had all I want of ship travel," said the sorcerer. "I'll be ready to continue my studies on dry land."

Daleel clamped a hand on his shoulder. "You won't find much dry land in Suderbod, but I'm sure that Solin will find a good place for you. Don't worry if he should ask you out on his barge. A large ship rides much easier. When you are the hemarch's personal wizard, I'm sure you'll never ride a vessel this small again."

"You're sure about this?" asked Aligarius. "That Solin will name me to the post?" He fingered the shiny, sleeveless tunic that Daleel had given him to wear when they left Berimish. "Won't a leader like Solin have sorcerers of his own?"

The Suder waved a dismissive hand. "A few conjurers may hang about, but which of them is a member of the Institute of Arcane Study? Your reputation is known from the wastes above Skollten to the deserts of Acapiston." He paused and chuckled. "You can be sure that Solin would never waste your skills on something so trivial as garbage disposal."

Aligarius nodded, but the words that had sounded so good back in Berimish seemed less comforting with every mile of landscape that slipped past. He was leaving his life and his studies behind, and all he had to balance that loss were the promises of a man he had known for a short time.

It took the Viashino crew only a few minutes to

transform the ship from a river craft to a seagoing vessel. The mast was locked into place. Long strips of supple wood were woven into loops on the back of the cloth sheets to stiffen the sails. The shallow rudder used for steering along the river was hauled on board, and in its place was put a short but deep tiller. Soon the sails were filled with the breeze from the west, and the ship leaned hard starboard as they tacked south and east toward the Suderbod coast.

They crossed the waves at an angle, driving spray into the air. Blue-headed gulls circled above, making loud rasping calls. As the musky scent of the river and the swamps was replaced by the cleaner, sharper scent of salt, Aligarius was surprised to find himself feeling better. The rocking of the sea waves did not bother his stomach as much as he had feared.

He turned and looked back at the coast. Already Tamingazin—the land where he had spent his whole life—was only a green line on the horizon. At the very limits of his vision, he could see a sliver of darkness jabbing into the silver-blue sky. Even from this great distance, the institute and its black volcanic mount gave an impression of power and purpose.

The thought of what he had done suddenly became very clear to Aligarius. He had betrayed not only Tagard, but the institute, a lifetime of study—and himself. He would never again sit in the crisp air of that magical peak and spend the day in contemplation of the treasure trove of artifacts. True, he had many of the most valuable pieces with him, but that only added to his guilt. He looked around the ship frantically, hoping to spy some means by which he could return to Tamingazin and make right all the things he had ruined.

But all he saw was a crew of Viashino and the open deck of the small ship. Tagard was dead, and it was far too late to save his own honor.

"Why?" he whispered to himself. Everything that had happened over the past days seemed like some horrible vision born of demon smoke. The riches and position he had been promised as a member of Solin's court seemed like nothing but baubles and an empty title. He could not understand what had made him such a traitor to everything he had lived for.

"Feeling better?" asked Daleel.

"Yes," said the sorcerer. "I mean, no. That is . . ."

"If your stomach has settled," said the ambassador, "then perhaps you might enjoy a bit of something to eat." He held out his hand, turned it palm up, and opened his fingers to reveal slices of dried fragaria. On each sliver of red fruit, there was a film of pale yellow syrup.

All memories of the institute, all regrets concerning Tagard, all rue for his lost honor vanished when Aligarius saw the food. He snatched the fruit from Daleel's hand like a pet casperjay taking seeds from its master, and popped them all into his mouth in a single bite. The juice ran down his throat and soothed both his hunger and his spirit. At once he felt more confident. He had betrayed Tagard, but then Tagard had only used Aligarius and his magic to get what he wanted. Everyone was out for themselves, that was very clear. Now, after a lifetime of denial, Aligarius would have the recognition and admiration that his learning and abilities deserved. He had done no worse than any other.

"Is there any more?" he asked.

"Of course," replied the ambassador. "We will have a larger meal near sundown. And, as promised, once we get to Solin's court, you will be able to eat to your heart's content."

That thought lifted the sorcerer's spirits even higher. Everything he had done was tied to the Suder's promises of an endless supply of the delicious food and a position of authority where he could continue his research. Once he had these things in hand, there would be no more reason to do things he didn't want. He could go back to studying the artifacts he had taken from the institute if he liked, or innovate new magics that were not allowed by the strictures of the institute. And he would have assistants to help him with his work. Daleel had promised that, as well.

The waters of the gulf turned a dark blue as the ship moved over deeper water, and the coast of Tamingazin dropped out of sight. Aligarius stood at the railing of the ship and watched the Viashino climbing up and down in the complex rigging. A sleek daggerfish found a place in the bow wave of the ship and slipped through the water near the sorcerer's feet, playing and flashing in the afternoon sun.

The sorcerer smiled as he watched the large fish glide along. The sun was warm at his back, and the rolling of the ship had settled to a gentle, pleasant sensation. Slowly, Aligarius's chin dipped until his silver beard rested against his chest. He jerked awake at a touch on his shoulder.

"Are you ready to come below?" asked Daleel.

The sorcerer shook his head to clear away the sleep. "Yes, I suppose." While he had stood nodding at the rail, the sky had purpled and the sea had grown dark. He followed the ambassador through the low wide opening and down a steep sloping board to the single cabin of the ship.

A pair of Viashino slept at one end of the long, low room, with their tails fitted through straps on the wall. A single lamp swung from a rope overhead, casting shifting, tilting shadows.

The room was too low for Aligarius to do more than crouch, and there was not a single chair to be found.

Daleel sat down on the rough boards and patted the wood at his side. "The appointments here are certainly not up to those on a Suder ship," he said, "but by morning we will reach port."

Aligarius folded his legs and joined the Suder on the floor. The familiar position put him in mind of the institute, but the damp, smelly interior of the *Harra* was nothing like the cool room where he had met with Tagard. His stomach rumbled, and he remembered Daleel's promise. "You said we would have a meal at sunset."

The Suder nodded. He reached into a pouch and pulled out more dried fruit and a few strips of hard, salted meat. "The food is no better than the quarters," he said. "But that will be remedied as soon as we reach Solin."

The handful of food did little to cut Aligarius's building hunger. "How long will it take?" he asked. The thought of holding out more than a few hours on the scraps that the ambassador offered was more than he could bear.

"As I said before, we will be there by dawn." Daleel leaned back, resting his head against the curving side of the ship. "Hemarch Solin will be very happy to see you."

Aligarius shifted his legs. The Suder had given him stiff trousers to match his tunic when they had escaped from Berimish. The clothing was not nearly as gaudy as that which the ambassador wore, but it was clearly not designed for comfortable lounging. "It sounds like a marvelous place, this Court of Solin."

"It is," agreed the ambassador. "Tell me about your institute. I saw little on our little visit. What's it like to be inside?"

"It's quiet," said Aligarius. "And there is enough for everyone, if no more."

"And how do you advance there?"

"Advance?"

"How do you choose your leaders?"

Aligarius shook his head. "We have no leaders. Everyone is free to study as they want. And everyone works to help the institute."

The Suder laughed. "Of course. Only some of you get a little more than enough, don't you? And some of you get to do more of your own work and less of others."

"Well, those of us that have been there for years . . . "

"You won't find us coy about these things in Suderbod," said Daleel. "To advance means power, and you'll have to look hard to find a Suder who doesn't want more of it." He popped a piece of the tough meat into his mouth and chewed it as he spoke. "The path that leads a man to the hemarch's throne is a twisty trail, indeed. You have to know when to serve, know who to trust, know . . ." The ambassador suddenly stopped and smiled. "Enough of this," he said. "You'll see it all soon enough."

Daleel's speech had done little but confuse Aligarius. "Well," said the sorcerer, "I'm sure it's a marvelous place."

"Oh, yes," said the Suder. Then he lowered his face and sighed dramatically. "I only wish we would be able to linger there as long."

Aligarius blinked. "Why not? I thought you said we would be staying there."

"I did, but our earlier discussion made me think."

"What discussion?"

"About Tagard's army," said Daleel. "Despite the steps I've taken, you may be right. There may be more of a force remaining to be dealt with than I expected." He shrugged. "In any case, it will pay us to be prepared."

"What has that got to do with me?" asked the sorcerer.

"As the hemarch's personal wizard, you will of course accompany him on this military mission," said Daleel. "Until Tamingazin is subjugated, he will probably want you at his side each day."

The sorcerer frowned. This was starting to sound like his relationship with Tagard. He had not given up everything he knew only to spend his time traipsing along after yet another ruler. Besides, his brief experience with Tagard's army had taught him that armies had poor quarters and even poorer meals. And if he was traveling all over the countryside, there would be no time for research and learning new magic.

"How long do you think it will take?" he asked.

"How long?"

"To bring Tamingazin under control," said Aligarius. "Will it be a matter of days? Weeks?"

Daleel shrugged. "Tamingazin is a relatively small land. Without the magewall to protect it, we might take it in a matter of only a few days. That is, all except Berimish." He sighed. "Capturing the city could require a siege of months, or even years."

"Years?" Aligarius was quite startled at the idea of spending months or years sitting in a tent, getting no work done. "Tagard took Berimish in a night," he said.

"Yes. Yes, that's right." The Suder smiled. "You were very helpful in getting Tagard into Berimish the first time," he said. "Now I think you may be just as useful to us. If you can put the whole city to sleep again . . . "

Aligarius nodded. "I could help you, as long as that meant I could get back to my work, and my assistants."

"And your riches and good food," added the ambassador. "Of course it would. In fact, I can assure you that we would not make the mistakes that Tagard made in taking the city." He shook his head briskly.

"Once we have taken the city, there will be no fear of it falling again."

"Why not?"

"Well, once you've put them all to sleep . . ." Daleel paused and drew his finger across his throat. "There's no real reason for any of them to wake up again, is there?"

The sorcerer's eyes went wide. "You mean to kill the whole city?"

Daleel pursed his lips. "Don't tell me that this bothers you. If you really want your riches and fame, you will have to live with the costs. Already, you have helped us get rid of Tagard. This is not so different."

Aligarius closed his eyes. "But Tagard was only one man. You want to make me responsible for the deaths of everyone in the whole city."

"Perhaps you can comfort yourself with the thought that it won't be you who slits their throats," said the Suder.

For a moment, there was no sound but the creaking of the rigging and the soft noise of water rushing past the wooden hull. The sorcerer opened his eyes and looked around the ship. Most of the crew was asleep. Ursal Daleel sat with his back against the wall, his dark eyes sparkling with the light of the swinging lamp.

Aligarius was on his way to becoming the most powerful sorcerer to the most powerful leader on the continent. Finally, his abilities and scholarship would be acknowledged. But already, just beyond the soft passage of the water and the creaks from the rigging, he imagined he could hear the screams of thousands.

Interlude

An Inductive Enchiridion to Thaumaturgic Artifacts
Surveyed During Initiatory Classes

There have been several requests of late that I
should take mercy on those students who, well-versed
they may be in other areas, are yet unfamiliar with the
collection of artifacts housed at the institute. To that
end, I have prepared the following monograph giving a
brief overview of the more prominent pieces housed
within our walls. Each entry in this list provides the
indicia required to locate more complete reference
materials within the appropriate library.

Item 1: Spheres of Le'Teng. Two spheres formed of
rhodium and wound copper. Diameter: 32d. Weight:
522j. These two spheres date from the period of . . .

.

.

.

Item 24: Magewall Hub. A cylinder of polished
lazulite and cyanine crystal. Length: 22d. Height: 47d.
Weight: 217j. This is an attractive piece and frequently
of interest to those new to the institute. Certainly, it is
worth a cursory discussion, but there is actually little
reason to probe further as the origin and use of the
hub is well understood. Through the actions of the
magewall, all those attempting entry into Tamingazin
are slowed to an average rate not more than 1/25th
their normal progress while crossing the 17Fd expanse
of the wall. This effect varies in strength by region, and
becomes more pronounced if additional people attempt
to pass through the magewall in the same area within a
short period of time.

Though it serves as a focus for the protective enchantments placed around the valley by the members of the institute, the hub itself contains no source of power and requires outside activation. Those interested in the establishment and maintenance of the magewall can find the relevant spells and treatises in Library A, level 4.

Item 25: Millstone. An oblate toroid of dark steatite malachite. Diameter: 57d. Opening in center has a diameter of 14d. Runes line the outside of this object whose use is poorly understood . . .

—*Timni, Aligarius. "An Inductive Enchiridion to Thaumaturgic Artifacts Surveyed During Initiatory Classes,"* Institute Bulletin, *Volume 17, pp. 123–144.*

CHAPTER
11

"YOU CAN'T MEAN TO KILL THEM ALL!" shouted Talli.

Karelon's face was hard as iron. "And why not?" she said. "The Viashino are at the root of every problem humans have had in this valley. We have the chance to end their threat forever."

Talli shook her head. "This isn't what my father wanted."

"Maybe not," admitted the dark-haired woman. "Excuse me for saying this, but where is your father now?"

"Because he's dead, do you think we should ignore all that he asked of us?" Talli slapped her hands against the council table. "Maybe my father is no longer here, but none of us would have ever been in Berimish without him. It was his ideas that brought us here."

The war leader nodded. "I agree, but how do we know what Tagard would have wanted now? If he had survived the attack . . ." Her face twisted with frustration and she raised a hand to point at Talli. "You. What if it had been you, instead? Would he have been so forgiving if it was his daughter that had been killed?"

"I don't know," Talli said through tight lips. "But it wasn't Viashino that killed him, anyway."

A pained look crossed Karelon's features. "I thought this was an area where we agreed. You have spoken frequently of your hatred for the Viashino, and I have always commiserated. Why should you change your feelings now, after they have killed your father?"

"I haven't changed my feelings," said Talli. "I'm only trying to do what my father would have wanted."

"He would have wanted justice," said Karelon. "It may not have been a Viashino that held the bow, but you can bet it was a Viashino that arranged it all. It is always the Viashino. You should remember that." She turned and swept out of the chamber with the clank of heavy armor.

Rael Gar rose from the chair where he had watched the exchange. "She is right, in a way," he said. "If your father had let us impose the punishments we wanted, much pain could have been avoided. We must still deal with this Garan family that has revealed themselves as traitors to both my race and yours. If we act quickly, perhaps others will think before they attack us."

Talli ignored him. She got up from the table and walked across the room, seeking the cool breeze from the window. It was not even dawn, and already she was facing the problems of another day—problems which seemed to double with every hour since her father's death.

The room was suddenly filled with red light as the sun cleared the city walls. The morning mists burned away in moments, leaving the air around Berimish unusually clear. From the window of the council room, Talli could see the snow-edged crests of distant mountains. They were not the familiar shapes of the round-shouldered mountains which surrounded Farson Hold, but she could still imagine how the wind would smell there—cold, clean, weighted with hard-driven snow.

More than anything in the world, Talli wanted to climb those peaks and open her arms to the bitter wind. She wanted to feel the icy tempest against her face until it cleaned the heavy, hot air of Berimish from her lungs and brought a welcome numbness to both mind and body. Her father's body had been carried there to be stripped and sundered. By now, hunting beasts would have torn away his flesh. His bones would be scattered. His spirit would be free from this world. He was with her mother now. . . .

An unwanted touch on her arm brought her back to the council room, and to the unpleasant list of tasks at hand.

"You asked Karelon to follow your father's wishes," said Rael Gar. "Now I'm asking you to follow the decision your father made." The Garan leader folded his muscled arms across his broad chest. "Let me carry out that decision. Let me finish off the boy and his family."

Talli sighed. "It seems like a poor way to remember my father by sending a family to its death."

"They are traitors," said the Garan leader. "You more than anyone should appreciate the need to deal with them promptly. If we had dealt with them more quickly, your father might not have died."

"All right." Talli gave a reluctant nod. "Go ahead and have the women brought in until we can make arrangements for an execution."

Rael Gar nodded. "I have already brought them to

the Splendent Hall. These traitors do not deserve a traditional Garan ceremony. We can kill them now."

If Talli didn't know better, she would have said there was a smile on the Garan's face. "Have the guards get them ready. As soon as we have a council meeting, you can go ahead."

"There's no need for a meeting. If you agree and I agree, we would win any vote."

"We have to do it correctly. We have to stay together."

A streak of irritation crept into the Garan's eyes. "All right, we'll preserve the appearance of the council. Just so long as it's done quickly."

Talli nodded. "What about the riders who were sent to the institute?" she asked. "Have they returned?"

"They arrived just an hour ago. Some wizards are with them."

"Aligarius?"

"No," said the Garan. "He is still missing."

"He's been missing more than three days," said Talli. "We could have taken this town apart by now."

"We have," said Rael Gar, "but we still haven't located the wizard."

"You're sure he didn't leave the city?"

"Karelon's guards were at their posts. They report no one leaving the gates after the ceremony."

Talli fingered the amulet around her neck. She had taken it from her father's body and had not taken it off since his death. Like the necklace she had held onto from her mother, it was a violation of tradition—a possible lure to her father's spirit. But Talli needed some token to keep her own spirit alive without Tagard's guidance. "Keep looking," she said. "And send the people from the institute to me."

As soon as the Garan left the room, Talli dropped

into one of the chairs beside the table and rested her elbows on the stack of papers that covered the polished wood. She could feel the power in the valley shifting under her feet. Her father had been the undisputed leader; now there was no leader. But it could not stay that way for long.

Talli noticed that one of the maps her father had been trying to explain to her was still lying on the table. She reached out a finger and pushed other papers aside to reveal more of the map. Lines and letters appeared. The writing ran close to a series of marks that didn't seem to match any streets or buildings she had seen. No matter how Talli squinted at the markings, the map made no sense. Like so many things, her father had been the only one who understood these papers, and now it was worthless.

"It shows how the water drains off after a rain," said a deep, rumbling voice.

Talli spun around and saw Lisolo's hulking form filling the doorway. Before she could think of what to say, the huge Viashino stepped into the room and tapped a claw against the map.

"This is very important," he said.

Despite herself, Talli backed away from Lisolo until the backs of her legs were pressed against the table. "What are you doing here?"

The Viashino tapped the map again. "The ceremony of the Eight Days is almost upon us, and with them come the annual rains," he said. His claw scraped across the paper. "These gates must be opened, or the southern portions of the city will flood." Lisolo looked up and his old, amber-colored eyes fixed on Talli. "But you must remember to close them again. The river will rise with spring, and then the gates will serve to keep it out."

Talli had always thought of Viashino faces as more

expressionless than the most constrained Garan, but there was something in the way Lisolo held his long muzzle that told more about his feelings than most human faces. "Is this why you came here?" Talli asked. "To tell me about the floodgates?"

The Viashino shook his head slowly. "I came here to talk to you about the boy."

"What boy?"

"Recin." Lisolo moved to the wall and leaned his bulk against the stone.

Talli shoved the map across the table and stomped back to the window. "There's nothing to talk about."

"There should be," said Lisolo. "Someone has to talk before this boy is killed for something he didn't do."

"He killed my father."

Lisolo made a rumbling sound that made Talli's skin crawl. "You know that isn't true," said the Viashino. "Do you really think he did it?"

"There were witnesses."

"Witnesses who saw him running across the rooftops, none that saw him fire the bolts which killed your father." Lisolo pushed himself away from the wall and stepped closer to Talli. "Recin says that a merchant can vouch for his innocence, and that he gave you the name of this merchant. Have you talked to him?"

"Yes."

"And what does he say?"

"He says that Recin was there with him, watching the ceremony from a building across the street. He says Recin climbed onto the roof after my father was killed."

"If this witness has told you of Recin's innocence, then why is he still being held for execution?" The huge Viashino drew very close, his head looming far above Talli.

She squared her shoulders and looked up into his

enormous eyes. "Because the witness is a Viashino," she said.

"And no Viashino can be trusted?"

"Not in this case," said Talli bluntly. "We know that some Viashino were calling for my father's death. You could hear it from the windows of this hall only the night before he died. This merchant might have been one of those who wanted all humans dead. Why should we believe what any of you have to say?"

"If the boy is killed, there will be trouble. His family is known by both the humans and Viashino of the city." The old eyes looked past Talli to the street. "They think he is innocent."

Anger flared in Talli. "It doesn't matter what they think. If we decide to kill him, we will."

The Viashino leader seemed to shrink down into himself. He made a long, low sound that was almost a moan, then he slowly walked back to the door. From there he stopped and turned. "There is blood ahead of us. This is a sad end to your father's dreams."

Talli clenched her teeth together so hard that her jaw ached.

"What do you know about my father's dreams?"

"I know what he told me. I know he believed we could all live together."

"And this is what you really want? That humans and Garan and Viashino should rule together?"

"No. I want you all to leave and never come back," said Lisolo. "But I will settle for peace." He pushed through the door and let the wide wooden panels swing shut at his back.

"I wish we *could* leave," Talli whispered to herself. She wondered what Karelon would say if she suggested they pack up and return to their homes, leaving Berimish to the Viashino. Somehow, she didn't think the idea would go over well.

There was a rap at the door, and a trooper only a year or two older than Talli stuck his head through the opening. Talli remembered playing catchstones with the boy back at Farson Hold, but since her father's death, he—and many of the other soldiers—had looked at Talli with a new and unsettling expression.

"You wanted to see the magicians?" he asked.

Talli nodded. "Send them in."

The door opened wide and two figures came through. One was a Viashino still young enough to be no larger than a human, the other was a human girl with jet black hair and pale skin. Talli was surprised to find that she recognized them both.

"Oesol?" said Talli. "And . . . Kitrin?"

The Viashino nodded. "You have a good memory."

The human girl was not nearly so restrained. She crossed the floor and wrapped Talli in a tight hug. "I was so sorry to hear about your father," she said. "I lost my own a few years back, and I know how awful it is."

Talli felt her throat tighten. There had been little chance to mourn her father. She had not realized how many tears she was still holding back until the girl from the institute came in. But she still could not afford to let those tears out, not when there was work that had to be done. She extracted herself from Kitrin's arms.

"I'm glad to see you," she said, "but I'm afraid I have bad news for you. Aligarius Timni has been missing since my father's death."

Oesol and Kitrin exchanged glances. "We have seen him since then," said the Viashino. "He came to us two days ago."

"He came to you?" Talli said. "What do you mean?"

"Aligarius showed up just after sunset three days ago—on the same day we now know that your father died," said Kitrin.

She moved to stand beside Oesol. "He was covered with dust from the trail and nearly exhausted."

"Then he's still at the institute?" asked Talli.

The pale-skinned girl shook her head. "He left only a few hours later."

"But I don't understand. What was he doing there?"

"He told us you sent him."

"Me?" Talli shook her head. "We've been searching for him everywhere. We had no idea he'd gone back to the institute."

Oesol made a hissing sound. "I knew it," he said. "We should never have let him leave."

Kitrin laid her hand against the base of the Viashino's scaly neck. "What were we going to do? It's against the rules of the institute to restrain anyone. You are the one who is always saying that the rules must be upheld."

"This time we should have made an exception," said Oesol. "Then at least he wouldn't have gotten away with the artifacts."

"Artifacts?" asked Talli.

"Aligarius was a specialist in studying magical relics," explained Kitrin. "There are a great number of such items at the institute. Most of them are powerless remnants of ancient spells. We study them to see if we can learn more about the magic that created them, and Aligarius was probably the best expert we had."

"And he stole these artifacts?"

"That's how it looks," said the girl. "At least, when we checked the next morning, he was gone and so were they."

Talli shook her head. "I don't understand. If all he can do is study these things further, why didn't he just go back to the institute and stay there?"

"I said that most of them are powerless, but not all. Some of these objects hold great abilities." Kitrin took a small square of parchment from a pouch at her belt. "This is a list of the things that are missing."

Talli looked at the scrap of paper, but none of the scribbled names meant anything to her. "What can he do with these things if he decides to use them for something besides study?"

Kitrin ran her finger down the list. "This one can summon the undead. This one has control over certain animals. This one, well, we don't know what this one does. Aligarius must have thought it was worth something, though." Her finger moved quickly to an item at the center of the list. "This is the one that concerns us most."

"The Magewall Hub," Talli said, reading the words at Kitrin's finger. She looked up and shook her head. "I know what the magewall is, but what does this object have to do with it?"

"Everything," said Oesol.

"But the magewall has been there for centuries," said Talli. "Aligarius can't really do anything to it, can he?"

"Those who have studied the hub don't think that Aligarius can dismiss the magewall," said Oesol. "But he may be able to change it so that it no longer protects Tamingazin from invasion."

Talli felt a tightening of her throat that had nothing to do with her father's death. Though Karelon and her father had complained about the magewall's effects on the valley, there was no question that the magewall had stood between Tamingazin and its aggressive neighbors for centuries. If someone had convinced Aligarius to remove the magewall, there was little doubt about the purpose.

"Was there anyone with Aligarius when he came back?" she asked.

"I saw no one myself," said Oesol. "But one of the

acolytes reported a man near the base of the tower that night."

"A man. Did this acolyte tell you what this man looked like?"

"No," said Oesol. "He didn't see him too well." He spread his clawed hands. "And to Viashino, many humans look alike."

Talli sighed. "All right. So we know that Aligarius stole artifacts from the institute two days ago, and that those artifacts included the one we need to protect the valley. What we don't know is where he is or what he's doing with them."

Kitrin reached into her pouch again and produced a fragment of glittering blue crystal. "We may not know what Aligarius is doing, but we can tell you where he is."

"That piece of rock will find Aligarius?" asked Talli.

"Well, not Aligarius," said the pale girl, "but it will show the way to the Magewall Hub." She fastened a loop of leather cord around the center of the crystal mass and stretched out her hand. For a few seconds, the stone swung wildly, but then the object began to move back and forth with more regularity. Finally it froze in one position, jutting almost straight out from Kitrin's hand.

"South," announced the girl. "That's what I got the first time I tried this, too. But this time, he's farther away."

Talli nodded. "So if Aligarius has the hub, that means he's still moving to the south. Still moving toward . . ." She hurried to the door and threw it open. The young trooper outside looked at her with startled eyes. "Go find the ambassador from Suderbod," said Talli. "And bring him to me right away." The trooper nodded and ran off down the corridor. Talli returned to the council room.

"Can you tell how far away the hub is?" she asked.

Kitrin shook her head. "Only that he's getting farther away with each hour."

"If Aligarius has gone to the south . . ." Talli went to the table and pulled off the map showing the floodgates, and the one under that, and the one under that. At the bottom of the stack was a map she had seen once before: a map of Tamingazin and the surrounding lands.

Both Kitrin and Oesol moved closer to the table and looked over Talli's shoulder as she pointed to the names on the map.

"He might be in the islands," she said, "but those are as much east as they are south from Berimish. My bet is that he's on his way to Suderbod."

"I've been to Suderbod," said Kitrin. "Can't say that I liked it much."

"I'm not sure even the Suder like it," said Talli. "From what my father told me, most of the country is low, wet, and miserable."

"That certainly describes what I saw," said Kitrin. "Not to mention the En'Jaga that the Suder use for hunting teams and soldiers." She wrinkled her nose. "There's not much good to say about the place. Why would Aligarius go there?"

Talli remembered the En'Jaga she had seen in the plaza. The idea of fighting against hundreds of the creatures as part of the Suder army was not a pleasant thought. She stared at the map. It was well drawn, and with a little effort she could interpret the intentions of the mapmaker. A dark gray swath between Tamingazin and Suderbod showed the location of the Great Marsh. The area of Suderbod itself was streaked with sloughs and bogs. From what she had been told, nowhere in the whole country did the ground rise more than a few feet above the water. The distance between this soggy land and Berimish was no more than a few days' march, or a full day's sail.

"The Suder have always wanted to take over Tamingazin. Even with the magewall in place, they've tried several times," said Talli. "Just a few days ago, the Suder ambassador tried to talk my father into letting some Suder settle in this valley."

"The Suder threat to the institute is well documented in our records," said Oesol. "They were the most immediate reason the magewall was put in place."

Kitrin pushed past her Viashino colleague and joined Talli at the map. "So if Aligarius still has the hub, and if he's heading to Suderbod, it probably means the Suder will try to invade Tamingazin."

"Exactly." Talli gripped the amulet around her neck and ran her fingers across the cool metal. "And with no magewall to slow them down, I'm not sure we have enough forces to stop them."

"Can I see that?" asked Kitrin.

"See what?"

The pale-skinned girl took hold of Talli's hand and pulled the amulet from her grip. She looked at it for no more than a second before turning to Talli with wide eyes. "Where did you get this?"

"I took it from my father on the day he died. Aligarius gave it to him. Look." Talli turned the amulet over and revealed a bright nick on the back. "One of the bolts glanced along it before going into my father. Maybe if it had been in just the right place, it could have saved him."

Kitrin shook her head. "This amulet didn't guard your father." She flipped the amulet over again and pointed to the rows of tiny characters inscribed in the oval housing. "This spell attracts bolts, pulls them to itself."

A strange whistling sound rose in Talli's ears and she felt a tingling wave sweep from her feet to her head. "You're saying that Aligarius killed my father," she said. She could barely hear her own words. Her heart was beating in her ears and her fingers twitched and tightened on their own. In many battles, she had heard some of the troopers talk of being swept along by a cold, angry wind—a wind that pushed them beyond pain, beyond reason. Talli had never felt that killing wind before.

Now it was a hurricane.

"Aligarius may not have fired the bolts," said Kitrin, "but if he put this amulet around your father's neck, then the worst shot in the valley could have hit the king from a hundred paces."

There was a knock at the door. A moment later it opened and the young trooper stuck his head inside. "We've had no luck finding the Suderbod ambassador," he said. "No one seems to have seen him in the last couple of days."

Talli nodded. "I thought you might have trouble locating him. Keep looking." The man raised his fist in a quick salute and closed the door.

"Well," Talli said to the two wizards, "I think we can be pretty sure that Aligarius and the Suder ambassador worked together to kill my father. And they're probably working together still."

She jerked the cord of the amulet sharply and the leather strap snapped apart. With a grunt of pure rage, she hurled the oval of burnished metal to the floor. "Suderbod has started a war with us, and my father is the first casualty. But he won't be the last."

"What should we do now?" asked Kitrin.

"Now we prepare for war," said Talli. She stared off into space for a long moment, her eyes focused far beyond the stone walls of the council chamber. When she spoke again, her voice was surprisingly gentle. "But first, I've got to make sure that an innocent man doesn't die."

She left the room at a dead run, and the two sorcerers hurried after her.

CHAPTER
12

WATER LAPPING AGAINST STONE WAS A gentle sound, but after three days and as many nights, the noise was beginning to drive Recin witless. Aside from the *hush, hush, hush* of the water at the foot of the docks, the only sounds in the dark chamber were the footsteps of the guards at the top of the ramp and the occasional leaping of a fish in the black water.

The only light came from a pair of swampglow balls that were two weeks past the time when they should have been taken down and thrown away. The murky orange light was barely adequate to shine on the surface of the water, and far from enough to light the dark corners of the vast underground hall.

Aunt Getin had once told Recin a long tale about a heroic tak who ventured into the dead world looking for the lost gar of his agnate. In the story, the dead world had been dark, warm, and wet. The story hadn't mentioned anything about a loading dock or a river full

of attalo, but after three days, Recin was beginning to
wonder if he hadn't already been executed and just
didn't know it yet.

When he first heard the babble of voices at the top
of the ramp, he thought it was only the guards changing shifts. They had a tendency to throw an insult or
two his way when they thought about it. But a few
moments later the voices drew closer, and with them
came the yellow glow of wicks floating in oil.

"Time for food," he said to himself. Talking to himself was already becoming a habit.

He was surprised to see three lamps instead of one
approaching, and more surprised at how those
approaching lights made his heart race. It didn't take
three guards to bring him his meager supper, but three
might be sent to bring him up for his execution. Three
days in the dark had not prepared him for that. He
struggled to stand, but his legs were stiff from inactiv-
ity and his knees grew weaker as the lights approached.
He sat on the cold stones, waiting for them to come
and take him to his death.

As the lights grew near, Recin had to shield his
dark-adapted eyes from the bright glow. "What did
you bring me?" he called, hoping against hope that
this might be only a very well-guarded plate of food.
The question broke apart and echoed from the unseen
walls. There was no reply.

The lamps stopped a few feet away. In the glare
that leaked around his fingers, Recin was surprised to
see the silhouettes of two women and a Viashino. He
couldn't see them well, but none of them seemed to
be wearing the heavy clothing of the human soldiers.

"I have to ask you a question," said a voice. With
the echoes and distortion of the room, it took Recin a
moment to identify the speaker.

"Talli?"

The human girl stepped forward. She lowered her own lamp to the damp stones and crouched a stride away from Recin. The light of the lamps behind her made a glowing nimbus of her blond hair. "Did you know Ursal Daleel?" she asked. The name broke and sounded around and around in the warm darkness.

"Daleel?" Recin thought for a moment. "I think I've heard the name," he said at last, "but I don't remember where."

"He was the ambassador from Suderbod."

Recin nodded. "He was the one who let you into the Splendent Hall. I remember now."

"Did you meet him any other time?"

"No."

"Did your mother know him?"

"I . . ." Recin shook his head. "I don't think so."

"What about Aligarius Timni?" asked Talli.

"The wizard? I think everyone in Berimish knows who he is."

"But did you ever meet him?"

"I saw him at the ceremony and on the night you first came," said Recin, "but I never talked to him, if that's what you mean." He squinted against the light. "I don't understand. Why are you asking me about him?"

Talli looked into his eyes and frowned. "I wish I knew if I could believe you."

"So do I," said Recin.

"I have a suggestion," said the girl who waited farther up the ramp. She came forward and bent down to set her lamp on the stone floor. As she hitched up her robe and lowered herself to the ground, Recin saw midnight dark hair gathered around an unfamiliar pale face. The girl reached into a pouch and produced a mass of blue-green crystals. "Hold this over him and ask him again," she said. "Then you'll know if he's telling the truth."

Recin leaned forward to get a better look at the crystals, but Talli pulled them away. "Kitrin is from the Institute of Arcane Study," she said gravely. She turned and pointed to the Viashino. "So is Oesol. Like Aligarius, they have a great deal of power and knowledge. Now they can use that power to show me what to do."

Talli started to hold the crystals over Recin's head, but Kitrin grabbed her wrist. "Be careful," she said. "If he does tell a lie, the magic might burn you, too."

"Burn?" said Recin. He pushed himself back from the two girls, but as he did one hand went off the side of the dock into the black water.

"That's right," said the girl from the institute. In the light from the lamps, dark shadows hovered around her eyes and her pale face hovered like a ghost against the background of her black hair. "If you lie in the presence of the truth crystal, the fire will surely take your life. Even the slightest untruth may bring on the fire."

Recin's gaze turned to the small green stone. "I don't suppose you can just take my word?"

Talli slowly raised the crystals toward his face. Recin had to hold himself steady to keep from flinching.

"Do you know Ursal Daleel?" Talli asked again.

"No. I don't think so."

"Have you ever talked to him?"

"No."

"Did you ever talk with the wizard Aligarius?"

"No."

Talli pressed the crystals hard against Recin's forehead. Though the stones were cool, he would have sworn that he could feel the burning energy just waiting to get out and roast him.

The human girl leaned toward him until they were almost nose to nose. "Did you kill my father?" she asked.

Recin shook his head slowly. "No," he said. "I tried to save him."

He closed his eyes and waited for either Talli's hand to move or death to come, but neither happened. He stood there feeling the sharp edges of the crystals against his skin. Slowly he opened his eyes again. "I didn't do it," he said. "And I don't know who did. I'm sorry." The chamber picked up this last word and sent it chasing round and round in the darkness.

Talli took the crystals away and handed them back to the Kitrin. "I think I believe you," she said to the boy.

Recin nodded at the girl holding the crystal. "I'm still alive. I must be telling the truth."

The young wizard smiled. "Well, maybe you wouldn't have *really* died if you told a lie."

He looked from one of them to the other. "You mean that thing isn't magic?"

"It's magic enough," said the girl, "just not that kind of magic."

Recin thought he should be angry, but the relief was too great. "Good trick," he said.

"Come on," said Talli. She stood, then reached down and helped Recin to his feet. "Let's get out of the dark and find a better place to talk."

Recin was happy to stumble after her up the ramp and out of the darkness. The guards at the top of the ramp stopped them for a moment, but they accepted Talli's orders and moved aside. Once in the upper halls, he was surprised to find that in the city outside it was actually still daylight. In only a few days without light, he had completely lost his sense of time.

Talli stopped at the door of the council chamber and spoke to the trooper stationed there. "Rael Gar is holding two Garan women somewhere in this hall," she said.

"Why are they—?" started Recin, but Talli held up a hand and cut him off.

"I want you to find them and bring them straight to this room," she told the soldier. "And make sure that everyone understands that these women are to be considered guests, not prisoners. I don't want either of them harmed."

The trooper touched his fist to the stiffened leather of his armor and hurried off to carry out Talli's orders.

"The women you were talking about have to be my mother and Aunt Getin," Recin said.

Talli nodded. "That's right. Rael Gar wanted to bring them in so you could all be executed together."

The fear that had lifted when he left the darkness settled back on Recin like a weight. "You aren't going to let him do that, are you?"

The human girl turned to him with a firm, unblinking glare. "My father gave orders that this was a Garan matter and that Rael Gar could act as he felt fit." She crossed her arms across her chest, and suddenly Recin could see the image of Tagard reflected in the face of his daughter. "But this is one time I think my father was wrong."

Recin released a breath he hadn't known he was holding. "You won't let him kill them?"

"Not now," said Talli. She raised a finger. "I won't let him kill you or them here in Berimish, but I will allow him to take them back to the agnate on midsummer day."

Recin started to protest, but caught himself and nodded. Midsummer was months away. There was still time to find a way to stop Rael Gar.

Talli led the way as they filed into the council room. The sight of an actual chair was enough to make Recin sigh in relief. He half fell into it and ran his hands along his aching legs. Though he had been sitting in the dark for three days, Recin had gotten barely any rest. Now that the threat of execution had been lifted, he felt like he could go to sleep in the chair and not wake up for a month.

"We're going to have to move fast," said Talli.

Recin struggled to shrug off his drowsiness. "I still don't understand," he said. "Why did you ask me all those questions about the wizard and this Dall person?"

"Daleel," said Talli. She pulled a chair from beside the table and sat down with not much more grace than Recin had shown. The dark-haired girl joined her at the council table while Oesol—who had not yet said a word while Recin was around—leaned against the wall at a spot some distance from the others. Even without talking, the Viashino had given an impression of being stolid and aloof.

"Daleel," repeated Recin. "Why is he important?"

"We can't find him," said Talli. "It looks like he's been missing since my father was killed."

"You think he had something to do with it?"

"I'm almost sure he did." She picked up a small bronze amulet from the table. "And I'm absolutely certain that Aligarius was part of it."

"How do you know?"

"Because of this," said Talli. She held out the amulet for Recin to see. He examined the bit of dull metal while Talli related what they had learned about her father's death and Aligarius working with the Suder.

"But why would the sorcerer turn against your father?" asked Recin. "What could the Suder offer him?"

Talli shrugged. "We don't know everything yet," she said. "We only know we have to do something before Aligarius removes the magewall and lets the Suder march across the border to take Tamingazin. We should go back to the institute. Maybe they can put the magewall back, or maybe we can get more magic to—"

Suddenly Oesol smacked his long stiff tail against the wall, making a crack loud enough to startle both Recin and Talli. "No," he said. "There is no need for you to return there."

"Why?" asked Talli. "Do you have magic that can help us defeat Aligarius?"

"Sadly, no," said the Viashino. "I have no magic to speak of. And I'm afraid there's no chance of restoring the magewall without years of research and effort represented by the hub."

"Then we have got to go to the institute and enlist the help of more powerful sorcerers," said Talli. "Aligarius himself said that he wasn't the strongest one there."

"That is true, and I'm sure that there are those at the institute with the power you need." He thumped his tail against the wall again, producing another sharp crack. "But there is no point in going, because I'm even more sure that none of them will use their powers to support your cause."

"Do they want the Suder to take over?" asked Recin.

Oesol shook his long head and neck. "No, but they will not violate the rules of the institute." He dropped his chin and scaly lids fell over his yellow eyes. "No matter how noble the goal may sound, the magics that we have learned must not leave our mountain. We have learned that lesson from Aligarius."

"But this is different," said Recin. "This is using magic to stop Aligarius. This could save the whole valley and repair the damage he's done."

"No. Not even if it means the fall of the institute itself," said the Viashino. "For the sake of all, we can't afford to let any more of the magic we have learned leak out into the world."

For a long moment, there was silence in the room. As relieved as Recin was to be out of the darkness, it now seemed that he had not evaded disaster, after all. The whole of Berimish might be as doomed as he had felt down on the dock. Tagard's army had been a powerful force in the valley, but Tamingazin was only a small, isolated place. Compared to the vast forces of lands like Suderbod and Acapistan, the humans and Garan elves who had marched under Tagard's banner were a relatively feeble company. Even if they somehow came up with a way to stop Aligarius and the Suder this time, they would never be able to hold out forever.

"We have to get the magewall back," he whispered.

"What?" said Talli.

Recin cleared his throat and spoke louder. "I'm no soldier, and I can't tell you how to fight this war. But even if we manage to get everyone to work together, I don't think it will be enough. The Suder will just attack again and again till they kill us all."

"So what do you want to do?" asked Talli. "Surrender?" There was anger in the human girl's voice.

"No," he replied. "We can't do that. What we need is the magewall to protect us. With the magewall there, the Suder might as well turn around and go home."

The look on Talli's face turned from anger to frustration. "What are you talking about? The magewall is gone, and you just heard Oesol say that we couldn't put it back."

"I heard him say that they couldn't put it back without the hub," said Recin. He turned to the Viashino. "If you had the Magewall Hub, could you restore the wall?"

"There should be no difficulty. Aligarius has written dozens of monographs on the hub, and the spells necessary to manipulate the magewall are both simple and well known."

"Good." Recin leaned forward in his seat. The sleepiness he had felt a few moments before slipped from his shoulders, and with it went the feeling of despair. In their place was a confidence that he knew what to do. "We have to go after Aligarius and take the hub away from him. Once we have it, everything will be all right."

Talli looked at him and her mouth dropped open. She whirled around to face Oesol. "Is he right? Would just taking the hub from Aligarius stop him from lifting the magewall?"

"If he has not yet effected the change, then taking the hub will protect the wall," said Oesol. "But if Aligarius has already deformed the wall, it will take magical action to restore the original state."

"Then we have to catch him before he does anything," said Recin.

"It'll be hard to catch him before he reaches Suderbod," said Talli. She stood up and began pacing around the map-strewn table. "Once he's there, he may well be out of our reach. We'd never manage to get a ship past the Suder fleet."

"Then I should go through the Great Marsh," said Recin.

"You?" Talli shook her head. "Why you?"

"Because you don't need me for anything else." Recin got to his feet and went to her. "Look, I don't know anything about war. I'm no good to you here. But I have been pretty deep into the marsh collecting ingredients for my mother. Let me do this."

The human girl shook her head hard. "This is not some day trip to gather berries." She reached across the table and pushed a large map toward Recin. "The Great Marsh is wider than the march from here to the institute. Even back at the holds we heard stories about the beasts that live there."

"Just stories," said Recin. "It's not as bad as you think."

"What about the En'Jaga? Don't several tribes live in the marsh?"

"Well, yes." Recin looked down at the map. On the paper, the gray expanse looked like nothing special. "I've met En'Jaga before. They're not as bad as the stories say, either."

Talli looked at him and frowned. "You've gone a hundred strides into the marsh, and sold bread to a few En'Jaga in the market. You think that qualifies you to cross the Great Marsh, sneak into Suderbod, and steal the Magewall Hub away from a powerful sorcerer and the whole Suder army?"

Recin shrugged. "Who else have you got?"

Before Talli could reply, Kitrin jumped to her feet. "Me," she said. "You've got me. I'll go after it."

"No!" shouted Oesol. "We must not—"

"Use our magic to help them," finished Kitrin. "I know. But I didn't say anything about using magic. I'm going to get the hub back. That's all."

"I don't think I should let either one of you go," said Talli.

"I've been to Suderbod," the dark-haired girl said quickly. "I know what it's like there. And if Aligarius uses the hub before we find him, I can fix it."

Recin moved around the table to stand beside the young wizard.

"I know the marsh, she knows Suderbod and magic. Between us, we can do what needs to be done."

Oesol smacked his tail against the wall again. He pushed himself away, stomped across the room, and put a clawed hand on Kitrin's shoulder. "Ever since you came to us, you've had trouble surrendering yourself to learning and solitude. Don't let your love for excitement bring you death."

The girl put her own hand over Oesol's claws. "This is the right thing to do," she said. "If the Suder take over this valley, do you really think they'll leave the institute in peace?"

The Viashino let out a long low rumble. "I won't try to stop you, but I still think this is a foolish effort."

Kitrin smiled. "When I get back to the institute, you can make me wash the floors for a month."

Talli looked from Recin to Kitrin. "Do you two really believe you can do this?"

"I think we should try," said Recin. "If we succeed, the Suder will be stopped. If we don't . . ." He shrugged. "If we don't, then you're no worse off than you are now."

Talli bit her lip. "All right," she said briskly. "Go to the western gate and talk to the supply master. Tell him to give you whatever you think you'll need for this trip."

Recin nodded. "There's just one more thing."

"What?"

"If we are successful, I want my mother and aunt spared from Rael Gar."

"I'm not sure I can promise that," said Talli.

"We're talking about the entire valley of Tamingazin," said Recin. "Isn't that worth two women who haven't done a thing to anyone?"

It took only a moment before Talli nodded in agreement. "All right. I'll do everything I can to see that they're left alone. But remember, I'm only one member of the council. If both Karelon and Rael Gar vote against me, my promise is worth nothing."

"It's worth something to me," said Recin. He went to the door and Kitrin came after him.

"When will you leave?" called Talli.

"We'll leave as soon as we have what we need," said Recin.

The blond girl nodded. "Go safely and come back as fast as you can."

Recin pushed open the door and went out into the hall. As soon as he was outside the council room, the confidence he had felt began to fade. Did he really think he could cross the Great Marsh? If they made it to Suderbod, how would they get the hub? For a moment, he thought about going back to tell Talli that he had changed his mind. But then Kitrin stepped into the hall. Though the dark-haired girl was only a few years older than Recin, she seemed very sure of herself and eager for this trip. They had a chance. That was all that mattered.

They walked in silence to a junction where several hallways met. Recin started to cross to the western passage, but familiar forms in the hallway ahead made him stop abruptly.

"What's wrong?" asked Kitrin.

"My family is there." He took the young wizard by the hand and led her down another passage.

Kitrin craned her neck to look back. "Don't you want to talk to them before you go?"

"I don't think it's such a good idea," said Recin. "If my mother finds out what I'm up to, she won't exactly be thrilled about the idea."

"Then you better hurry," said Kitrin, "because she's sure to find out from Tallibeth."

Recin doubled his pace. When they were almost to the door of the Splendent Hall, he heard the distant sound of footsteps crossing the junction behind them. He turned, but whoever it had been was already out of sight.

It wasn't until that moment that he realized he might never see his mother again.

Interlude

IN YOUR TENTH YEAR
LISTEN.
Part of any discipline is the discipline of remembering. You must remember how to perform a task. You must remember how to deliver a blow in combat. You must remember which parts of a plant may be eaten. You must remember your past if you hope to reach the future. We Garan remember.

The humans in their stone forts cannot tell you where they have come from. The names of their fathers and mothers are lost in a handful of lifetimes. They are a rootless people.

The Viashino in their walled towns and in their great city keep their memories on paper and parchment. They do not tell these things from mouth to mouth, and they do not strengthen themselves with the need to keep all these things in their own mind. Their priests do their remembering for them, and their discipline grows lax.

I know the name of my mother and father, and theirs, and theirs, and theirs. I can name them all back to those who left the point in the ice, where the Garan first became Garan. In your tenth year, you will have to learn these things as well.

You have already learned to carry yourself without showing anger and to keep all the secrets of your heart hidden from other eyes. This is also part of discipline.

Now you must know something of your past. Use it to find our future.

—Traditional Garan Instruction

CHAPTER
13

KNOTS OF MUSCLE BULGED FROM THE COR-
ner of Rael Gar's jaw. Red and gray boiled together in
his eyes. "Tell me where they are," he said.

"Why?" asked Talli. "If all you want to do is hold
them until time for trial, I can do that as well as you."

The Garan's hand sliced through the air an inch
from Talli's nose and struck the stone wall beside her
head with enough force to send cracks radiating out in
all directions. "We didn't agree to a trial, we agreed on
an execution. I want those traitors. Now."

Talli did her best not to flinch, but her heart was
racing like a stone rolling downhill. There was something wrong with the Garan. Not only was he showing
more anger than he ever had before, there was something unsteady and unbalanced about his movements.
If Talli hadn't known it was against Garan traditions,
she would have said Rael Gar was drunk.

"Don't threaten me," she said. "I said there would
have to be a meeting. If you want something from me,
you can ask at the council meeting tomorrow."

The Garan lowered his hands, but considering how fast he could move, the gesture didn't make Talli feel safer. "There's no reason to wait for a meeting," said Rael Gar. "The boy has already been sentenced to die. So were the women. Both you and your father had already agreed to that."

"That was before I found out that Aligarius and the Suder were behind my father's death. Recin and his family had nothing to do with it."

"So you say," replied Rael Gar. "Tell me where to find this boy and we can discuss what you have learned."

"I'm only one member of the council. Before I make a decision, I think I should talk to Karelon and Lisolo." Even in Talli's ears, this political argument sounded weak. But she could think of no better reason to postpone the Garan leader from looking for Recin and his family.

Rael Gar shook his head. "This is a Garan matter. Your father understood that, and so should you."

"My father also understood that the races of this valley had to work together if we were going to survive," she said. "That means the Garan have to listen to the law just like everyone else."

Rael Gar's eyes went from green to night black in an instant. "I am gar. Only I can say what happens for the Garan."

"These women have lived in Berimish for years," said Talli. "They no longer consider themselves part of the agnate."

"They're traitors. What they say doesn't matter."

"Take it to the council," said Talli. "That's all I asked before and it's all I'm asking now."

The Garan leader shook his head slowly. "You're asking too much."

Talli gritted her teeth and raised her chin. "If you

want your answers sooner, then call a council meeting sooner." She looked straight ahead and pushed her way past Rael Gar. The shoulder of the Garan felt hard as stone as she pressed around him.

Striding along quickly, she turned down another hallway, swung through a door, and stepped into the forechamber of her own quarters. She shut the door—grateful that the Splendent Hall was one place in Berimish where there were doors were made of real solid wood—and pressed her forehead to the cool stone wall. There were no lamps burning in her chamber, and the darkness was almost complete, but that suited Talli fine. She was exhausted. She needed time to rest, to mourn her father, to consider what she should do next. But no one was giving her time.

The door to the bedroom creaked open, spilling yellow light into the forechamber. "Is it you?" said a soft voice.

Talli turned and nodded. "Just me. But you should be more careful. What if it had been someone else?"

Recin's Aunt Getin stood in the bedroom door with a cone-shaped candle in one hand. The flickering flame of the candle reflected from her metallic golden eyes. "Sorry. But Janin has an ear for these things."

"Be careful anyway."

Talli crossed to the bedroom feeling like her legs weighed ten shalu apiece. As she stepped past Getin, she saw Janin sitting at a small table in the corner of the room with a knife and a small piece of wood in her hands. Slivers of light-colored wood littered the floor beside her chair.

The Garan woman rose and nodded a greeting. "Have you heard anything from my son?" she asked. "Did your people manage to stop him at the mage-wall?"

"No," Talli said with a shake of her head. "I sent the

Viashino wizard, Oesol, to talk to them as you asked. But they were already through the wall and into the marsh before he arrived." She sat down on the edge of the bed and began removing the braided cord which held back her blond hair. "Frankly, I'm glad that Oesol arrived too late. What Kitrin and Recin are doing may be our best hope for saving the valley."

"If this is your best hope, then it's a very slim one," said Janin. "My son isn't trained either to fight or to navigate the dark paths of the Great Marsh." She dropped her half-formed carving onto the bed and paced around the room. "Is there nothing you can do to get them back?"

"It would be hard for me to send someone through the magewall," said Talli. "The army is nominally under Karelon's command, and while she may not mind me ordering a few soldiers about, she'll certainly object if I try to send her troops into the wilderness."

"But his life is in danger," said Janin.

Talli shook out her hair, stood up, and shrugged off her leather vest. "If Karelon objects, then it's likely that Rael Gar will know. If Rael Gar knows, then I don't think you'll have to worry about someone going after Recin. Rael Gar will see to that."

Janin looked away. Though the expression on the Garan woman's face was as composed as ever, the candlelight picked up tears brimming in her eyes. Their golden color had been replaced by midnight blue. "I can never go back to my people. Recin and Getin are all I have."

Before Talli could reply, there was a knock at the door of the forechamber. "Stay here," Talli whispered to the two Garan women. She slipped back out of the bedroom and carefully closed the door before answering the knock.

An older female trooper with a scar across her forehead

THE PRODIGAL SORCERER

213

was waiting in the hallway. Talli recognized the woman as one of the handful of soldiers who had been with her father all the way from Farson Hold.

"Sorry to disturb you," said the woman, "but a council has been called. Some sort of emergency. The rest of them are already in the room waiting on you."

Talli nodded. "All right," she said. "Tell them I'm on my way."

The trooper nodded, but made no move to leave.

"Was there something else?" asked Talli.

"No . . ." said the woman. "That is, I don't know." She frowned and pushed her short hair back from her face. "It's just that they've been having meetings today, and they've kept us out of them."

"What meetings? And who is being kept out?"

"The army. They've been bringing in the officers and making command changes all day. A lot of promotions are being handed out. Only none of us from Farson have been asked in."

"I see," said Talli. "And you're thinking that without my father, you might get passed over."

The woman looked down. "Meaning no disrespect, but we are worried. Some of us have been in the ranks for six years now. Seeing green troops put in command doesn't sit too well."

"Well, don't worry," said Talli. She gave the woman the most confident smile she could muster. "Bring the Farson troops to the dining hall in the main western corridor. I'll come there and let you know what I've learned as soon as the council is over. And I'll do everything to see that any promotions go where they should."

The soldier nodded in reply. "That's all we want." She raised her fist in a quick salute and marched off down the hallway.

Talli slipped back into her chambers and went to the

bedroom. "It looks like Rael Gar is in a real big hurry to see you two."

"What's going on?" asked Getin.

"I told him that if he wanted you, he would have to call a council meeting. It looks like he didn't waste any time." Talli picked up her sword belt and started to strap it back on. Then she thought better of it. She wasn't even going outside the Splendent Hall, and with the tightened security, no assassin was likely to be found inside.

Janin stepped out of the shadows. "This council will hold a vote about us?"

"Yes."

"And what if they decide to turn us over to Rael Gar?" In the darkness Talli could not read the color of the Garan woman's eyes. "Will you give us up?"

"There's not much chance of that. With me and Lisolo both on the council, we can block any vote."

"But if it should somehow happen?"

"No," said Talli. "No, I won't turn you in."

"What will you tell them?"

"That you've left the city. That I don't know where you are." Talli shrugged. "I don't know, I'll think of something." She walked to the door. "Even if the council doesn't vote to imprison you, we're going to have to find you some other place. You shouldn't have to spend your days hiding in the dark."

Janin stepped into the pool of light near the candle. "We owe you more than we can repay," she said.

"Your son is risking his life to save this valley. That's payment enough." Talli slipped on her vest, walked across the floor, and put her hand on the older woman's arm. "And I hope I have your friendship. There are few enough people I can talk to in this city."

Janin covered Talli's hand with her own. "I've had

few friends over the last six years. I'd be glad to number you among them."

Talli repeated her warnings to the women to remain hidden in the bedroom. Then she marched off for the council room with renewed intentions of never turning them over to Rael Gar. Along the way, she stopped in at the kitchen and picked up a heavy mug filled with steaming hot caltino. She sipped it as she walked, hoping the acrid brew would keep her alert during the meeting.

A whole maniple of guards waited outside the council room doors. Talli thought it was a ridiculous amount of troops for security, but Karelon had been keeping more and more men around her since Tagard's assassination. Inside, Rael Gar and Karelon were already seated at the long table. Talli was relieved to see Lisolo in his place by the wall. Only a few days before, the sight of the huge Viashino would have filled her with revulsion. Now Lisolo was the only hope she had to keep Rael Gar from having his way.

"Welcome," said Karelon. "I know it's late, so I hope we can get this taken care of quickly."

"I told Rael Gar to call a council meeting," said Talli, "but it never occurred to me he would call it in the middle of the night." She pulled a chair out and sat down. She took a long drink from her mug, then rested it on a corner of the table.

"Despite your opinion," said Rael Gar in his flat emotionless voice, "the matter between us is not something to be settled by the council. I didn't call this meeting."

"Then who did?"

"I did," said Karelon. The thin woman leaned back in her seat and smiled. "There are some decisions to be made that can't wait for tomorrow."

"What decisions?" asked Talli.

"Decisions about the structure of this council. When Tagard was here, the leadership was quite clear." Karelon looked from one face to another around the room. "Now the situation is confused."

"I've had many of the same thoughts," said Talli, "but can't this wait? With the Suder getting ready to attack, we can't afford to spend our time fighting over positions."

They were interrupted by a knock at the door. A soldier pushed it open, then stepped inside. In his hands was a tray holding four tall pottery cups. "Your drinks," he said.

"What drinks?" asked Talli.

"Ahh," said Karelon. "I was concerned that this might be a long meeting, so I asked that we be provided some refreshment." She took the tray from the man and passed the drink to each member of the council. Both Rael Gar and Lisolo took a long swallow from their cups.

Talli sniffed at the warm cup. The spiced smell of the brew was enticing, but with the bitter tang of caltino already in her mouth, she didn't feel like drinking anything else. She put the cup down on the table and continued to sip at the caltino. "We need unity," she repeated. "That's the only way we can face the Suder."

"If you are right about the Suder coming," said Karelon, "then that's all the more reason we should settle this quickly."

"Just what is it you want settled? You are already war leader, the army is in your hands."

Karelon placed her hands on the table. "There are too many people in this council to run things efficiently."

Talli had been worried that this would come up so soon. "My father thought Lisolo was important on this council. Now that my father is gone, he's even more important."

"I disagree," said Karelon. "But we don't have to start with Lisolo." The war leader turned to Talli and gave her a broad smile. "Let's start with you."

A sour, burning taste rose in Talli's throat. "What are you talking about?"

"There's no need for you to be on the council," said the older woman. "Your command experience with the army is limited to raids, and we have no more need of such raids. There is no group you represent."

A furious blush swept over Talli's face. She felt as though Karelon had struck her with a club. "I don't understand," she said. "Why are you doing this? I thought you were my—"

"Friend?" Karelon shook her head. "Or were you going to say mother?" The war leader rose to her feet. "Tagard is dead. Without the sponsorship of your father, you would have never made the council on your own merit, and now that your father is dead, there's no reason for you to be here."

Lisolo made a rumble as deep as a distant thunderstorm. "I protest," he said. "This young human has been very helpful. She has worked hard to keep this council working for everyone."

Karelon's smile grew wider. "I said I would start with this whining child," she said, "but that doesn't mean I'm going to stop there." She stood, and the smile dropped from her face as fast as it had come. "I am not sharing this room or this council with some foul, reeking lizard."

The Viashino opened its long mouth and revealed rows of shining white teeth. "You have no interest in this council or this city," he said. "Your only interest is in yourself."

Karelon moved her hand, and suddenly there was a

gleaming iron blade in her grip. Talli pushed herself to her feet, sending her chair tumbling. From the corner of her eye, she saw Rael Gar rise and bring his hands to the ready.

Talli felt her blood begin to surge and roar in her ears the way it had before battle. "You don't want a council at all," she said. Her own voice seemed distant and muffled. "You want to be ruler alone."

"And I will be," said Karelon. "Your father had a chance to rule with me, but he was greedy; he wanted all the power for himself. This valley needs only one hand to lead it. This council is meaningless."

Rael Gar took one slow step forward. Colors played across his eyes in strange erratic pulses. "What of the Garan?" he asked. "Tagard promised us a say in how this land was governed. We will . . ." He paused for a moment and swayed on his feet. "We will not submit to rule by humans."

Karelon shook her head. "No, I didn't suppose you would. But your troops are scattered across the valley from the Skollten border to the Great Marsh. How many warriors do you really have within a day of Berimish? One hundred? Less?"

Rael Gar's eyes stopped changing and settled on a deep bruised purple that Talli had never seen before. "My people are guarding the borders of this land."

"But mine are not," said Karelon. "Guards!" she shouted. "Now!" The door to the council room burst open and a dozen human troops tried to squeeze through the door at once.

Rael Gar made a high trilling call and leaped. His movement was so fast that he was only a dark blur as he swept past Talli and lunged across the table. For the briefest moment, he seemed frozen in the air over the table, then he fell. His head struck the hard table like a hammer ringing on stone. From the front of his soft black clothing, an astonishing bright flow of blood appeared, spilling across the table, soaking through all the carefully drawn maps. The cup that Karelon had given to Talli fell from the table and shattered on the floor.

Rael Gar's open eyes slowly changed to silver, then faded to a pale, lifeless gray.

Karelon reached out and wiped her blade on the cloth just below Rael Gar's neck. "I always wondered just how quick you were," she said. "It seems that with enough amarit in your drink, you're not quick enough."

Talli looked at the sprawled body of the Garan. For days, she had worried about how she would defeat his plans. Now he was dead, and all she could feel was horror.

"You gave him amarit to slow him down," Talli said slowly. "You planned for him to die."

"It wasn't necessary that he die," said Karelon, "but it does simplify things. There is amarit in the drink, of course, and there was more in his supper this evening." With a flip of her hands, the small blade flew across the table and buried itself nearly to the hilt in the back of Talli's overturned chair. "Either way, my plans would have gone forward."

A thought went through Talli's head that was almost too awful to even consider. But once it had come, she knew it was right.

"You planned well for my father, too, didn't you?" she asked. "You decided where the platform would be. You made sure it was in just the right spot for the assassin. And it was your guards at the gates of the city. You made sure that Aligarius and the Suder made it out of Berimish."

Karelon looked across the table with a steady remorseless gaze. "I gave your father a hundred chances to do as I asked, but he insisted on throwing away all that we had worked for."

Talli gripped the side of the table so hard that the wood popped between her fingers. Rael Gar's warm blood washed against her hands. "It was my fault. I should never have tried to bring you and my father together."

The war leader laughed. "You flatter yourself. Though I did appreciate your help."

"You couldn't live with my father in charge, and you really think the Suder will be better?"

"The Suder won't be the ruler here. I will." Karelon waved one hand through the air. "A few Suder families will be allowed to move into the valley, but they will be under my control."

"And you really believe that?" asked Talli. "You really think that when the magewall goes down, the Suder won't take over everything?"

Karelon smiled again, and Talli saw that there was real joy on the thin woman's face. "Yes. Yes, I do believe it. The army is loyal to me. Even if the Suder try to betray me, they'll find me prepared. And whatever the Suder do, at least they will be human." She turned her gaze toward Lisolo. "Together we will cleanse the Viashino from this valley forever."

Though anger tightened every muscle of her body, Talli felt a terrible urge to cry. Her father was dead, and his dream of bringing peace to Tamingazin had been perverted into something much worse than the situation they had started with. "You seem to know all about betrayal," she said in a choked voice. "What happens now?"

"Now?" Karelon reached out and stroked Rael Gar's brown hair. "Now I explain to everyone how our friend Rael Gar was killed by the loathsome Viashino king and Tagard's renegade daughter."

"You can't expect anyone to believe that," Talli said. Her hand went to her waist, and her heart leaped as she realized her sword belt was missing.

"Perhaps not everyone," said Karelon, "but I've planned for that situation, as well." She looked past Talli to the soldiers who were still standing just inside the door. "March Leader, have you taken care of the troops from Farson?"

Talli whirled around. She had been blind to Karelon's ambitions, and now the people who had followed her father from his mountain home might be the first to pay for Talli's mistake with their lives.

But the march leader shook his head. "We went after them," he said, "but their barracks is empty."

"It seems someone may have anticipated our actions," said Karelon. "All the more reason to end this right now." She waved to the soldiers. "Take them down to—"

Talli flung the mug of scalding hot caltino into Karelon's face. The thin woman screamed and raised her hands to cover her ruined skin. Talli jerked the knife from the chair at her side, turned, and plunged the blade into the chest of the nearest guard. She felt the blade catch between the man's ribs as he collapsed against her.

As the first trooper fell, the others surged forward. An enormous man with a bright red beard loomed over Talli. He raised his sword to start a swing that would surely tear Talli in half.

A huge dark muzzle shot down and engulfed the man's arm from elbow to shoulder. Lisolo grunted, and blood poured from around his teeth. With the ease of a child lifting a doll, the great Viashino raised the man from the ground, shook him, and dropped him at Talli's feet. He pivoted, and his tail knocked two more troopers from their feet.

"Hold on," he said. His clawed hands grabbed Talli by the shoulders, and with a single leap he was past the remaining soldiers and into the hallway. Shouts and screams followed them down the hallway as Lisolo carried Talli toward the heart of the Splendent Hall. His pace was rapid, and in a few seconds both sight and sound of the council room was lost.

Beads of blood welled up around the points of Lisolo's claws where they dug into Talli's shoulders. "Put me down," she said. "I can walk on my own."

Lisolo loosened his grip and lowered her feet to the floor. "We must go to my chambers," he said. "Officers of the city guard are there, and we can rally a defense against Karelon."

Talli raised a hand to her aching shoulder. "You go and gather your people. I think I have another force that can help."

"I will see you on the south side of the hall at the edge of the central plaza." Lisolo pounded off down the corridor.

Talli hurried to her own quarters. Going there was a risk, but she would not leave the two Garan women alone.

When she reached the door to her quarters, she was surprised to find it already open. She stepped into the room slowly. Sprawled on the floor were a pair of Karelon's troopers. One of them appeared to be simply unconscious, but the frozen staring features of the second marked him as clearly dead.

"They came in here only minutes after you left." Janin stepped out of the shadows. "I'm afraid they searched too thoroughly for us to stay hidden."

"We have to leave," said Talli. "More troops will probably be here any second." She ran into the bedroom and grabbed her sword belt, then hurried back to the forechamber, where Janin and Getin were waiting by the door.

"What's going on?" asked Getin. "Why are your own soldiers after you?"

"They're not my soldiers," said Talli. "At least not anymore."

She ran from the room and headed down the western corridor with the two Garan women close on her heels. As she neared the dining hall, she had a moment of fear—the room would be empty, or it would be filled with the fallen bodies of the Farson troopers—but when she opened the door, almost two hundred men and women were seated at the long tables, talking and drinking.

The scarred woman that Talli had spoken to before saw her at the door and stood up. "Are you done already? Will Farson be given its due?"

"Not from Karelon," said Talli. She raised her voice and shouted to the troopers. "Karelon has betrayed us."

"You mean we're not to get promotions?" asked the woman.

"It's far worse than that."

Every head in the room turned toward Talli, and every voice went silent. She stepped farther into the room and walked between the rows of tables. "Rael Gar is dead by Karelon's own hand. Her treachery was behind my father's death. Now she means to kill us all and turn the valley over to the Suder."

Voices erupted again into an angry roar. Curses of anger mixed with despairing cries.

"What do we do?" shouted one young trooper. "Should we leave?"

"That's up to you," Talli replied. "If we try, we can probably fight our way out of the city and make it back to Farson Hold."

A murmur of agreement ran through the troops. For centuries the humans of Tamingazin had depended on the stone walls of the holds and the rugged terrain around them for defense. Though they had been in

Berimish for some days, it was still an uncomfortable, alien city.

A tall, rawboned soldier stood and waved his sword over his head. "Let them come against us along the walls of Farson Hold!" he shouted. "Then they'll know what we're about!"

More shouts of agreement joined in. Several of the soldiers stood and started for the door.

"Wait!" cried Talli. She paused for a moment, letting the noise decrease before she spoke again. "We can retreat to Farson, and they will attack us on the old stone walls. But it won't only be Karelon's troops that come for us there. The Suderbod army is marching toward us with thousands of men and almost as many En'Jaga. Maybe we can hold onto our traditional lands. Maybe not."

She stopped again and turned to look at every face in the room. "But even if we could, that's not enough for me. We've fought more than six years to win this valley. Are you ready to surrender it in one night?"

"What else can we do?" called the scarred woman soldier. "There are no more than two centrame of us here, and Karelon has nearly ten."

"Lisolo is waiting in the plaza with the city guard," said Talli. "With his numbers, we should be a match for Karelon."

"Fight with the scaleheads against humans?" said the woman. "That doesn't sound right."

"How does it sound to give the whole valley to traitors?"

The woman hesitated for a moment, then nodded. "I'm with you."

"And me," shouted another trooper.

In a moment the scattering of support turned into a single great shout of approval. Talli led the soldiers from the dining hall, down the corridor, and out of the Splendent Hall without encountering Karelon's forces.

The streets outside were filled with chaos. Viashino ran through the streets. The wooden slats over shop windows had been shattered and the cloth door coverings were torn from their frames. Two Viashino lay dead near an overturned cart.

Everywhere figures hurried through the darkness and shouts echoed down the streets and alleys.

On the south edge of the plaza, Talli found Lisolo waiting with a group of perhaps three hundred Viashino.

"I'm glad to see you made it this far," called the Viashino leader.

Talli looked at the Viashino behind Lisolo. Most of them seemed armed with poles or clubs. Few of their powerful crossbows were anywhere in sight.

"Where are the rest of your people?" Talli asked. "I thought the city guard numbered over a thousand."

"It does," said Lisolo, "but ever since you came to town, Karelon has been disbanding units of my people and replacing them with her own."

"And your weapons?"

"Most of them were impounded."

She cursed under her breath. Karelon had planned this better than Talli wanted to admit. "We can't win this with no more than five centrame—and most of those poorly armed."

Janin stepped out of the crowd at Talli's back. "Wait. The other guard have been dismissed by Karelon, but they haven't ceased to exist. When they know what is going on, we will have more people coming to our side."

Lisolo looked down at the Garan woman. "It seems we share mutual friends."

There was a shout from behind, and Talli turned,

expecting to see Karelon's troops coming down on them, but the plaza was empty of all but a few running figures. "What is it?"

"There!" shouted a trooper. "Look there."

A plume of red sparks streamed upward from the center of the Splendent Hall. Talli remembered that Karelon had once said she would burn down Berimish. It seemed she was starting with the hall.

CHAPTER

14

KITRIN HELD OUT THE MASS OF GREEN crystal and watched it swing at the end of its cord. "He's still to the south, but closer."

"He should be," replied Recin. He paused to slap a fat black fly that was biting his arm. "We've been walking for days." He lifted his hand and scowled at the smear of blood and bug that mingled with streaks of gray mud on his arm.

The pale girl shook her head. "He's closer than he should be," she said. "We're not walking that fast." She put the stone back into its pouch and started off down a faint animal track between the looming trees.

Recin had to agree with her statement. Their progress through the Great Marsh was anything but speedy. A jabbing pain came from the back of his neck. He yelped and swatted at the site of the most recent insect attack. "If these flies get any bigger, maybe we can catch them and use them to fly to Suderbod."

"Flies?"

"The ones that are biting me to pieces!"

"Oh," said Kitrin. "They don't seem to bite me."

"No," Recin grumbled under his breath. "Of course they don't."

From the moment they entered the shadows of the ancient gray trees, there had been one obstacle after another. Sloughs of black water cut across their path and forced them to detour hours out of their way. Mud rose up to their knees. Fresh tracks of an En'Jagan band would send them scurrying in another direction. When they did find what looked like a good path, the ground might drop out from under their feet to reveal that it was no more than a thin mat of mud and vegetation over dark murky water. If Recin had to make an estimate, he would have bet they were no more than one day's march from the magewall.

All of the detours would have bothered Recin less if they hadn't bothered Kitrin so little. Recin had always thought of himself as quick and agile. He could climb the ropes and poles of Berimish as fast as any Viashino. He could leave the bakery with five coils of snake bread on a rod and reach the southern market while they were still warm. But in the Great Marsh, it seemed like every root was out to trip him and every vine was determined to snare his arms.

"We'd better keep moving," said Kitrin. "We need to get in as much distance as we can before dark."

"Sure." Recin waved another fly away from his face. "Let's keep walking while I still have some blood left in me." He took one step, slipped on a mass of wet leaves, and fell face-first into mud the consistency of cold gruel.

"Are you all right?" asked Kitrin.

Recin wiped the mud away from his eyes and mouth. "Just keep walking."

She nodded and walked off between the trees. Nothing in the marsh seemed to bother Kitrin. She was always in the lead, moving lightly over the unsteady ground. She never complained about Recin's slowness. In fact, she took that and every other hardship of the trek through the swamp with unfailing good cheer. She smiled as she showed Recin how to rig a bed in the branches of a tree and how to dry kindling for a fire. She smiled while she explained the best way to extract the long barbed thorns of a misery vine.

Her smile was beginning to get on Recin's nerves.

When he had offered to go to Suderbod, he had pictured himself as the valiant lone hero, braving the terrible swamp to help the beautiful and exotic Tallibeth. Now he was only an afterthought, plodding along behind a girl who knew better than he did where they were going and what to do when they got there. He felt worse than useless. But he got up from the mud, shouldered his pack, and followed.

Mottled sunlight slipped through the canopy of vegetation overhead. On the previous days, noon had come and gone without bringing more than a gray twilight, but since morning trees had been drawing apart. Frills of fungus and pallid flowers on the moist ground gave way to gray mire and stubborn brown weeds. Lizards with rows of spines along their backs hurried up the tree trunks as the two travelers passed.

Soon the trees dropped away completely, and they found themselves walking across a muddy plain covered in grass that rose above their heads. A low drone of insects came from all around them, and yellow-green forms leaped away as they pushed through the grass. Though the sun was fierce out in the open and the saw-toothed grass cut at Recin's arms, it was by far the easiest walking they had experienced since entering the marsh.

"If this keeps up, we really will make some progress," said Kitrin.

Recin nodded, but just then his feet found a particularly slippery spot of mud, and he landed on his rump in the muddy grass. The contents of his pack, mostly tough round pieces of dried attalo meat and slices of hard bread, spilled onto the ground. "Great," he said. "Now what am I going to eat?"

Kitrin came back and helped him pick up the fallen food. "I'd eat this stuff if I was you." She wiped a chunk of dried meat across her brown trousers. "I'd rather eat a little mud than anything else I've seen around this place." She handed the last of the spilled supplies to Recin and walked away.

He got to his feet and got the pack situated quickly. Kitrin walked fast, and he didn't want to add to his embarrassment by having to search for her in the tall grass. This time, however, Kitrin had stopped only a few steps away. She stood with her back to Recin and her black hair fluttering in the warm wind. Just from the way she was standing, he could tell there was something wrong.

"More En'Jaga tracks?" Recin called.

Kitrin shook her head. "Looks like we've got a long detour ahead."

A few more steps revealed what the tall grass had been hiding.

Water stretched out left and right as far as Recin could see. Unlike the sloughs they had come across before, this water was clear and blue. But it was also wide. The far shore was almost out of sight.

Recin squinted left and right, but the water didn't seem to narrow in either direction. "Which way do we go?"

"I don't know." Kitrin untied a waterskin from her waist. "At least this gives us a chance to get some water. This is the first stream we've come to that looked like it wouldn't kill you to take a sip." She bent and cupped a handful of the clear water. But as soon as she raised it to her face, she spit it out.

"Foul?" asked Recin.

The girl shook her head. "Salty. This water had to come from the ocean."

"Which ocean?" Recin stood on tiptoe and peered over the water again. "We're almost in the middle of the marsh. The water could have come from the gulf or from the western sea."

"We'll just have to pick one direction and stick with it," said Kitrin.

"And if we pick wrong?"

"Then we turn around and go the other way."

Recin frowned. "We can't walk the entire width of the Great Marsh. That would take as long as the whole trip to Suderbod."

Kitrin held a hand up to hold back her blowing hair and squinted against the sun. "I didn't manage to fit a boat into my pack, and we don't have the tools to build one. Unless you've got another suggestion, we've got no choice but to start walking."

"I do have a suggestion."

"What?"

Recin shrugged. "Why not swim?"

The girl's blue eyes went wide. "Swim?" She looked down at the water. "What if there are attalo in there? Or something even worse?"

"Attalo like fast-moving water," said Recin. "They wouldn't live in a place like this."

Kitrin shaded her eyes and looked across the blue water. "But it's so far."

"It's not so bad. We can swim it in an hour."

"I can't swim," said Kitrin.

"What? I thought you came from a fishing village? How can you work on boats and not learn to swim?"

"My village was north of Skollten," said the young

wizard. "We went into the water sometimes to use the nets, and I learned to keep myself above the waves, but you just don't do much swimming when the sea is colder than snow."

"I guess not." Recin looked at the water, then at Kitrin. "I'm a good swimmer," he said. "I can pull you across."

"Are you sure?"

"Sure. I swim all the time back in Berimish, and I've even taught others. Just because I have trouble walking doesn't mean I can't swim." Recin stepped out of his reed-soled shoes and put them in his pack, then he handed the pack to Kitrin. Carefully, he stepped into the water. It was warm, and the bottom was soft, fine sand that held up well under his weight. Around Recin's muddy legs, the clear water fogged with silt. A few small fish, no longer than his fingers, darted away, then returned to investigate this intruder in their domain, but no monster rushed up to eat him.

"We should take our clothes off," he said. "That will make it easier."

"Take our clothes off?" The girl crossed her arms and shook her head. "I don't think so."

Recin shrugged. "Come on, then," he said. He raised his hands to Kitrin. "It's fine."

"It's not fine, it's water. People drown in water."

"I'll hold you. Besides, you said you had waded in the water before."

"That doesn't mean I liked it." The girl set her jaw determinedly. "You better not let go of me." She stepped out to meet him. Kitrin was not tall, and the water rose to her shoulders within a few steps. "What now?"

"Can you float?" asked Recin.

"Float?"

He moved to her side and put one hand behind her back. "Let your feet come up off the ground."

She raised her feet for a moment, but as soon as her head swung back toward the water she flailed out with her arms and splashed until she was upright again. "No," she said firmly. "You are going to drown us both. I'm getting out and walking before it's too late."

"If we walk, it will be too late—too late to help anyone." Recin kept his hand against the small of the girl's back. "Don't worry, I won't let you slip. Just let your feet swing up and keep looking at the sky."

Hesitantly, the girl complied. She struggled for a moment, and water splashed across her face. Fear flashed through her eyes and Recin was certain she was going to put her feet down, but slowly she relaxed.

Moving slowly to avoid making waves, Recin stepped into deeper and deeper water. Soon the bottom was gone beneath his feet and he had to kick against the water to stay up. Kitrin stiffened as he moved his hand from her back to her side. Then he got his other hand into position. His chest pressed against the girl's shoulders as he kicked out with his legs. They glided out onto the dark blue water.

"Are we swimming now?" asked Kitrin.

"We're swimming." Recin found the going harder than he had expected. He had played with the human children in the pool beside the Splendent Hall, but this salty lake was far wider than the pool. Long before they were halfway across, his legs and arms were beginning to tire.

He twisted his head and saw a hummock of sand and saw-toothed grass emerging from the water a few lengths away. With a twist of his shoulders, he adjusted his course, and within a few minutes, he was able to put his feet down on the sandy bottom. "We need to stop here for a moment," he said as he helped Kitrin get her feet pointed down.

She looked around at the water stretching out

around them and stepped up onto the sand of the little island and sat down with her feet in the lake. "This isn't nearly as bad as I thought," she said. "It's actually nice to feel the warm water sliding past."

"It's a lot more work for me," said Recin, but the girl's words made him feel better. He had finally found something that he could do better than Kitrin.

He sat down beside her on the sand. "As soon as I'm rested, we'll go the rest of the way across."

Kitrin nodded. She closed her eyes and turned her face up to the sun. "A warm lake is so much better than a cold ocean," she said.

Recin looked over at the girl. Soaked with water, her clothing did little to disguise her form. She was not tall and slender like Talli. Kitrin was small, with smoothly muscled arms and legs. Except for her rounded face and unchanging blue eyes, she looked much like a Garan.

The girl opened her eyes slightly and looked over at him. "What's wrong?"

"Nothing." Recin looked away, hoping his embarrassment didn't show. "So, if you didn't swim in your village, what did you do?"

"Fished, mostly." Kitrin kicked her toes in the water. "And took care of the boats. In the winter village we mended nets and got things ready for the next year's fishing."

"Doesn't sound like there was much time for games."

"Oh, there was fun," she said, "but it was mostly indoor fun. Outside was too cold."

Recin thought about asking more about "indoor fun," but decided that might be pushing things. "Did your parents have their own ship?"

"Boat," said Kitrin. "They weren't big enough to be called ships. My father had one. He was the best pilot in the village."

"And your mother?"

"I don't know. She died when I was born."

"I'm sorry."

"Me, too," said the girl.

"Is your father still a fisherman?" asked Recin.

"No, he's dead, too. Viashino killed him."

Recin wished he had never said a word. "I didn't . . . I didn't know Viashino lived that far north."

Kitrin bent forward, wrapped her arms around her legs, and rested her chin on her knees. "They don't," she said. "Some priests were looking for some ancient chunk of stone. They forced my father to take them to where it was hidden, then killed him."

Recin winced. "Sorry," he said again. "If anyone has a reason to hate the Viashino, it should be you."

"I don't hate them," she said. "Another Viashino saved my life, and Oesol's been one of my best friends at the institute." She turned to face him, and Recin was surprised to see that the girl's smile was back. "Are you rested yet?"

"Yes." Recin jumped up, glad to be out of the conversation he had started.

He splashed in the water and waited for Kitrin to join him. In a moment they were again moving backward across the smooth water. Recin was more acutely aware of the girl's body close to his. He tried to concentrate on swimming smoothly and easily. There were no more islands between them and the far shore, and if he tired before they reached it, they would both be in trouble.

"What's that?" said Kitrin.

"What?"

She raised one arm from the water and pointed with a dripping finger. "That."

Recin moved his head to see over her shoulder. A dozen lengths away, a rough brown lump floated in the water. At first glance, it looked to be the exposed top of a water-soaked log. But it was a little shinier than it should be, the ridges and knots transparent around the edges, like a tree carved from dark amber.

There was a ripple at one end of the log. An armored head rose from the water. Red eyes looked at Recin from sockets of heavy bone.

With a wild flailing of his legs, Recin surged backward. "Kick!" he screamed. "Kick hard!"

"What is it?" Kitrin said.

"It's an attalo. A really, really big attalo. Kick!"

Her legs started to move, though Recin couldn't tell if it added anything to their speed. "But you told me that attalo didn't live in water like this," she said.

The beak at the end of the beast's mouth gaped open. Attalo had no real teeth, but the edges of their jaws were all one piece of razor-sharp yellowed bone designed to shear great chunks of meat from the attalo's prey. Recin got a wonderful view of the long killing surface, and of the dark open gullet beyond.

"I was wrong," he said. "Keep kicking."

Kitrin twisted in his arms, kicking her legs hard enough to foam the water at her feet. Recin kicked just as hard below the surface. The distance between them and the attalo stretched to a dozen lengths. To fifteen.

The attalo's head submerged. Slowly the great hump of its shell turned round in the water. It began to move toward them at a frightening pace. The distance between them began to disappear.

Recin's legs began to cramp. He kept kicking, but the muscles only knotted tighter and tighter until they felt like a bowstring cranked far too tight. Even with his body in the water, sweat poured down his face.

The attalo closed to within ten lengths.

Recin lost the feeling in his legs. He thought he was kicking, but he could no longer be sure. He squeezed his eyes shut against the sting of sweat.

When he opened them again, the attalo was only five lengths away.

He wanted to scream, but he had no breath left for it. Bolts of pain shot up his sides. He still could not feel his feet.

He wondered if he would feel it when the attalo started to feed. He closed his eyes again, certain that they would be dead in a moment.

Then his back scraped across sand.

"We're here," he cried. He tried to stand, but his tortured legs wouldn't obey.

Kitrin twisted out of his grip. The water came only to her waist. "Come on," she said. "Get out."

Recin swung his arms at the grassy shore only a few feet away. He was too tired. "Get away from the water," he said. "Leave me here."

The attalo's head burst from the water almost close enough for Recin to touch. Its armored skull was as big as his chest. Its long leathery neck stretched out from the protection of its heavy shell. Its open mouth was wide enough to swallow Recin's head in one bite.

Strong fingers bit into the aching flesh of Recin's shoulders and dragged him up onto the grass. Two more pulls and his limp legs slid from the water just ahead of the surging attalo.

His head lolled at the end of his neck as he watched the animal plant its short legs on the bank and heave itself up onto shore. The claws at the end of its broad webbed feet dug grooves in the soft ground. The neck stretched out, and the red eyes gleamed with hunger. Recin's bare toes were only a hand's width from the end of the slicing beak.

He was quite astonished when he began to move slowly but steadily backward. The attalo seemed to be even more surprised. Its head shot out, and its jaws clacked together just shy of Recin's feet. It took one

clumsy step onto land, glared at Recin with its shadowed red eyes, then turned and slid back into the
water.

The painful grip on his shoulders disappeared, and
Recin slumped to the muddy ground. Kitrin dropped
down at his side.

"Are you all right?" she asked. The dark-haired girl's
face was flushed redder than the attalo's eyes and wet
hair was plastered to her cheeks.

Recin struggled to raise his head from the ground. "I
think so," he said. "I just can't move."

"I feel the same way," said Kitrin. She took a deep
breath, and her face began to loose some of its ruddy
stain. "Tell you what. Next time, no matter how far it
is, we walk."

"Sure," said Recin. "We walk."

Kitrin reached to her belt and pulled out the tracking crystal. "I lost my pack out there somewhere, but at
least I didn't drop this." She let the stone dangle at the
end of its cord. Almost immediately the cord grew taut
and the crystal hung in the air almost level with
Kitrin's hand. "That can't be," she said.

"What?"

"We're close. Really close." The girl shook her head.
"We can't have come that far."

Recin sighed and let his head fall back to the soggy
ground. "I don't know," he said. "We were swimming
pretty fast."

"Aligarius must be moving toward us," said Kitrin.
She stood up.

"That's good," mumbled Recin. "Then we won't
have to go so far." The lids of his eyes felt as if they
were heavier than an attalo's shell. "I'm sorry I made
you swim. I almost got us both killed."

Kitrin smiled. "You did fine." She said something
more, but whatever it was, Recin was too exhausted to

understand it. There was a light touch against his cheek, and Recin smiled in his sleep.

Then Kitrin was holding him by the shoulder and shaking him. "Get up," she said in a harsh whisper. "We've got to move."

Recin groaned and rolled onto his side. The sun, which had been high overhead when they came out of the water, was now lying low and red above the saw-toothed grass to the west. Recin could feel his legs and feet again, but he almost wished he couldn't. Everything from his hips to his toes seemed to be on fire.

"What's wrong?" he asked.

Instead of answering, Kitrin reached down and hauled him to his feet with astounding strength. "Let's go," she said. "Now."

They took a few steps along the path with Recin leaning heavily on Kitrin. Shots of pain went up his legs at each step. Within a dozen lengths, massive trees again surrounded them and the fading light of the sun was reduced to a vague rusty glow.

Recin stumbled over a root and cried out as his abused muscles jerked in response.

Kitrin clamped a hand over his mouth. "Quiet," she whispered.

"They'll hear."

"What is it?"

"En'Jaga," said Kitrin. "There's a whole tribe of them coming this way."

"How far away?"

"Not too . . ."

There was a deep-throated growl and two huge dark figures stepped from between the dark boles of the trees.

"Pretty close," said Recin weakly. Kitrin turned and began pulling Recin away from the En'Jaga.

"Stop, hairy people," said an En'Jaga in a grating voice. "Hairy people, stop."

Kitrin moved faster, forcing Recin to a hobbling trot. "Maybe we can make it back to the water. If there are no attalo around, we could get away."

"I don't think so," said Recin.

"Why?"

The third En'Jaga caught them both with one back-handed sweep of its huge scaly hand and knocked them to the ground. "I catched you," it rumbled. "You, I catched." It leaned over them and held up its hand for another blow.

Recin rolled over and stretched up his hands. "Don't!" He shouted. "We're catched. We're catched."

CHAPTER
15

TALLI'S SWORD CUT THROUGH THE trooper's leather vest. The man staggered back, a look of astonishment on his weather-beaten face. Beads of blood welled up from the shallow cut in his chest. Behind him flames licked at the dry walls of a tannery and sparks drifted up into the night sky.

"Drop your weapon," said Talli.

The man's face hardened. Sweat shown red in the firelight. "Surrender to the scaleheads? Never!" He leaped forward, slashing at Talli with his notched sword.

She was tired, but she managed to catch his blade with her own and turn his blow to the side. Before he could withdraw, she disengaged, turned her wrist, and thrust the point of her blade into the center of his chest. The man made a single strangled cough and fell to the street. Talli pulled her sword free and raised it high overhead. She gritted her teeth and swung the blade hard at the dead soldier's neck. Then she did it again, and again, until finally his head rolled free in the street.

Talli lowered her sword and stood panting beside the body. "Now your spirit can go on," she said. She wiped her blade on the man's back.

The sundering might have assured the man's happiness in the next life, but it did little to bring happiness to Talli. He was the ninth man she had killed since leaving the Splendent Hall. Maybe the tenth. The fighting and dying was beginning to merge into one endless, smoky nightmare.

There was a long creak from her right, and Talli dashed back just in time as the wall of the nearest building collapsed. A tower of smoke and fire roared up into the predawn sky. Talli coughed and covered her eyes against the stinging smoke.

"They're leaving!" cried a Viashino voice. "We've beaten them!"

Talli rubbed the smoke from her eyes and squinted across the plaza. It did seem that Karelon's forces were retreating. She wished she could believe they were defeated, but she knew better. Karelon was only testing them. She had not thrown a third of her strength into the midnight battle.

"Hold your positions!" Talli shouted to the humans and Viashino near her. "Don't chase them!"

The troopers quieted and faced north across the plaza. Where the Splendent Hall had stood, there was only a mass of soot-stained stones and still-glowing ashes. The air was full of the sounds of burning, the screams of the wounded, and the cries of Viashino who had lost everything to the torches carried by Karelon's troops. Talli wished she could order her men to help put out the fires, but they could not fight the fires and Karelon at the same time.

Finally the eastern sky began to gray. Talli staggered away from the smoking ruins of what had been a Viashino home and went down to splash her face in the waters of the river. She knelt down on the sandy bank, cupped water in her hands, then paused.

Amid drifts of scorched timber and a scum of ash, a human soldier floated facedown in the stream. Talli stood quietly and watched the sodden form drift past. Clouds had rolled in during the night, bringing the gray sky close to the earth and making the scene even more forlorn. Though the man was one of Karelon's troops, it felt wrong just to let him float by. Maybe one of the Viashino had a boat that they could use to retrieve the body. Maybe . . .

She shook her head. There were attalo in the river. Soon enough the trooper's body would be torn apart and his spirit would be freed. And this was not the time for ceremonies. She kicked a piece of charred wood into the ash-stained water and went to join the others. As she picked her way through the destruction, the first fat irregular drops of the spring rains began to fall.

She found Lisolo and the officers of their two forces standing together at the corner of the ruined house with Janin close by. The Garan woman had been invaluable during the last few days. She seemed to have more knowledge of how to move and motivate troops than either Lisolo or Talli's most seasoned officers. Every one of them, human and Viashino and Garan, was stained with soot and their clothing was tattered. They looked more like the refugees of a burned-out village than any army. Talli supposed she looked as bad as any of them.

In a day and a night of fighting, Karelon's forces had burned most of the buildings immediately south of the great plaza. All through the night, troops armed with both swords and torches had raged through the streets, forcing Talli's smaller army to fight both the soldiers and the flames they spread. Their retreat with the dawn could only represent a brief respite before the next attack.

Lisolo raised his chin in greeting as Talli approached. "There is enough food cooking down in the south market to feed all our people," he said. "You've been up all night. Why don't you go have a warm meal and some sleep?"

"Yes," said Janin. "Getin is down there helping. I'm sure she could find something for you."

"I'll go when you do," said Talli. She removed her padded cap and ran her fingers through her scorched, filthy hair. "What have we learned from our agents?"

The Viashino leader looked down at her and gave a toothy smile. "Things are better than they may seem," he said. "Karelon's forces hold the north half of the city and the buildings around the great plaza, but they have not taken the eastern gate or come close to the southern market."

"That doesn't sound so good," said Talli. "They've got far more of the city than we do, and they have many more troops."

"We're still getting more Viashino with each passing hour," said Lisolo. "And they may have most of the city, but we hold all the gates and the access to fresh supplies. If we can keep a grip on our positions, they'll soon be getting hungry."

"If we can find weapons—" Talli began, but she was cut off by a sentry calling her name. She turned to see two troopers leading a Garan warrior between knots of weary soldiers and stacks of debris.

The trousers of the Garan's black clothing were dusty from the road, and his eyes were a confused, cloudy gray. He was an older man, with streaks of white in his brown hair. His narrow, sharp-chinned face showed the effects of many years of sun and wind.

"I'm looking for Rael Gar," he said as soon as they were within a few strides.

Talli stepped through the ashes to meet him. "What is your place in the agnate?"

"I'm Samet Tak," said the warrior. "I was sent by Rael Gar to lead those who guard the southern border. Though we were forbidden to enter the city, I have news I must pass on."

"Rael Gar is dead," said Talli. "I'm sorry."

The warrior's expression did not change, but his eyes went a murky brown. "How did this happen?"

"Karelon killed him. She had a hand in killing my father, as well."

The old Garan placed his hand against his forehead and made a sharp downward gesture that Talli had seen before when Garan fell on the battlefield. "I told Rael Gar that we should never trust humans. This alliance has cost us dearly."

"Not all humans are untrustworthy," said Talli. "My father held to his word, and so will I."

The warrior stood among the ashes, drops of rain rolling down his face. If there were tears mixed with the rain, Talli saw no sign of them. "Here is the message which I was bringing to Rael Gar," he said. "The magewall is gone. The valley is open."

Though Kitrin and Oesol had warned her of the possibility, Talli was shocked by the words. "When did this happen?"

"Yesterday at dusk." Samet Tak turned away. "I will be gar now," he said. "As gar, I will take my people and return to the mountains. We will have no more to do with either humans or Viashino."

"But the Suder—"

"Are your concern now." The warrior stepped over the remains of a fallen building and started down the street.

"Samet Tak!" Janin stepped out of the mass of soldiers.

The Garan warrior's stoicism had not been visibly shaken by the news of Rael Gar's death, but at his first sight of Janin, his mouth dropped open and he fell to his knees. His eyes went a deep, swirling green. "Janin Gar," he said in a hoarse voice. "How can this be? Am I dead? The stories do not speak of cities in Tarak Ah."

"You're not dead," said Janin, "and this is not the life that comes after."

Samet Tak shook his head. "But you have been dead for almost two decades."

"Who told you this?"

"Rael Gar," said the warrior. "He told us of your mate's shame, and of how you had taken your own life. He said he tried to stop you, but you insisted that honor must be preserved."

Janin kicked a piece of scorched furniture out of her way and moved to stand over the kneeling Garan. "You were on the council," she said. "Did Rael Gar come to you and ask you for your sentence?"

Samet Tak shook his head slowly. "Who was there to sentence? Rael Gar said you were all dead."

Talli was startled to see the hair on Janin's head rise like a billowing brown cloud. When the Garan woman turned around, her eyes had gone beyond the red of anger. They blazed the color of hot coals. There had been times when she thought Garan looked much like humans, but this was not one of them. In her anger, Janin was more alien than even the Viashino.

"He lied," said the fire-eyed fury. "He lied to me and to all the Garan." She turned and lashed out at a beam of wood which had survived the fire. The thick board snapped cleanly and tumbled into the ash.

"That's why he was so insistent on having you executed here," said Talli. Though she was frightened by the Garan woman's actions, she walked across the rubble to Janin's side. "He didn't actually go to the agnate, and you were never condemned. He wanted to get you out of the way before the rest of the agnate learned what he had done."

"He cost me everything," said Janin. "He stole my life, and that of Getin and my son."

Talli put her hand on the woman's shoulder. "You still have a life. You still have Getin and Recin."

Samet Tak climbed to his feet. "If you are alive," he said, "then who is gar?"

Janin looked at him and her eyes gradually lost their fiery glow. The nimbus of her hair settled. "It cannot be me," she said. "It's been too long since I was part of the agnate. I cannot serve as gar."

Talli hurried to Janin. "Wait," she said. She stood close to the woman and spoke quietly. "If you take your position as gar, you can order the Garan to stay at the borders. We need them there to stop the Suder."

"I could order them," said Janin, "but I won't. I've been away too long. The younger warriors will know me only as a name and a memory from their childhood."

"Then who . . ." started Samet Tak.

Janin spoke quickly. "You will be gar."

"But it was Rael Gar that named me tak," said the warrior. "If he took his position through a lie, then I don't deserve mine."

"You're a good man," said Janin. "You will be a good gar." She took Talli's hand from her shoulder, squeezed it for a moment, then let it go. "Though I'm not gar, I ask that you listen to these people and help them. Their fight is our fight, as well."

Samet Tak's eyes swirled with many colors. "Will you come with me? You are not forgotten. There are many who would wish to see you again."

"No," said Janin. "At least not today. But there is one more thing I will ask of you." She slowly went to her knees and looked up at the black-suited warrior. "Samet Gar, I and my family are without position. Will you give us the honor of a name?"

This time, Talli was sure that the moisture on the Garan warrior's face was more than rain. He placed one hand on Janin's head and raised the other to the cloudy sky. "You are Janin Esgar, the respected leader who has stepped down. Your sister is Getin Pak, a member of the march. Your son . . ." He stopped and looked down at Janin. "What is your son's name?"

"Recin."

"Your son is Recin Kan, the young warrior." He took his hand from Janin Esgar's head.

"Thank you, Samet Gar," said Janin.

The new leader of the Garan nodded. "I need to go now," he said. He looked at Talli. "The borders must be guarded." Samet Gar turned and headed down the street at a steady run.

Janin stood and watched him go. "Now I have a life again," she said.

Thunder crashed overhead and the spring rains began in earnest. Talli and Janin ran to join the others as they sought shelter in the surrounding buildings. Within a few minutes, they had set up their headquarters in what had been a potter's workshop.

"This is a sad way to start the Eight Days," he said, "but the rain should help us. Karelon's troops won't be able to start so many fires, and it might prevent them from attacking again."

Janin stirred the embers in the fire grate at the center of the room. "Let's hope so. A few more days like the last ones, and there'll be no city to fight over."

Talli stood in the doorway of the shop and looked across the empty plaza at the smoldering ruins of the

Splendent Hall. The gleaming white walls that had so impressed her on first sight were black with soot. The arched roof had collapsed, and dark pillars of smoke still rose into the rain. With the lowering clouds, noon was almost as dark as midnight.

"We can't wait for them to attack again," she said. "We have to attack first."

Lisolo grumbled in surprise. "How can we attack them? As you have already said, they have more people than we do and they are well fortified in their positions."

"It doesn't matter," said Talli. She bent and picked up a discarded crossbow bolt from the wet cobblestones outside the door. "The magewall is down. Either we defeat Karelon's forces now and go defend the border, or we might as well surrender."

The great Viashino lowered his head. "There is an alternative," he said.

"What?"

"We could leave Berimish to Karelon."

Talli looked at him with astonishment. "Karelon would burn the city," she said.

"Maybe not," said Janin. "The Suder probably want to take this city intact."

"Karelon hates the Viashino," said Talli. "I wouldn't count on her letting the Suder stop her from showing that hate." She shook her head. "No, we need to think of a way to end this quickly so we can get to the real war."

There was a flash of lightning outside. As thunder echoed around the plaza, Talli saw a lone Viashino sprinting across the wet stones.

"Looks like we have another recruit." She stepped through the doorway and waved her arms.

The Viashino spotted her and changed its path to come her way.

"You must be Recin's blond human," he said as he drew close.

"I know Recin, said Talli, "but I don't belong to him. Who are you?"

"Heasos," said the Viashino. "I was in the city guard."

"Yes, Recin talked about you, too." Talli stepped out of the doorway. "Come in out of the rain."

As soon as Heasos spotted Lisolo in the room, he leaned down until his clawed hands touched the ground. "Bey Lisolo," he said. "I was hoping to find you."

"Get up," said Lisolo. "This is no place for such displays."

"If you've just come from the northern part of the city," said Janin, "what do you know of the human forces there?"

"How to avoid them, mostly," said Heasos. He raised his head high and bared his teeth in a Viashino smile. "I think they must be scared of you. They've made their headquarters in the dockmaster's building and they've barricaded most of the streets. I barely got out before they blocked the last one."

"It sounds like they've decided to wait for the Suder," said Janin. She gave the embers a final stir and stood up. "They'll let the Suder and En'Jagan troops kill us when they get here."

Talli returned to the doorway and stared through the rain. "If we could capture Karelon, the others would surrender."

"Are you sure?"

"They've always followed a leader. From the holds all the way to here, they've marched under someone else's banner. I don't think there's another among them who could take her place." She leaned out the door and looked at the rain splashing in the river.

"Could we take a ship up the river and land at the docks?"

"We could," said Lisolo, "but we don't have any ships."

"We don't have enough people to force our way past a barricade," said Talli. "We need some way to go around. Some way that . . ." She whirled about and looked at Lisolo. "The map!"

Lisolo blinked his huge amber eyes. "Map?"

"The map of the city that you gave my father."

"It was in the council room," he said. "I suppose it's burned now."

"Yes," said Talli, "but on those maps there were markings for storm sewers that ran beneath the street. Tunnels large enough to handle the spring rains."

"That's right," said Lisolo. He raised his head so quickly that it smacked into the ceiling. "You can't mean to move troops through those."

"That's exactly what I mean to do." Talli paced around the room, her excitement too great to stand still. "We had nothing like those tunnels in the holds. Karelon won't expect us to go under the streets. She'll be completely surprised."

"But the spring rains have begun," said the Viashino leader. "Those tunnels will soon be choked with water."

Talli put her hand to the pommel of her sword and gritted her teeth. This might be their last chance to end Karelon's rebellion and get to the border. She was not going to let it pass. "If they'll soon be filled with water, then we had better move fast."

It took a little more than an hour to assemble a team of thirty humans and young Viashino and get them roped together near the entrance to one of the larger tunnels. The water at the bottom of the tunnel was only ankle-deep, but it was swift enough to make keeping a footing on the slippery stones difficult. Talli held out her torch and saw the tunnel curving away to the north.

"All right," she said. "We'd better get moving."

Lisolo looked on from above as first Janin, then the human and Viashino soldiers, stepped down into the tunnel mouth. "I wish I could go with you," he said.

"You'd never fit," said Talli. "Keep them busy down here. Make some noise. I don't want all of Karelon's forces gathered around her headquarters when we come out."

"Don't worry," said Lisolo. "We'll have them dancing." He reached down and touched her lightly with his huge, clawed hand. "Good luck."

Talli nodded and plunged ahead into the tunnels.

One of the Viashino who cared for the tunnels had given them careful instructions, and aboveground it had seemed simple enough. But once they were in the maze of interconnecting drains, it was much harder to tell north from south. The light reflected from the brown water at their feet, casting crazy shadows on the moss-encrusted walls. Ribbons of translucent fungus which had grown through the dry seasons hung down and brushed against Talli's face like half-rotted rags.

With a rope stringing them all together, progress was a slow, twisting shuffle. Each time the soldiers slipped and fell, everyone had to wait while they got back to their feet. Talli's first torch guttered, and she lit the second with its last tongues of flame. She had one more, but she sincerely hoped they were out of the tunnels before she had to use it.

"Are you sure we're going right?" asked Janin.

Talli hesitated, then nodded. "I'm having trouble remembering all the turns, but that gate we just passed through was something I was told to look for. Thus far, we're on course."

They passed through a tunnel so small they were forced to walk bent over like aged washmaids. They entered an underground galley large enough to hold a row of houses. Here the water flowed in from other tunnels and split to follow several routes to the river.

A small attalo scurried across the floor and made for Talli's feet. Its beaked head darted out from its shell and snapped at her toes. She lowered her torch and waved it at the beast. "Go on," she said. "Go on before I eat you."

The creature made a whistling yelp and hurried away down a small passage. "I hope you don't have larger relatives down here," Talli muttered.

They left the large junction and entered a tunnel which angled northeast. It was tall enough to stand in, but narrow. The water was deeper than it had been in other passages. It pressed against the back of Talli's knees, threatening to send her tumbling with each step. Her second torch began to sputter, and she lit the last of her three.

"I hope we're almost there," she said. "I wouldn't want to try to navigate the tunnels in the dark."

"Neither would I," said Janin. "There were caves in the mountains where I was born, but we seldom ventured beyond the entrance. If they were like this, I can see why."

"We're almost there," said Talli. "We have to be."

There was a strangled cry from behind them, and another on the heels of the first. Talli tried to twist around, constrained by the narrow passage and the rope. "What's . . ."

A wall of brown water swept over her. It lifted her from the floor and pushed her down the tunnel. The torch dropped out of Talli's hand, hissed in the surging water, and went out. She tumbled through the

blackness. Her head went under and her mouth filled
with the foul water. She flailed out with her hands,
but the walls slipped by under her fingers. The noise
of the water was like a great beast roaring in her ears.

Interlude

ALWAYS CHECK

When your enemy asks for the death rites, be gracious. Say them yourself. See that the body is treated well.

But first make sure he is dead.

—*A Suder Proverb*

CHAPTER

16

THE GREAT MARSH WAS DARK, RAINY,
upside down, and it moved backward.

Strapped as he was to the back of an En'Jaga, with
his feet and hands firmly tied and all his blood pounding in his dangling head, it was hard for Recin to concentrate on any details. Trees went whipping past.
Saw-toothed grass lashed at his face. Water splashed
over him as the creature bounded through pools. A few
times he caught a glimpse of another En'Jaga with
Kitrin similarly affixed to its back. He passed out for
hours at a time. Twice his captor removed Recin from
his straps and held him skyward in one hand while it
swam across stretches of deeper water.

The attalo did not seem to bother the En'Jaga.

It had been dusk at the time of their capture. All
through the night the En'Jaga stayed on the move, running or swimming without pause. Occasionally they
exchanged a grunting word with each other. Once,
Recin made the mistake of trying to ask a question. For
an answer he received a casual backhanded blow

which left him reeling for hours. Once was enough to teach him to be quiet.

Dawn came late and brought with it rain and wind from the north. Drops of chill water rolled across Recin's face and dripped from his sodden hair. Flickers of lightning leaked through the canopy. Though he had been hot ever since entering the marsh, Recin now found himself shivering against the cold damp. If the rain made a difference to the En'Jaga, they didn't show it. The day became only a gray extension of the night as they ran on and on.

Finally, when the day was beginning to shade toward night and Recin was quite certain that his head was going to come off from hanging upside down so long, the En'Jaga stopped. Another of the creatures walked up, unlashed Recin from his captor, and dumped him on the ground. One of them produced an ugly black iron knife and hacked through their bonds.

"Stay here," said the En'Jaga. "Stay." The creature opened his mouth and revealed a line of teeth each as long as Recin's hand.

"I'm not going anywhere," said Recin. He sat on the ground and rubbed the back of his aching head. Though he was sitting still, the scene around him seemed to be lurching up and down, up and down in a sickening rhythm.

Another En'Jaga approached and dropped Kitrin at his side. She hit the ground with a yelp. Her normally pale skin was an unsettling shade of gray-green.

"You alive?" asked Recin.

Kitrin looked at him with eyes that rolled around in their sockets, and she moaned. "I'm alive," she replied, "but I don't think I want to be. You have any idea where we are?"

Recin looked around. There were broad flowers as wide as a human and the color of bruises spread over the ground to the left. The smell that came from them was like meat that had sat in the sun for days. Just beyond was a cluster of knobby fungus that coated the ground with a layer of tan and yellow lumps. On the right a narrow slough of black water wound through the exposed roots of marshwood trees. A fat gray serpent slipped out of the water near their feet and vanished under one of the massive flowers before Recin had time to do more than cringe.

"Well, we're still in the Great Marsh," he said. "As long as we were on the move, we might be almost in Suderbod. I wonder why we stopped here?"

"Maybe they got tired." Kitrin rested her head on the soggy ground. "I know I did."

A fat black fly darted up, landed on Recin's cheek, and buzzed away before he could slap it. "You'd think after all that walking, they'd take at least a little while to find me," he grumbled.

The En'Jaga wandered in and out among the dark trees. None of them seemed to be paying very close attention to their captives, but Recin had no doubt the creatures would have little trouble catching them if they tried to run. He put a hand against the slick bole of the nearest tree and climbed to his feet. His wrists and ankles had been rubbed raw by the straps. Between the torture of the frantic swim and the long bondage on the back of the En'Jaga, Recin's legs felt about as effective as damp string.

A distant noise caught his attention. At first he thought it was more thunder from a far-off storm, but this sound lingered in a protracted hiss that was unlike anything Recin had ever heard from a storm. There were a few seconds of silence, then the noise came again. This time it brought with it a flock of green scatgliders, who tilted their leathery wings and drifted away between the trees. The third time the noise came, it was noticeably closer.

"What do you think that is?" he asked.

Kitrin raised her head slightly. "What?"

"That noise."

It sounded again. This time, it was loud enough that it seemed to shake the ground. Tiny ripples rose in the slough at their side.

"It's magic," said Kitrin.

"Magic?"

"Somebody's using magic." The girl sat up and felt for the bag at her waist. "Thank goodness they didn't take this."

As soon as she opened the bag, Recin could see a pulsing blue-green glow from inside. And as soon as she reached inside and took hold of the cord, the mass of crystal swung up and hung quivering well above the level of Kitrin's hand. The cord was pulled so tight that it vibrated in the air.

"He's close," she said. "Really close."

"Aligarius? What would he be doing here?" Recin asked.

The noise sounded again. More scatgliders went whirling away between the trees. Brown leaves drifted down from above and settled on the surface of the slough.

Kitrin drew a deep breath and shoved the finder stone back into its pouch. "Maybe the army is coming through here on its way to Tamingazin," she said. "The En'Jaga might have brought us here so they could hand us over."

Recin shook his head. "There's no way you could march an army through this swamp. It would take them a long month to get here."

The noise sounded again. More leaves and debris fell

from the canopy above. This time there was something more—through the gloom of the marsh, a dull red glow flared.

"What kind of magic makes sound and light like that?" asked Recin.

"Big magic." Kitrin stretched up a hand and Recin helped her to her feet. "The artifacts that Aligarius stole from the institute are among the most powerful items known. Many of them have powers that aren't well understood."

Another rumble shook the marsh, stirring the slough into a lather of waves and mud. The ground shook hard enough that Recin had to brace himself against a tree to stay on his feet. Bloodred light shown brightly from the direction of the sound, casting long shadows from trees. Above the overbearing roars, Recin could make out the pop and squeal of breaking wood.

As the noise settled down, one of the En'Jaga appeared beside them. "This way, hairy people. Hairy people, come this way." He gestured with a clawed hand half as big as Recin's body.

Half sick and wholly exhausted, Recin and Kitrin struggled to comply. The En'Jaga didn't lead them far. Several of the huge scaly people had gathered in a small clearing. Once they had reached it, they again ceased paying attention to their two captives.

When the sound came again, there was no question of their staying on their feet. The ground heaved and humped like a riding beast gone wild, dumping both Kitrin and Recin to the ground. Even the En'Jaga were staggered. An immense tree to Recin's left sprang upward, revealing a tangled mass of roots. Then it tumbled down with a noise so loud it temporarily eclipsed the rumbling sound. Another tree let go with a screech of wood tortured beyond its limits. Another crashed down. Cracks opened in the earth and steam rose up from the ground.

With a final earsplitting roar, the curtain of trees parted and the army of Suderbod was revealed.

The great force of men, wagons, riding beasts, and En'Jaga stretched out beneath the gray sky. Recin had thought that Tagard's army was impressive on the night it entered Berimish, but now he could see they were no more than a ragged collection of hill humans. There had to be ten thousand men in the forces of Suder, maybe twenty—and that was even without counting the hundreds of hulking En'Jaga.

The vast Suderbod army marched forward to the sound of rattling drums and stepped between streaming banners. Unlike the armies of either the Garan or humans in Tamingazin, the Suder army seemed to contain only males. Rank after rank, they stood in neat rows, their gleaming steel armor chased with swirls and stripes of all colors. Their clothing was more vivid than a casperjay. Even their helmets were decorated with puffs of feathers and colored crests.

Mixed with the neat ranks of humans were ragged knots of En'Jaga. Some were the plain gray creatures Recin had seen in the market, but many of them wore streaks of red or blue paint on their bodies to match the patterns on the Suder armor. Bands of metal decorated their massive arms. The claws on their hands and feet had been extended by sharp caps of steel.

A single human figure stood in front of the army. He wore an oversized tunic with stripes of midnight black and glittering gold, and breeches of searing scarlet. On his head was a floppy hat in a shade of pink run through with veins of crimson. His white beard was trimmed short and forked in the Suderbod style.

Kitrin drew a sharp breath. "Aligarius."

Recin looked again at the small figure in garish clothing. The man didn't look much like the gray-robed figure he had seen in the streets of Berimish. "Are you sure?"

"I worked with him every day for better than a year," said the girl. "I'm sure."

The sorcerer held out a clenched fist and the ground began to throb and dance again. Beams of crimson light leaked between his fingers. Ahead of him trees twisted and writhed; pools of water vanished in clouds of steam. When the noise ceased, the area in front of Aligarius was a flat, treeless path, as smooth and solid as any street in Berimish.

Through the gap where the trees had been Recin could see low rolling hills of grass and the mouth of a wide river.

"I think that settles the question of where we are," said Kitrin. "I recognize that river."

"Is that Suderbod?"

"No," she said, "it's Tamingazin. That's the mouth of the River Nish."

Recin moaned. "Great. After all this walking we've managed to end up where we started."

The En'Jaga around them began to move forward. One of the creatures walked to Recin and Kitrin and waved them toward the army.

"You come this way," it said. "Come." The En'Jaga herded them into the path of the advancing army.

As they drew close to Aligarius, the sorcerer turned and faced them. Even for Recin, who had seen the man only from a distance, the change in Aligarius was startling. His cheeks were hollow and sunken. His dark eyes were dry and dull.

"Kitrin Weidini," the sorcerer said in a hoarse voice. "I'm surprised to see you here."

Kitrin drew herself up and faced him with a grave

expression. "Aligarius Timni, you have broken your oath to the Institute of Arcane Study, and you have taken objects which do not belong to you. Return what you have stolen and come with me to face your peers."

Aligarius sniffed and raised his nose in the air. "Peers? I have no peers. Why should I listen to you?" he said. "You . . ." He blinked and swayed on his feet. "You're nothing but an unschooled apprentice."

Kitrin shook her head. "I'm here representing the institute, not myself. You owe everyone there a debt of honor."

"The institute owes me far more than I owe to it," said the sorcerer. "For nearly a hundred years I taught and studied and wrote papers. What did it gain me?"

"Respect," said Kitrin.

Aligarius snorted. "I saw no respect." He opened his hand to reveal a small mass formed from what looked like strands of gold interwoven with copper. "This is the Heart of the Mountain. Do you know how to draw it's power? Does anyone at the institute?" He shook his head. "Half the artifacts in the collection would be no more than curiosities without my lifetime of research."

"That doesn't give you the right to take them," said Kitrin.

Aligarius glared at her down his long nose. "Who are you to tell me what is right and wrong?"

There was a shrill whistle and a series of shouted commands. The Suder ranks split apart and teams of soldiers hurried around in what looked like near chaos. Within seconds, tall poles began to rise in the air. Moments after that, circles of cloth were flung over the poles and the rows of soldiers began to disappear behind a sea of conical tents.

A group of men left the growing camp. Most of them wore the shiny armor plate and plumed helmets of the Suder soldiers, but the two in front were dressed much as Aligarius, in a variety of clashing colors and stripes.

One of the men was thin, with a dark forked beard. Recin thought he recognized the man as the Suder who was always hanging around the Splendent Hall back in Berimish. He had to be the ambassador who had taken Aligarius from the city. The other man was fat and clean shaven, with a sash of golden cloth across his chest and numerous chains of gold around his neck.

"Who is this?" called the fat man. From a distance, he had the jolly look of an old grandfather, but as he drew nearer Recin saw bags and lines around the man's eyes that gave him a look that was anything but jolly. His skin was a sickly yellow spotted with florets of broken blood vessels.

"The girl is named Kitrin," said Aligarius. "She is from the Institute of Arcane Study."

"Really?" The fat man pursed his equally fat lips. "Hmmm. Another sorcerer might be useful." He stood directly in front of Kitrin and ran a finger down her soiled cheek. "Even if she is filthy."

Aligarius grunted. "She's of no use," he said. "She's been studying only a year. Even the most basic spells are beyond her grasp."

"Pity." The fat man moved to stand near Recin. The man's eyes were a faded, milky brown. His gaze made Recin feel dirtier than any amount of mud and water. "Who is this one? I've never seen his like."

"I don't know," said Aligarius. "I . . ." He staggered again, and for a moment Recin thought he might fall. "I've never seen him before," the sorcerer finished. He blinked, and beads of sweat rolled down his forehead.

If either of the Suder noticed anything wrong with Aligarius, they didn't show it.

"I believe I have seen this boy before," said the ambassador. "I think this is one of Lisolo's pet Garan."

"A Garan?" The fat man's mouth dropped open slightly. He lowered his face until it was only a finger's length from Recin's. "Yes, he has the eyes, doesn't he?" he said. "Those marvelous shifting eyes. Hmmm. And the features, too, though he's not so muscular as you said in your reports, Daleel." The fat man's tongue appeared for a moment between his lips. "We have no Garan in Suder. I've heard very interesting things about you. Very interesting. Are they true?"

The man's breath had an odor that was both sweet and foul—like bread overgrown by mold. Recin had to struggle to keep from flinching away. "I don't know," he said.

"You don't know," repeated the fat man. "Hmmm." He looked over Recin's shoulder. "You, Jah!" he shouted. "Come here."

One of the En'Jaga bounded over and dropped onto all four limbs before the fat man. "Yes," it said. "Yes, you wish?"

"Where did you find these two?"

"Hairy people by the blue waters," said the En'Jaga. "By the blue waters, there were hairy people."

The fat man turned his attention back to Recin. "I would ask you why you were in the center of the Great Marsh," he said, "but there seems little point." He smiled, revealing teeth that were filed to points and painted all the colors of his garish wardrobe. "A sorcerer and a warrior. They sent you to kill me, didn't they, hmmm?"

"Kill you?" Recin said. "Why?"

Recin blinked. He was sitting on the ground, looking at the fat man's knees. How he had gotten there was something of a puzzle. It took several seconds for him to associate the ringing in his head with his position and realize that he had been slapped with a force and speed that were entirely unexpected.

"It seems the stories of a Garan warrior's agility and strength are only that. Hmmm," said the fat man. "Only stories."

"I'm not a warrior," said Recin. His lips felt swollen, and a warm trickle of blood ran down his chin.

"Not a warrior." The fat man tilted his head. "A Garan, but not a warrior. Hmmm." He looked over at Kitrin. "You are from the northern islands, aren't you?"

"Yes," said Kitrin. "From Umber."

"I have already known people from your land," he said. "But only a few. Hmmm. You are still of some interest to me." He looked down at Recin and smiled his frightening, colorful smile. "I have never known a Garan."

The fat man turned around, moving with much more grace than his bulk would suggest. "Daleel, take these two and clean them up," he said to the ambassador. "Then we'll see if they are as interesting as they appear, hmmm?"

"Yes, Hemarch," said the ambassador.

Recin watched the fat man walk back to the rest of the army, trailed by the knot of attending soldiers. "That was Solin?" he asked.

"Of course," said the ambassador. He reached down and offered Recin a hand. "You'd best come along quickly. The hemarch is not the most patient of men." He smiled.

Like the hemarch, Ambassador Daleel looked like a friendly man at first glance, but there was something buried in his narrow features that Recin didn't like. He avoided the man's hand and got to his feet under his own power.

"I must go and lie down," said Aligarius. "If we're to make Tamingazin tomorrow, I must be rested." The sorcerer's pinched face looked pale.

"Of course," said Daleel. "And don't forget to eat."

The wizard hesitated a moment, then gave an uncertain nod and walked toward the still forming camp.

"Now let's take care of you two," said Daleel. He brought his hand down on the shoulder of the prone En'Jaga with a force that might have broken a human's bones. "Thank you, Jah. Go back to your people. There will be a treat for you tonight. Amaranth."

The creature rose on its three-toed hind feet. "Yes, amaranth," it said. "Yes, a treat." It hurried away.

"Amaranth is a poison to Viashino and En'Jaga," said Kitrin. "It kills them."

Daleel clapped his hands together and smiled. "Yes, well, but they do enjoy it so. Come on, let's get you clean enough that you don't offend Solin's delicate nose."

He led them between the ranks of tents while Suderbod troopers looked on with little apparent interest. They passed hundreds of soldiers and dozens of tents before the ambassador stopped beside an odd-looking pair of wagons pulled by teams of harnessed riding beasts. Two shirtless men stood by with folded lengths of cloth thrown over their shoulders.

"We need these two prepared for Solin."

One of the men touched his palm to his forehead. "Right away, Archval Daleel."

"All right," said the ambassador. "Take off your clothes."

"What?" Recin and Kitrin said together.

"You have to get cleaned. And that means removing your filthy clothes."

Kitrin shook her head. "I'm not getting undressed in front of an army of men."

"Suderbod is filled with public baths," said Daleel. "These men have seen naked women most every day of their lives."

"They haven't seen me," said Kitrin.

Daleel laughed. "No doubt a sight which would leave the whole army stunned. Cleaning Master, do you think we can arrange some sort of screen for our modest guest?"

Recin thought of asking for the same sort of covering, but decided after a moment that he would be more embarrassed to ask than to submit to the Suder's cleaning. While preparations were made for Kitrin, Recin was stripped of his clothing and plunged under a stream of water from the truck. After a round with scouring brushes and aromatic oils, there was another wash of water. Finally Recin was handed one of the pieces of cloth to dry himself and given a set of Suder clothing to wear.

"Isn't all this a lot to carry with you?" he asked as he slipped into the sky blue and orange tunic. "These wagons and oils. Why try to clean a whole army?"

"We don't clean the whole army," said Daleel, "only the officers."

"Why even do that?

Daleel leaned against the cleaning wagon. "Suderbod is a low and muddy land. Cleanliness and rank are tied together for us."

Recin finished dressing and looked down at himself. His breeches were of bitter yellow, and his shirt striped with blue and orange. He wasn't sure if the Suder clothing was less embarrassing than no clothing at all. "What now?"

"As soon as your friend is ready, you'll both be going to see Solin." The ambassador flashed his broad smile. "I'm glad to see that you're alive. You gave me quite a chase across the rooftops back in Berimish. I was afraid you might have been badly injured."

Recin looked at the small Suder in amazement. "It was you? You're the one who killed Tagard?"

"It was a team effort, really," said Daleel. He closed one eye and mimicked firing a crossbow. "But it was my finger on the trigger. A shame, really. He was the only man in the kingdom that showed a glimmer of potential."

Kitrin appeared from behind her screen. Except for the pouch holding the tracking crystal still belted at her waist, she was dressed identically to Recin.

"Why, now you two look like brother and sister," said Daleel with a laugh. "Solin will probably enjoy that."

He led them to a sprawling construction of green and yellow cloth that was supported by dozens of poles and many times bigger than the other tents. Inside, the space was broken into rooms by hanging sheets of cloth. Recin was surprised to see that these rooms were furnished with heavy wooden chairs and tables. There were even thick rugs spread on the ground and portraits suspended from the cloth walls.

"It's like a portable palace," said Kitrin.

"It does make the privations of the field a bit easier to tolerate," said Daleel.

Recin's gaze swept around the giant tent. A pair of soldiers stood near the door, but he saw no sign of other guards as they went deeper into the maze of rooms and hallways. If they could get to the outer walls of the tent, it should be simple to slip under the cloth. Perhaps in the dark of night . . .

"I wouldn't be thinking about escape," said Daleel,

apparently reading his mind. "The hemarch has resources that you may not expect."

They passed through a long hall to a room where couches sat against the walls and a fire burned in a metal brazier. Low tables beside each couch held bowls of food and carafes of some yellow fluid. If Recin had not known they had entered a tent, he would have sworn the room was in the middle of an elaborate building.

Hemarch Solin lolled on a couch of shimmering purple, his bulk half-submerged in the soft cushions. The ornate clothing he had worn outside had been replaced by a rainbow-striped robe.

"Well, now," he said, "don't you two look better?"

"What are you going to do to us?" asked Kitrin.

"To you? Hmmm. Nothing *to* you," said the fat man. He bared his multicolored teeth. "I'd much rather do things *with* you."

Daleel bowed to the man. "If you don't mind, Hemarch, I'll leave you to your delectations. I need to go make sure things are ready for tomorrow."

"Of course, my friend." Solin spread his meaty hands. "Tomorrow we will be in Berimish, and you can show me all the things that you have written about in your marvelous dispatches."

"It will be an honor, Hemarch." The ambassador bowed quickly and exited, leaving Recin and Kitrin standing alone at the end of the room.

"Come, come," said Solin. "Take a seat, rest. You must have had quite an exhausting trip getting here."

Recin was too tired to argue. He selected the couch most distant from the fat Suder and dropped onto the cushions. Kitrin sat down at his side and the couch sagged under their combined weight. Almost immediately, Recin's eyelids drooped. Being unconscious while strapped to the back of a running En'Jaga had not provided much rest. He figured three or four days of solid sleep should be just about enough.

"You two are certainly an attractive pair," said Solin. "Are you mated?"

"No," said Kitrin. The firmness with which she said the word made Recin frown.

"You should be," said the hemarch. "You have that look about you. Hmmm. Now, tell me, was it Tagard who sent you to kill me?"

"Tagard's dead," said Kitrin. "You know that."

The fat man shook his head. "One can never be too sure about these things. A great many dead men tend to turn up again if you don't check the body yourself." He made a sweeping gesture with his meaty hands. "Please, eat. Enjoy yourselves."

Recin opened his eyes and looked down at the table. His stomach reminded him that it had been a long, long time since he had eaten. He reached toward a bowl.

Kitrin grabbed his wrist. "No," she said. "You don't want to eat anything while you're here."

Hemarch Solin laughed. "What is it, island girl? Don't you like Suder cooking?"

There was a commotion from elsewhere in the tent. Someone leaned against the wall at Recin's back, causing a bulge in the cloth. There were muffled shouts. Then Aligarius Timni appeared in the doorway.

His colorful tunic was half open, and his pink hat was gone, revealing a skull that was shaved clean. In his hand was an empty bowl. "I need more," he said. "Mine has gone bad."

"Has it?" Solin looked at the sorcerer with a flat expression. "Hmmm. Feel free to take what you need."

Aligarius dropped his bowl to the carpet and raced to the table in front of Kitrin and Recin. The sorcerer plunged his hand in, came out with a fistful of cubed meat, and thrust it into his mouth. Immediately, his face twisted with despair.

"This is bad, too!" he cried.

He went to the next bowl and pulled more food from it. And the next. Finally he fell on his knees and faced Solin.

"It's all bad," he said in a trembling voice. Yellow syrup ran over his lip and trickled down his chin. "Please," said the sorcerer. "Please, I need more."

"Hmmm." The fat Suder rose slowly from his padded seat. He lifted a bowl from the table near his own couch and carried it to Aligarius. "I'm afraid that the food you've been eating will no longer satisfy your appetite. Why don't you try some of mine?"

With shaking hands, Aligarius took the bowl. He reached inside and pulled out a small piece of some unidentifiable bit of food dripping with a viscous red fluid. As soon as it touched the sorcerer's lips, his head snapped back sharply. Tremors ran over his thin body.

"I . . . I can't eat this," said Aligarius. "This is too strong. This is not what Daleel promised me."

"Your tastes have changed." Solin shook his head. "Soon you will find that even this new spice has become too mild." He reached down and patted the top of Aligarius's bald head. "But don't worry. Hmmm. There are many flavors yet to try. Many stronger spices."

Aligarius reached into the bowl and took out another piece of food. He put it in his mouth and was wracked by another bout of shivering and twitching. Thick tears ran down his hollow cheeks.

Recin looked at the food in the bowls. No matter how his stomach complained of being empty, he was very glad that Kitrin had stopped him from eating.

"Why don't you take this food back to your chamber?" said Solin. "There you can eat in peace."

Aligarius got to his feet and shuffled toward the door. He suddenly seemed very old and fragile.

Solin clapped his hands. "Now," he said. "Food and the pleasures of the bed are all that matter in this world. I have food. Hmmm. Let us see what kind of entertainment you two can provide." He approached the couch where Kitrin and Recin sat. He reached toward Recin.

Recin tried to flinch away, but once again the fat man moved with impossible speed. His thick fingers locked into Recin's hair and pulled him forward.

"You shouldn't try to fight me. Hmmm. Some spices give more than flavor," said Solin. His moldy breath washed over Recin with sickening strength. "Some give strength. Some give speed. I indulge in both. I could fight a dozen such as you and still be untouched." He smiled his gaudy smile. "True, there is a price to be paid in years and pain." His other hand went to Recin's tunic and his fingers worked at the ties. "But the compensations are worth it."

Though the man's fingers were fat, their grip could not be denied. Recin threw himself from side to side, but no matter how he strained, Solin's grip did not loosen. He kicked out, but his foot glanced off the Suder's fat leg and brought only laughter.

Kitrin jumped up from the couch. "No," she said. "Let me be the first to entertain you."

Solin turned his large head. "I have already been with your people. Do you have anything new to show me?"

Kitrin nodded. "Aligarius said I knew no magic," she said. Then she reached up and began to loosen her own tunic. "But Aligarius doesn't know all kinds of magic. Magic can happen in other places than the temple or the battlefield." The first tie came loose under her fingers and she moved to the second. "Some magic happens in the bedroom." She paused, her bare white shoulder peeking through the open top. "Would you like to see?"

The Suder made a rumble deep in his throat. His hands left the ties of Recin's shirt and he laced his thick fingers together. "What magic do you have, little wizard?"

"Don't," said Recin. "You don't have to do this."

"Quiet," replied Kitrin. Her hands went to the pouch at her waist and she loosed the leather cord. Using both hands, she lifted out the blue-green tracking stone. The glow of the stone was so bright that it filled the room with green light.

Solin's small eyes glowed with the light of the stone. "What is this?" he said. "What does it do?"

"This stone can provide an experience like none you've had before," said Kitrin. "An experience that will make you forget everything else." She held the crystal out in her shaking hands and moved slowly around the room to stand across from the hemarch. "Would you like to see?"

Solin turned to face her. "Show me," he said.

Kitrin opened her fingers and the finding crystal flew from her hands. It struck the Hemarch in his wide forehead with a sound like an ax biting into the trunk of a tree. Then it glanced off and ripped through the cloth wall above Recin.

Recin scrambled out of the way as Solin tumbled back against the couch. Blood poured from a deep gash on the Suder's face and into his open staring eyes.

Solin's blood was black.

"Hmmm," said the hemarch. The dark blood flowed down his heavy face and dripped from his round chin. "That was . . . hmmm." His hands reached out.

Recin scuttled back and stayed away from the man's grip. "What do we do now?"

"Now we run," said Kitrin.

Solin rose from the couch. "Oh, no," he said. "No. You have to stay. We haven't. Hmmm. Haven't . . ." He spread his arms and took one step forward. Then the hemarch of all Suderbod fell facedown on the ground.

Kitrin stared down at the dead man with a sour expression. "I'd like to think things will be better in Suderbod without him," she said, "but there are a thousand more just like him."

Recin moved to the opening at the front of the room and looked toward the front of the tent. "I didn't see anyone coming. Let's get out of here while we can."

"Not without the Magewall Hub." Kitrin jumped over Solin's body and grabbed the edges of the hole through which the crystal had disappeared. With a strong pull, she ripped the cloth wall open and stepped through into the room beyond.

Recin went around the fallen hemarch, being careful to stay out of reach in case the man was not quite as dead as he looked. The next room was not as luxurious as that of the hemarch. A small table stood in the center of the room, flanked by a pair of simple wooden chairs. In the center of the room, Aligarius Timni sat on the floor, his face and hands stained with scarlet sauce. The bowl in front of him held only a few small scraps of food. He looked up at them and blinked his dark eyes. "Kitrin Weidini," he mumbled. Sauce was smeared across his lips and cheeks like a child indulging in some forbidden treat. "Are you here for a lesson?" His voice was soft and far away.

"Yes, that's right," said Kitrin. She bent over the sorcerer.

"You were going to teach me about the Magewall Hub. Remember?"

"Magewall Hub?" Aligarius rolled on his side. "Not very interesting. Just a pretty rock."

Recin spotted the tracking stone lying on the floor. It was no longer pulsing with light, and when he picked it up it rested cool and motionless in his hands. Then he noticed another object on the floor, a cylinder about the size of his hand that seemed made from the same crystal as the tracking stone. He lifted it and held it out to Kitrin.

"Is this it?" he asked.

Kitrin took the cylinder from his hands. "Yes." She looked around the room. "Now, if we can just find our way out of here, it's all over."

"It is all over," said a voice from the next room. Ursal Daleel stepped through the tear in the wall. "Though perhaps it hasn't ended in quite the way you wanted."

Recin snatched up a wooden chair and held it over his head. "You're not going to stop us."

Daleel smiled. "You're absolutely right," he said. "I'm not. In fact, I have riding beasts waiting outside to make sure you escape."

"Why would you do that?" asked Recin.

The former ambassador to Tamingazin laced his fingers together and put his hands behind his head. "You don't know what a joy this last year has been for me. War, war, and rumors of war. There is nothing quite so lovely to the ambitious man."

Recin looked into the man's dark eyes. "And you're ambitious."

"Of course," said Daleel. "Solin was hanging on much too long. Without a bit of a push, he might have remained hemarch for years to come. And besides, under normal circumstances there are a good number of people with a better claim to the throne than me. I had to move very carefully to ensure that his death came about at just the right moment."

Kitrin slid the Magewall Hub into her belt pouch and straightened her clothing. "You started the war in Tamingazin so you could get Solin out of the way?"

"I had to do something. Patience is rarely the companion of ambition."

Recin felt as dizzy as he had when strapped to the En'Jaga. "All this killing just so you could take over Suderbod? You used Aligarius, and Tagard, and us, just for this?"

The Suder smiled. "Suderbod politics are seldom clean," he said. "If I had made some move on Solin myself, the army would have seen to it that I was sliced into pieces and dropped in some mud hole. But since it was Solin's own vices which brought on his fate . . ." He shrugged.

"So what now?" asked Recin. "Do you go back to Suderbod?"

The Suder's smile grew wider. "Of course I do. But first I have to cement my position as hemarch."

"How?"

"Why, by securing Tamingazin for the empire, of course. None of those pretenders back in Grand Sudalen will stand a chance once I have put that dish on the empire's plate." He turned and pointed back through the torn wall. "Now, if you'll simply go back the way we came and straight out the door. You'll find two riding beasts tethered just at the edge of camp. The attendant has instructions to help you get on your way."

Recin glanced over at Kitrin. The girl patted the pouch where the Magewall Hub now rested. "All right," he said. He lowered the wooden chair to the floor. "Let's go."

"There's just one more minor matter before you leave," said Daleel. He stretched out a hand to Kitrin. "I'll take the Magewall Hub."

The girl opened her eyes widely and blinked. "Hub?" she said. "What hub?"

"I'm not an idiot," said the Suder. "Give it to me, or I'll take it."

"I don't—" started Kitrin. Daleel reached forward, slid his fingers into the girl's black hair, and jerked her head down. At the same time, he raised his knee. Her face met his kneecap with a solid, sickening crunch.

Recin leaped forward, but Daleel delivered a backhanded slap that sent him flying across the room.

"Don't test me," he said. "Solin wasn't the only one who takes special spices. Now, give me the Magewall Hub."

Kitrin raised her head, and Recin saw that her nose was twisted to the side and her lips swollen. "What hub?" she said.

The Suder snarled. "On second thought, killing Solin's assassins might help secure the army's help. When you're dead, I can search you at my leisure."

Behind the Suder, a thin trembling figure rose. Aligarius Timni held out a shaking hand and moved his red-stained lips.

Slowly, a ball of light began to grow above his palm.

"This is your last chance," said Daleel. "Give me the Magewall Hub, and I may still let you live."

Recin snatched up the chair at his side. "Get away from Kitrin."

The Suder shook his head. "I'm going to take that chair apart, then put it down your throat one piece at a—"

The ball of light leaped from Aligarius's hand and enveloped the Suder's head. The force of the spell was not enough to fell the Suder, but it did stagger him. He started to turn toward Aligarius.

As he did so, Recin took one step forward and brought the chair down hard across Daleel's head. The floppy pink cap fell onto the floor and the Suder's knees sagged. Recin raised the chair and swung again. This time Daleel fell like a bag of sticks. He moaned, but he did not get up.

"Are you all right?" Recin asked.

Kitrin sniffed and nodded. "Yes." She looked over at Aligarius. "Thank you. Why did you help us?"

"I . . ." The old man shook his head. "I can't do this anymore."

Recin looked down at the man on the floor and frowned. "We should kill this one."

"Why?"

"You heard what he said. He's the one who killed King Tagard, and the one who got Aligarius to betray the institute, and the one who started this whole war," said Recin. "We can't just leave him here to plan something else."

Kitrin looked down at the crumpled form. "Are you really going to kill him?"

A black surge went through Recin's thoughts. The man on the floor had killed Talli's father just as Rael Gar had killed Recin's. Almost every bad thing that had happened since the humans captured Berimish could be laid, at least in part, at the feet of this little man in his ridiculous clothes.

Recin let out a long breath. "No," he said. "I'm not going to kill him." He dropped the chair. "Come on, let's go."

Aligarius put a weak hand on Recin's arm. "Take me with you."

"What?"

"I helped you," said the sorcerer. "Now take me with you."

"You're a traitor and a murderer," said Recin. "You deserve to stay here."

Aligarius looked down. "Please," he whispered.

CHAPTER
17

TALLI TRIED DESPERATELY TO PUSH HER
head clear of the water, but she could no longer tell
which way was up, which was down. Her lungs burned
for air.

There was a sharp jerk. Her tumbling motion
through the tunnel became more violent. The roaring
grew louder. Heard through the dark water, it was so
strong that Talli could feel the sound on her skin. The
blackness began to take on a different quality, filled
with sparks that flared behind her eyelids each time her
head struck the stone walls. She wanted to scream, but
she didn't have any air left in her lungs.

Then gray light was all around her. She flew from
the tunnel in a column of foam and landed in the boiling waters of the River Nish. Another form went by
her. And another.

Talli gasped for air as her head came above the surface of the crashing water. The bank of the river was
no more than a length or two away, but it was slipping

by all too quickly. Talli desperately wished that she had taken Recin up on his offer to teach her how to swim. She clawed at the water, trying to make the same kind of motions that she had seen others make in the water.

She swallowed a mouthful of water, coughed, sputtered. The land was drawing no nearer. She wasn't going to make it.

"Talli!"

She raised her head, looking for the source of the shout.

"Talli! Put your feet down!"

She obeyed and found that the muddy bottom of the river was only a few feet below the surface. With a few sloppy steps along the bottom, she lunged forward and threw herself on the muddy shore. There was a pile of huge empty attalo shells to her left, and dozens of wooden posts reared up all around her. Talli realized that they were under the Berimish docks.

A figure crouched by her in the rainy twilight. "Are you all right?" asked Janin.

Talli nodded. "Go help the others," she said.

By the time she caught her breath and got on her feet, Janin had located another half-dozen sodden troopers and gathered them together on the shore. They were split evenly: three Viashino and three humans. Twenty-three others were missing.

"Where are the rest?" Talli asked.

"I don't know," said Janin. "I was roped with three others. Maybe the rest are all still together somewhere."

Heasos, who was among those gathered on the bank, stood up and walked to where the storm drain emptied into the river. "Are they still underground, or have they washed down the stream?"

Talli stared out at the tumbling river. Bits and pieces of debris went past on the curl of every wave, but none

of them seemed large enough to be either human or
Viashino. "Does it matter?" she said softly. "In either
place, their spirits will soon be free."

"What do we do now?" asked a human trooper.
"Can we sneak back along the riverbank?"

"Sneak back?" Talli shook her head. "We're here.
We're not going back."

"But there are only eight of us!"

"Quiet." Talli walked over to the edge of the dock
and held a hand over her eyes to block out the slashing
rain. The imposing side of the dockmaster's building
loomed over the river front. Through the sheets of rain,
she could see lamps burning inside its shuttered windows. "There are only eight of us, but that's eight more
than they're expecting."

She moved back to the center of the group. "Karelon
may be no more than a hundred strides from us right
now, and I don't see a single guard in our way."

"You really think we can do this?" asked Heasos.

Talli nodded. "I think we have to."

They spaced themselves close together in a line and
moved up the sloping bank to the street above. Only a
few blocks away, a bonfire burned bright enough to
survive the rain. It appeared that Karelon's forces had
taken most of the furniture in the area and heaped it in
the center of the street. There it had been set ablaze. In
its orange glow Talli could see more furniture that had
been formed into a barrier across the street. Dozens of
human fighters moved back and forth behind this wall
of debris, and shouts echoed between the buildings.

"It looks like Lisolo has them excited," whispered
Heasos.

Talli hushed the Viashino, but she agreed with his
assessment.

It looked like Lisolo was doing everything he could
to keep the attention of Karelon's forces turned to the

south. Beyond the flaming barrier, they could see figures running back and forth, and the echo of distant shouts echoed up the street. Talli hurried across the empty avenue and pressed herself against the side of the dockmaster's building. Janin was quick to follow. A second later, they were all in place.

"How do we go in?" asked one of the humans.

"I don't know," said Talli. She slid over to a window and peered through the shutter's slats.

A smoky oil lamp sat in a niche on the wall. Other than that, the room was empty. It was a large room, with ceilings high enough for the tallest Viashino, or even an En'Jaga. Talli was surprised to see a staircase on the far side of the room, one of only a handful she had seen in Berimish. The dockmaster's building served the mixture of races who brought their ships to the city, and it seemed designed to accommodate them all. There were doors at both ends of the room. Both were closed.

She moved down the wall and peered through the next window into another room. This time Talli saw a dozen soldiers gathered around a long table, drinking and talking. They made broad gestures with their hands and their faces were animated, but the sound of the rain and river snatched away their words before Talli could hear what they were saying. Behind the men there was a closed door.

"I recognize these men," said Talli. "They're all from Karelon's hold. If they're here, she probably is, too. And if Karelon is here, then she must be in the back."

"What if she's not here?" asked Heasos.

"Just pray that she is."

Janin joined Talli at the window. "There are more of them, but we'll have surprise with us. Look how they move. Some of these humans have had too much wine to fight well."

"I hope you're right," said Talli.

She moved around to the front of the building. Like the Splendent Hall, the dockmaster's building had solid wooden doors. For once Talli wished for the cloth door coverings of most Viashino buildings.

"All right," Talli whispered. "Everyone stand away from the doors. Stay where they can't see you."

Talli pulled the sword from her belt and raised it to rap the pommel against the door, but at the last moment something caught her eye. A notched pole leaned against the wall a few paces to one side of the door. Talli walked over to the pole and stared up into the falling rain. As far as she could tell, the pole continued beyond the second floor all the way to the roof of the building.

She turned to the troops. "Wait here," she said. "I'm going up."

"So am I," said Janin.

Talli nodded. "All right."

"You should have at least one Viashino," said Heasos. "If there is any climbing to be done, then we're the ones to do it." Before Talli could say a word in protest, the young Viashino curled his clawed hands and feet around the pole and moved upward at an astonishing speed.

"What about the rest of us?" asked a human soldier.

"Stay in the shadows," said Talli. "If you hear us shout, come as fast as you can." She returned her sword to its scabbard. "Let's go."

The pole thumped against the edge of the roof as they climbed.

Talli looked down several times, expecting to see the door burst open. But Karelon's officers must have been enjoying their drinks and their conversation too much to notice. Lightning flashed close by as they climbed and the claps of thunder shook all of Berimish.

Heasos was waiting to lend a hand as Talli stepped off onto the rain-slick roof. "There's a door up here," he said, "and it's open."

Talli closed her eyes and breathed a sigh of relief. It was the first thing to go right in the whole long, wet day. A moment later, Janin reached the top of the pole and joined them on the roof. Then both women followed Heasos to the door. Talli drew her sword again as they prepared to go in.

"Ready?"

Janin nodded.

"I lost my bow in the tunnels," said Heasos. He flexed his clawed fingers. "But I can still fight."

A gentle push, and the door swung open with a squeal of old hinges. The room beyond was dark. More lightning flashed overhead, revealing glimpses of dusty boxes and overturned crates. Talli stepped through the door. The room stank of old fish and stale spices.

"Doesn't look like anyone's been up here for a while," she said.

Janin joined her in the room and eased the door closed. Only a faint glow from the staircase in the corner kept the room from being as dark as the underground tunnels. Together they crept across the floor to the head of the stairs.

"Looks like there're no other rooms up here," said Janin.

"Right. Then I guess we go down."

Talli winced at each creak and squeal from the warped wooden steps, but they reached the second floor with no cry of alarm. This level was larger, and there were barrels and boxes of all sizes stacked along the wall. Rolls of sail canvas filled one end of a huge room.

"Looks like they left here in a hurry," said Heasos. He pointed to a table where stacks of coins lay. More bits of copper and silver were spilled across the floor.

Talli saw a dark stain on the floor. It might have been old wine, or oil, but she suspected it was not. "There's nothing here," she said. "Let's go on."

Another flight of steps led them to the ground floor and the empty room Talli had first seen through the window. From the door to her right, Talli could hear the muffled voices of the officers in the front room. She turned to the left and pressed her ear to the smooth wood of the second door. At first she heard nothing, then a low moan and a sound of movement. There was someone inside. Someone spoke.

It was a man's voice. She couldn't make out the words, but someone was definitely in the room.

"I think this is it," whispered Talli. "Be ready." She held the grip of her sword in her sweaty hand and pushed against the door. It didn't open. She took the handle and pulled. It still refused to budge.

"It must be barred from the inside," said Janin. She put her hand against the wooden frame and eyed the door. "I can open it." She pulled back her hand and tightened her fingers into a stiff blade.

Talli caught her by the arm. "Wait. They'd be bound to hear that in the front room. Let's try something a little more direct." She leaned past Janin and rapped her knuckles lightly against the door.

"What?" said a sharp voice from inside. Karelon's voice.

Talli knocked again. She took a deep breath and made her voice deep and rough. "You're needed," she called.

"Not now," shouted Karelon.

"It's Tagard's daughter," Talli called through the door. "We've caught her."

Immediately there was a thump from inside the room, then a scraping noise as the bar was lifted. A man's voice spoke again, and though his words were still unclear, they carried a tone of complaint. Karelon cut him off with one word. A moment later the door was flung open and the dark-haired woman stood before them.

"Where is . . . ?" she started. Then she saw who was in front of her, and her brown eyes widened. The thin woman was wearing nothing but a cloak, which she held closed at her neck. Her long back hair spilled over her shoulders in disarray.

"I'm right here," said Talli. She jumped forward, pushing Karelon back into the room. Janin and Heasos came behind her, closed the door, and dropped the bar into place.

The room was small, with only a table and a narrow bunk. Clothing was scattered on the floor. On the bunk, with a spread pulled up to his chest, was a young man with delicate features and tumbling curls that framed his frightened face.

The shocked expression on Karelon's face gave way to a disdainful smile.

"Well," said Karelon. "Here you are along with a Garan and a Viashino. Wouldn't your father have been proud."

"Who are they?" said the man. His accent revealed him as a native of Berimish.

"No one of importance," she said.

"Surrender to us," said Talli, "and we'll let you live."

Karelon shook her head. "I don't think so." She looked Talli up and down and her nose wrinkled. "How did you get here, swimming in the river? You look like a drowned plodger . . . and you smell even worse."

Talli leveled her sword and directed it at her father's old advisor, at the woman she had so long thought of as her friend. "If you don't surrender, I'll kill you."

"You?" Karelon stepped across the floor and sat

down on the edge of the bed. "Have you ever killed a human?"

"Not yet."

"It's not like killing a Viashino," said the thin woman. She leaned back and tangled her fingers in the hair of the young man who shared her bed. "It's not as easy to slice a throat when it's so like your own."

"You are nothing like me," said Talli.

Karelon smiled. "Here you are with a Garan and a Viashino. One happy little group." The smile dropped and her face creased in a sneer. "Bringing these monsters with you to kill another human. You're as bad as your father."

Her arm came back from the other side of the reclining man's head. Talli had only a moment to see the glitter of steel in the woman's fingers, then the knife was whistling through the air.

Talli dropped to the floor and rolled. The knife stuck the wooden wall behind her and quivered.

Janin leaped across the room, her fingers raised to deliver a killing blow. Heasos was close behind.

"No!" shouted Talli. She scrambled to her feet. "Don't touch her. This is something I have to do."

"There is more at stake here than your honor," said Janin. Her eyes throbbed red.

"Please."

Janin stood frozen for a moment, then nodded and backed away.

Heasos lowered his head and hissed, but he backed away from the bed.

Karelon laughed. "You should have let them try me. At least they might have stood a chance."

"Surrender to me," said Talli, "or die."

From somewhere in the bedclothes, another blade appeared in Karelon's hands. "You really are a terrible fool, aren't you?" said the thin woman. She shook her head in mock sadness. "What a disappointment you must have been to your poor father."

Talli screamed and charged.

Karelon aimed and threw her blade.

Talli didn't try to dodge. She raised her left hand and the knife went deep into her forearm. Red streaks flashed across her vision, but she didn't stop.

Her sword passed down through Karelon's body, through the straw-filled mattress, and through the thin slats of the bed.

By the time the tip of the sword buried itself in the floor, Karelon was already dead.

The young man in the bed pulled back from the body and squeezed himself against the wall. He sobbed wordlessly.

Talli tried to remove the throwing knife from her arm, but each pull only brought on another wave of agony. Janin took her by the wrist and looked at it.

"It's buried too deep," she said. "The point is lodged in your bone and will have to be cut free."

There was a pounding at the door. "Karelon!" called a voice. "Is everything all right in there?" More pounding. "Karelon?"

Heasos looked at the door, then at Talli. "What do we do?"

There had been a time when Talli thought the Viashino were hard to understand, but she could see the fear in Heasos's face as clearly as she could in any human's. "Open the door," she said.

"There are a dozen humans out there," warned Janin. "We may surprise them, but you are badly injured."

"Open it."

Heasos raised the bar, and at once the door was battered open.

The leaders of Karelon's army crowded into the

room. A burly man, a head taller than Talli and twice as broad, stepped in with his sword drawn.

"What's going on in . . . ?" His gaze fell on Karelon's body, and the blood drained from his face.

"Karelon?" he said in a voice that was barely more than a whisper.

Talli grasped the pommel of her sword and jerked it free. There was a grating sound as the steel slid past broken wood and shattered bones. She raised the bloody weapon and leveled it at the man's eyes.

"Karelon is dead," she said. "Now it's your turn. Join me, or join her."

The soldier dropped his sword to the floor.

CHAPTER
18

"THERE'S NO USE," SAID KITRIN. "THE LEG IS badly sprained. It's not going any farther."

Recin kicked at the muddy ground in frustration. "We're no more than a good arrow shot from the Suder camp. If they come after us, they'll have no trouble finding us."

Kitrin patted the injured riding beast. "We'll have to walk."

"It'll be hard to walk fast enough to stay ahead of mounted troops." Recin kicked the ground again. Carrying three people was a lot to expect of any riding beast. To try it in the dark, in the rain, in the middle of a swamp—it was no wonder their trip had been a brief one. But there had been only one mount waiting outside Solin's tent, and they hadn't exactly been in a good position to complain.

The injured beast snorted and took a limping step, its damaged leg held off the ground. On the other side of the animal, Aligarius Timni sat among the weeds and vines. The sorcerer hadn't said a word since leaving the Suder camp. Recin wasn't even sure the old-man knew where he was.

He looked back along the path they had followed. Rain had been falling since they left Solin's tent; between the trees and the sheets of rain, he could see nothing of the Suderbod camp, but he knew it was out there. "Shouldn't we go ahead and use the Magewall Hub?" he asked. "That way, even if we don't get away, Tamingazin will be safe."

"You're probably right," said Kitrin. She moved away from the riding beast and fished the hub from its place in her belt pouch. She looked around, then walked to a huge fallen tree that lay on the undergrowth. She placed the Magewall Hub on the wet bole of the tree and pushed her dripping hair back from her face. "The ceremony should only take a few minutes, but it can't be interrupted."

Recin nodded. "I'll keep a look out," he said.

Kitrin spread her hands above the cylinder of green crystal and began to mutter in a language Recin had never heard before. Just the sound of it was enough to raise the hairs on the back of his neck. He could feel a tension grow in the air like the feeling before a summer lightning storm.

A flicker of light moved among the trees. It was faint, and after a moment it was gone. Recin squinted against the rain.

On their first few nights in the marsh, he and Kitrin had seen strange lights dancing above the black waters, but those lights had been blue, and the spark that Recin had just seen was yellow. He was about to dismiss it as his imagination when it came again. This time it was closer. A moment later, another light could be seen behind it. Then another.

A knot clamped down on Recin's empty stomach. He turned toward Kitrin. "They're coming," he said. "The Suder are hunting for us."

The girl nodded, but didn't pause in her mumbled

chant. On the fallen tree, the Magewall Hub had begun
to glow with a green light of its own. The verdant light
grew brighter with every arcane word; it began to
dance and pulse like the beating of a heart.

"Yes," said Aligarius Timni from his place in the
mud and weeds. "That's it. Almost there."

Recin swallowed and spun around. The torches of the
Suder troops were closer and seemed to be coming in
their direction. He hoped that they were only following
the signs along the trail and hadn't yet spotted the light
from the glowing hub. "Hurry," he whispered. "Please."

Kitrin's voice gradually rose in pitch, the words
becoming clearer and louder. Around her the creatures
of the swamps ceased their night calls. Even the rain
seemed to pause.

". . . argin vigil talech!" finished the young wizard.

A burst of wind swept through the trees and the
light from the Magewall Hub flared a brilliant
green-white. Then the light died and the marsh was
again dark. Within a few seconds, the insects, amphib-
ians, and reptiles of the marsh resumed their interrupted songs.

"Is that it?" asked Recin.

The pale girl nodded. "That's it," she said.
"Tamingazin should be protected." She frowned and
picked up the hub. "Only it didn't seem to go quite
right."

"What?"

Kitrin turned the hub over in her hands. "I should
feel the difference in the connection with the wall, but
I can't. I'm not sure it worked."

Aligarius stood on wobbly legs and gave a tittering
laugh. "I'm sure it didn't," he said. "The magewall isn't
restored."

"But I followed your ritual!" Kitrin cried. "I did
everything you said to do."

The sorcerer nodded. "But that was all just dry research, wasn't it?" He staggered a few steps and leaned against a mossy tree. "When I actually used the hub, I found that several portions of my theory were incorrect. The transitions were different than I expected. You see? It took me the better part of two days just to lift the wall."

"But what about putting it back?"

The sorcerer shook his head. "I haven't worked that out yet."

"We don't have two days," said Kitrin. "The Suder troops are only an hour's march from the border."

Recin looked over his shoulder. The torchlight was close enough now that he could see the brilliant colors of the Suder armor. He stepped to where the injured riding beast stood and delivered a hard slap to its side. The animal squealed in protest, then limped quickly away.

"Come on," said Recin. "If you're going to figure this out, you'll have to do it on the run." He took Aligarius by the arm and pulled the old man into the darkness.

Talli fingered the bandage on her arm and squinted into the mists that shrouded the Great Marsh. "Are you sure they're out there?" she asked.

Samet Gar nodded. "Our scouts saw them at evening. Over twelve thousands of humans, and almost two of En'Jaga. They will be on us at any minute."

It was almost ten times the force Talli had been able to muster. Even with the surrender of Karelon's forces, there were still skirmishes in Berimish with the more stubborn troops. Lisolo was in his city, fighting to extinguish fires both metaphorical and literal. Those who had ridden to the defense of the border were exhausted from days of fighting.

Talli peered up and down her own lines. The humans, Garan, and Viashino who made up her force had been preparing throughout the night. They were tired, but they were also anxious, ready to fight. They had been expecting the Suder attack since the first gray glow of dawn. Talli felt it herself: a cold band across her chest and a tightness in her gut; the pressure of battle that could cause the bravest to sneak off the field, or cause cowards to charge the enemy. In all the long war to unite the valley, they had never faced odds so great or a situation so desperate.

She looked down the gentle slope that led to the Great Marsh. Midway along the hill was a band of bare red clay that slashed across the path where the mage-wall had once stood. Broken lengths of white bone showed where previous invasions had been halted while they struggled within the wall. But the ancient protector of Tamingazin would provide no help today.

"Maybe we should attack them first," Talli whispered to herself. "If we move in the darkness, they may not know how few we are. It worked in Berimish. And then at least the waiting would be over."

"The Suder are accomplished soldiers," said Samet Gar. "There will be pickets and scouts between our lines and theirs. We won't catch them unprepared."

Talli scowled. Her people were running on nothing but excitement and determination. If they had to wait for the Suder, she hoped that the wait would be short.

She scarcely finished the thought before a shout came from her right. "There!" cried a Viashino voice. "Movement in the fog!"

Long seconds passed before Talli saw what had caused the alarm. Through the mists that rose from the swamp and the fine rain that still fell from the clouds, dark gray shapes moved. At first there were only a few, but then there were hundreds, thousands.

"Get the archers ready," said Talli. "I want a volley as soon as they come in range."

There was a creaking as three hundred Viashino tightened the abex hide straps of their bows. Talli saw Heasos in the center of the line. The mud of the Berimish sewers was still on him, but both he and Janin had insisted on accompanying Talli to the border. She thought of what Karelon had said before she died. The dark-haired woman had been making fun of them, but in a way she was right—Tagard would have been proud to see Talli fighting alongside these two people from the other races of the valley.

The figures in the fog grew clearer. And larger. The front ranks of the Suder force were not humans, but towering En'Jaga. Even in the dim gray light, Talli could see the gleam of steel armor on their bodies. More and more of the giant creatures emerged from the mists until there was an unbroken row of them spread out from the mouth of the Nish to the edge of Talli's lines. With a great roar, the monsters surged up the hill into Tamingazin.

Within seconds, the first flight of iron bolts soared over the heads of the humans kneeling in the front rank. Talli was too far away to see the bolts strike the enemy, but she could see their effect. Dozens of the En'Jaga tumbled into the mud. Dozens more threw back their massive heads and screamed at the sky.

"Again," said Talli. "Keep firing."

The crossbows groaned again as the Viashino prepared another shot. It caught the first En'Jaga just as they passed the site where the magewall had once been. Again the bolts drove a hole through the ranks of advancing enemy, but the line wasn't slowed.

"It's not going to be enough," Janin called from her position a few strides away. "They will be on us in a moment."

Talli nodded. It would come to a fight, and she could see no way that they would win. "Hold your positions," she said firmly. "Those with spears get ready to use them."

The mass of En'Jaga reached the red clay—and fell. Others stayed upright, but their huge feet could find little purchase on the slick wet ground.

"Out from behind the defenses!" called Talli. She drew her sword and leaped in front of the lines. "Up troops, we're going to them."

"What about the archers?" called Heasos.

"Keep firing."

"Over our own people?" asked another Viashino. "But—"

"Keep firing!" shouted Talli. She turned toward the En'Jaga and raised her sword. "Attack!"

In a moment a thousand humans, Viashino, and Garan were on their feet and racing down the hill. Flights of crossbow bolts sang over Talli's head. The wet grass slapped against her legs. By the time she reached the clay band, the first En'Jaga were past. Those coming across in the tracks of the first ranks were having much less trouble with the sloppy ground. Talli's momentary advantage was disappearing fast.

She gave a hoarse cry and threw herself at an En'Jaga. Great claws rent the air at her back. Teeth snapped close to her head. Talli slashed left and right with her sword, cutting into massive limbs, laying open wounds the length of a human.

From the corner of her eye she saw a Garan strike one of the creatures with a flying kick. The blow was delivered with such force that the huge beast was sent sprawling. Before it could rise, a young Viashino rushed in and sliced its broad throat. The Viashino was still proclaiming its victory when a second En'Jaga caught it and crushed it within its great jaws.

Another of the beasts reared over Talli. Its head lunged down, and her padded helmet crunched between its yellow teeth. She ducked, spun, and jumped away. The creature tried to turn after her, but Talli was faster. She came up behind it and drove her sword into the joint of its scaly leg. The En'Jaga hissed and twisted. Talli jumped away again. This time she cut at its tail, then at its armored back. In thirty seconds of combat, she left the monster bleeding from a dozen wounds. It made a guttural roar and fell on its side in the mud.

Another En'Jaga rushed her with its head held low to the ground. Talli dodged its first thrust, pivoted, and threw herself onto the creature's back. It reached for her with clawed hands. Before it could get a grip on her, she brought her sword down through the bones at the top of its skull. It fell to the ground with a crash like thunder. But as it fell, Talli's iron sword snapped in two. She drew out the broken stump and searched the ground around her. Two human bodies lay close by. One of them had to have dropped a weapon.

She was still looking when a claw slashed down from above, cut through the leather back of her armor, and opened a line of deep slashes on her back. Talli screamed and rolled over. She held up the broken stub of her sword, helpless as the En'Jaga leaned down for the kill.

Then a crossbow bolt whistled down the hill and ran through the creature's eye. The heavy head fell across Talli's legs as the En'Jaga tumbled to the ground.

"They're running!" shouted a Viashino. "They're going back into the marsh."

Talli turned her head and saw that it was true. All up and down the line the En'Jaga were retreating from the fight and hurrying down the hill. To her left and right, hundreds of the creatures lay dead or wounded on the muddy ground. It would have been a great victory, but mixed with the bodies of the En'Jaga were at least as many fallen humans, Garan, and Viashino.

She pulled her legs from under the dead En'Jaga and got painfully to her feet. She could feel warm blood flowing from the cuts on her back, but couldn't tell how bad the wounds really were. "Get everyone up the hill!" she called. "Bring the wounded with you."

She found a fallen sword on the ground and took it. It was not as well made as the weapon she had carried for years, but at least it was in one piece.

Samet Gar approached her across the trampled slope. "They have lost nearly half their En'Jaga," he said. "Your decision to attack them here was a good one."

Talli nodded weakly. "How many did we lose?"

"I'm not sure. Over a hundred dead, perhaps three times that in wounded."

"So they still have a thousand En'Jaga and many thousand humans, while we have lost a third of our forces."

"Yes."

Talli felt a wave of dizziness. Whether it was from her injuries or from sheer exhaustion, she couldn't tell. "We can't stand against another attack," she said. "We'll have to move back."

"To where?" asked Samet Gar.

"Berimish. With the city walls we might hold out against a force this size." She looked across the hill at the wounded soldiers moving slowly up the long slope. Getting them back to Berimish would be difficult. "Get the troops who aren't injured busy loading the wounded on the riding beasts. I want everyone out of here as soon as possible."

A shout sounded from up the hill. "They're coming again!" cried a trooper. "The En'Jaga!"

Talli turned and saw the huge forms emerge from the mist.

"It looks like we won't have time to reach Berimish," said Samet Gar. He raised his arms and curled his fingers into attack position.

Talli stood beside him and raised her borrowed sword. She was weary right down to her bones.

But it would all be over soon.

"Hurry," said Recin. He peeked out through the thick vines that hung between the nearest trees. There was a glimpse of scarlet cloth as one of the Suder troops passed nearby. The rain and darkness had slowed the pursuit and allowed the three fugitives to find a secluded spot behind a screen of trees along the edge of a twisting bayou. But with the coming of dawn the soldiers were rapidly closing in on their hiding place. "They're getting closer."

Aligarius grunted. "Don't rush me," he said. "I'm thinking."

Recin crept over to Kitrin. "Can he do it?" he whispered.

The girl shrugged. In the daylight it was clear that Daleel's blow had broken her nose. Vivid purple and blue bruises spread across her cheeks and she sniffed back a flow of blood that showed no sign of stopping. "He's the expert on this piece," she said. "He did manage to get the wall down, that should help in figuring out how to put it back."

Recin looked at Aligarius and frowned. The old sorcerer seemed a little more alert than he had when they had first escaped from Solin's tent, but that didn't mean he was in any shape to be solving complex magical problems.

"The magewall is not down," said Aligarius.

"You've fixed it?"

"No, no." The old man patted the green crystal in his hands. "This thing could not dismiss the wall. I only moved it."

"To where?"

"Straight up. It's hovering a few hundred feet above where it has been these last few centuries."

"Great," said Recin. "If the Suder decide to fly into Tamingazin, they won't stand a chance."

The sarcasm was lost on Aligarius. "I don't think they'll fly," he said.

Recin lowered his head and gritted his teeth. "Can you put it back?"

"Yes," said Aligarius. "I think I can." He pushed the hub toward Kitrin. "You. Hold this."

The human girl frowned, but took the stone and held it in both hands.

Aligarius rubbed his hands together and placed his fingers just above the surface of the crystal. "This should only take a few minutes." He closed his eyes and began to mumble in the strange language Kitrin had used before.

"Good," said Recin. "I'll keep a watch out." He went back to the vines and pulled them apart.

On the other side stood Ursal Daleel and a Suder soldier.

Recin screamed in surprise and dropped the vine. Daleel's hand shot out and caught him by the wrist. With one quick tug, Recin found himself facedown on the muddy ground. A hard boot came down on his back.

"It seems you were right, Picketleader," said Daleel. "They did come this way."

Recin struggled to turn his head and look up at the Suder. "I thought you'd be in the middle of your war by now."

"Oh, we are." Daleel smiled down at him with a frighteningly real imitation of warmth. "At this moment, the En'Jaga troops are attacking the pitiful resistance at the border." He cupped a hand to one ear. "If you listen closely, you can probably hear the sounds of your friends there being eaten."

Across the small clearing, Aligarius waved his hands. The Magewall Hub glowed brightly in Kitrin's hands. "You haven't won yet," said Recin.

"Haven't I?" The Suder gestured at the two magicians. "Go fetch that lump of stone," he said to the soldier. "It belongs to me."

"No!" Recin pushed free of the Suder's foot, reached up and pulled down on the back of Daleel's tunic. At the same time he got his knees under him and pushed up with all his strength.

The leader of the Suder was strong, but he was not as heavy as his predecessor. Recin's surge flipped Daleel from his feet and sent him tumbling down the slope to splash in the muddy waters of the bayou.

The soldier spun around and pulled a curved sword from its scabbard.

Recin saw Kitrin tense to jump at the man. "Wait," he said. "I'll take care of him."

"You?" sneered the soldier. He raised the sword to strike.

Recin jumped up and grabbed the vines above his head. By the time the soldier's arm came down, Recin was ten feet above the man's head.

The armored soldier looked up at him and scowled. "Come down here and fight."

"I really think I'd rather climb."

The soldier grunted. "Climb all you want. It won't help your friends." He turned and began to advance on Kitrin and Aligarius.

Recin let go of the vine and dropped onto the soldier. The Suder was faster than he had expected. The curved sword whistled through the air, passing just over Recin's head and severing the vine he had been holding. But as the man lunged forward to strike again, his feet caught in the tangle of vine now lying on the ground.

He toppled forward, waving his arms. As the soldier fell, Recin rolled out of the way. He raised his arms, wrapping the length of severed vine around the soldier's throat.

Before the man could rise, Recin turned and straddled his armored back. He pulled on the vine as hard as he could.

A thin squeal came from the soldier's constricted throat. He tried to reach back for Recin, but the joints of his armor would not allow it. The sword dropped from his fingers and he beat his hands against the ground. Recin leaned back as hard as he could and gave the vine a savage jerk. There was a solid snapping sound, like a twig underfoot.

When Recin relaxed his grip on the vine, the soldier lay still.

Ursal Daleel splashed out of the bayou and stood dripping on the shore. "Very impressive," he said. "Now, move out of my way."

Recin glanced over his shoulder. Kitrin was staring at him, her bruised face creased with worry. Aligarius's movements were growing more energetic, his words louder; the light from the hub pulsed and flashed.

Recin came up off the ground and lunged at Daleel. The momentum of his jump carried them both into the bayou. He managed to get one arm around the Suder's throat and wrapped his other around the small man's chest.

"Let go, you fool!" shouted the Suder. "Let go before you drown us both!"

Iron fingers bit into Recin's arms. Recin screamed, the cry turning into a stream of bubbles as his head rolled underwater. He did not let go. Daleel kicked against his shins, but Recin held on. Slowly, they sank into the murky water. Recin's lungs began to burn. Soon the desire for air was so great that he could barely feel the effects of Daleel's blows. Recin held on.

Just before everything went dark, he thought he saw a flash of green.

The En'Jaga were only a few strides away when they froze. Yellow light played around their bodies and ran over their bared teeth. Within the grip of the magewall, their movements were slowed to a hundredth of their normal speed. As more and more of them tried to breach the wall, the effect became stronger and stronger.

The iron bolts of the Viashino crossbows were not bothered by the wall. Volley after volley, they struck and penetrated the bodies of the frozen En'Jaga.

Talli sat down on the blood-soaked grass. All around her were the bodies of humans who had followed her father from the holds, Garan who had come down from their mountains, and Viashino who had left their city to fight at her side. For a moment she felt like sobbing at their loss.

Instead she began to laugh. The sound of her laughter mixed with the whistling of the crossbow bolts as the remaining En'Jaga retreated down the hill.

Recin coughed and opened his eyes. He found himself looking up into the bruised face of Kitrin. "What . . ." he started, but the attempt to speak only brought on another bout of coughing.

"Lie still," said the young wizard. "You almost drowned."

"Daleel?" Recin managed.

The girl shook her head. "There's nothing left of him. The attalo are already feeding."

"He'll probably make them sick." Recin raised his head and looked around. "Where's Aligarius?"

"He's keeping a lookout in case more Suder come near."

"Who got me out of the water?"

"I did," said Kitrin.

Recin laughed weakly. "I thought you couldn't swim."

"I just needed some incentive," she said. Then she smiled.

Recin decided that he didn't mind her smile after all.

"Stay here," Talli called to those around her. "We don't know what they'll try now. Don't let them pull you out of your positions until we see the form of their attack." She walked over to the lookout who had shouted. "What do you see?"

"People coming this way," said the Viashino. He raised a hand and pointed one claw at the billowing mists. "There."

It took Talli a moment to see what the Viashino's yellow eyes had picked out. Dim shapes moved: gray forms in the lighter gray of the fog. She saw one, then two, finally three: humans, all of them, or at least human-sized. She waited for the wall of forms that would represent the front of the Suder attack, but no more appeared.

The Viashino beside her raised its crossbow and put its eye to the sight. "I can drop them before they even reach the magewall."

Talli reached over and pushed the front of the weapon down. "No, wait."

Colors became visible through the fog. The three people were all dressed in the colorful stripes of Suder clothing. Then faces became visible. Recin. Kitrin. And . . . Aligarius?

Talli broke from the lines and dashed across the torn, blood-soaked ground. The three figures reached the magewall and their motion slowed to a fraction of normal as the yellow light played around them. Talli waited just inside the track of bare earth. For the moment, her exhaustion and injuries were forgotten.

As soon as they emerged from the magewall, Talli caught Recin with one arm, Kitrin with the other, and locked them both in a tight hug.

"What's happened?" Talli asked as she released them. "Where are the Suder?"

Recin jerked a thumb over his shoulder. "Right back there."

"We'd better get up the hill. If they attack again, the archers will need a clear line of fire."

"I don't think there's any attack coming," said Recin. "Not today."

"Are you sure?"

"As far as we can tell, they're leaving," replied Kitrin. She fished in her pouch and produced a cylinder of green stone. "Looks like this thing did what it was supposed to do."

"Yes," said Aligarius. His voice was thick, and a smile sat crookedly on his face. "If you know how to use it."

Talli stared at the sorcerer. He looked as thin as death. The Suder clothing sagged away from his frame and his floppy hat hung low on his head. The whites of his eyes were stained a bruised mixture of yellow and purple.

"What are you doing here?" she said.

Aligarius turned to her. "Now," he said, "let's see if

you know how to constrain a twelfth order Transcendental."

"What?"

"He's been talking like that ever since he managed to put the wall back," said Recin. "The Suder gave him some kind of spice that makes you want more all the time. I think it's affected his mind."

Kitrin nodded. "That's part of why he betrayed your father," she said.

Talli looked into the sorcerer's muddy eyes. "That doesn't excuse what he's done," she said.

"No, of course not," said Kitrin. "When we get him back to the institute, we'll see that—"

"The institute?" Talli shook her head. "He'll have to go back to Berimish for trial."

"We sort of made a promise," said Kitrin. "He helped us, and we told him he'd go back to the institute."

Talli pressed her lips together. "Promises are important," she said. She nodded. "All right. Aligarius goes with you. Just make sure he stays put this time."

Recin stepped forward and put a hand on Talli's arm. "What about my mother?" he asked. "Is she all right?"

"Your mother is fine. She's right up the hill tending to the wounded. Getin's still in Berimish, but she was in good health when we left. Rael Gar is dead."

"How did that happen?"

Talli looked around. The troops behind her were staring at them from their positions along the line. "Come on," she said. "Let's go somewhere where we can talk more comfortably."

"And eat," said Recin.

"Sure," Talli said with a laugh. "And eat."

The four began to walk up the gentle slope. Kitrin led Aligarius by the hand.

"A lot of things have happened in a short time," said Talli. "When you get back to Berimish, you may not recognize the place."

"I was thinking Recin might want to come to the institute with me instead of going to Berimish," said Kitrin.

"To the institute?" said Recin. "Why?"

"I don't think we have any Garan there. You could be the first Garan magician."

Recin blinked and shook his head. "I don't know. Do you really think I have any talent?"

"Come and find out."

Talli smiled. She suspected that Kitrin's desire to have Recin come with her had little to do with magic— at least, not the kind of magic that involved spells and artifacts. Recin shook his head again. "I never thought about that."

"That's the way things are after a war," said Talli. "You get to the peace and you don't know quite what to do with it." She paused in front of the of line soldiers that had assembled for a battle that would not be fought. "Maybe this time we'll figure it out."